Witches *and* Wedding Cake

A Magical Bakery Mystery

Bailey Cates

BERKLEY PRIME CRIME
New York

BERKLEY PRIME CRIME
Published by Berkley
An imprint of Penguin Random House LLC
penguinrandomhouse.com

ISBN: 9780593099223

First Edition: July 2020

Printed in the United States of America
1 3 5 7 9 10 8 6 4 2

Cover art by Monika Roe
Cover design by Katie Anderson

PRAISE FOR THE *NEW YORK TIMES* BESTSELLING MAGICAL BAKERY MYSTERIES

"Katie is a charming amateur sleuth. . . . With an intriguing plot and an amusing cast of characters, *Brownies and Broomsticks* is an attention-grabbing read that I couldn't put down."
—*New York Times* bestselling author Jenn McKinlay

"Cates is a smooth, accomplished writer who combines a compelling plot with a cast of interesting characters."
—*Kirkus Reviews*

"Fun and exciting reading." —*USA Today*

"[The] sixth of the Magical Bakery Mystery series remains as entertaining as the first, with a mythology that is as developed as Katie's newfound talent and life within the Savannah magical community." —Kings River Life Magazine

"If you enjoy . . . Ellery Adams's Charmed Pie Shoppe Mystery series and Heather Blake's Wishcraft Mystery series, you are destined to enjoy the Magical Bakery Mystery series." —MyShelf.com

"With a top-notch whodunit, a dark magic investigator working undercover, and a simmering romance in the early stages, fans will relish this tale." —Gumshoe

"As a fan of magic and witches in my cozies, Cates's series remains a favorite." —Fresh Fiction

"Ms. Cates has most assuredly found the right ingredients . . . a series that is a finely sifted blend of drama, suspense, romance, and otherworldly elements."
—Once Upon a Romance

"Sure to cast a spell on you and keep you enchanted and entertained." —Cozy Experience

ALSO AVAILABLE BY BAILEY CATES

Chapter 1

"Anytime the afternoon of the sixteenth will work," I said into my cell phone. "Just shoot me a quick text when you're on your way, so I can make sure someone is there to meet you." The Honeybee Bakery's landline rang on the desk. I quickly reached over to lower the volume, knowing Aunt Lucy or Uncle Ben would answer the call out front. "And you'll return to pick up everything on Monday, then? Okay. Oh, I wanted to make sure you're supplying an extra-long table for the caterers as well. And the tablecloth for that, too? Perfect. Thank you so much!"

I ended the call and spun the office chair to face Mungo. My Cairn terrier—and witch's familiar—had been listening to my end of the conversation with interest. "Well, that's the last detail, little guy! Stick a fork in it—the wedding planning is officially done." I grinned, almost giddy with relief.

It had been a whirlwind three months after Declan and I had finally set the date. But now the carriage house renovations were finished—well, except for the interior of the garage, but that could wait. The new sofa and chairs had been delivered the previous afternoon, so our guests wouldn't be wandering around an empty living room during the reception, which was doubling as a house-warming party. The ceremony would take place in the evening, and the weather was predicted to be on the cooler side for August in Savannah, with highs in the eighties. Add in plenty of awnings and cooling drinks, and most of the party would be in the backyard. Finally, I'd just recon-firmed the delivery of the outdoor furniture and linens from Vintage Event Rentals.

Briskly, I brushed my hands together. "Done, done, done. And Mama said I couldn't possibly get it all orga-nized in three months. Ha! Everything's going off with-out a hitch."

Yip! Mungo agreed softly, then gave me a brown-eyed look of affectionate approval before settling into his club chair for his third nap of the day.

Never mind that my father had to travel from my hometown in Ohio to work with the contractors on the carriage house. Never mind that one of the bakery's cus-tomers had been murdered a month ago. Never mind that I'd come close to permanently losing the thing that was most precious to me as a result.

No, that's not true. Declan is the most precious thing to me.

Still, July had been a pretty darn bad month.

But that was over now. I rose and retied my tartan plaid chef's apron, reflecting on the last two and a half years. I'd left a broken engagement and my low-paying job at a bakery in Akron to move south and start up the Honeybee Bakery with Aunt Lucy and Uncle Ben. I'd made wonderful friends, found the man I was truly supposed to spend the rest of my life with, and had embarked on an unexpected journey of self-discovery.

Unexpected and, at first, definitely unwanted. When Lucy had calmly informed me that I was a witch, specifically a kitchen witch with an affinity for accessing the magical powers inherent in herbs and plants in cooking, just as she and my mother and all the women in our family had been, I'd laughed. My aunt had called us *hedgewitches*. I mean, that had to be a joke, right? She'd been dead serious, though—more than figuratively, since Mavis Templeton had just been killed and my uncle Ben was the prime murder suspect.

It had taken me a while, but eventually I'd come to realize my inherited powers explained a lot about my life growing up that I hadn't understood before. And those wonderful friends I mentioned? Four of them happened to be members of the spellbook club, a casual coven of six witches who practiced various types of magic—all on the light side, of course—and discussed spell books. Lucy and I were the other two members.

I shut the office door behind me and walked through the Honeybee's open, shining kitchen. Our part-time helper, Iris Grant, looked up from where she was mixing fresh parsley, chives, and oregano into a batch of savory muffins.

She grinned. "Katie, you look like the cat who ate the canary." Then her expressive face morphed into a frown. "Though come to think of it, I don't really like that saying. It's one of Patsy's." Patsy was Iris' stepmother, whose basement she lived in while studying graphic design at the Savannah College of Art and Design, or SCAD.

I shook my head. "I don't think I'd care for canary, but I have to admit, I'm feeling pretty self-satisfied right now. Just tied up the last loose end for Saturday."

Five days. In five days, I'll be a married woman.

I'd decided to keep *Lightfoot* as my last name rather than taking Declan's surname, *McCarthy*. Plus, Declan and I had been more or less living together for months. A part of me wondered whether our relationship would feel any different after the ceremony.

Another part was sure that it would.

"Ha! That's awesome." Iris looked down at the bowl of batter, and I saw she'd managed to plait her chin-length bob—bright royal blue these days—into two tight French braids to keep it out of the way while she worked. "Do you think I should add some thyme to this?"

I walked over and inhaled the redolent scents of the herbs that flecked the rich muffin batter. "Hmm. No, I don't think so."

"Too many notes?" she asked.

"Something like that. Oregano for joy and chives for breaking bad habits. And focus on the strengthening aspect of the parsley when you invoke its power." After all, parsley could also be triggered to help communicate with the dead, and I didn't think our customers would appreciate that side effect.

She nodded. "Okay. Maybe mix in a little Asiago cheese, though?"

"Oh, that would be lovely." She'd been coming up with more of her own recipes lately and had been learning how to include the something special Lucy and I added to the Honeybee pastries. Iris wasn't a hereditary hedgewitch as my aunt and I were, but she had a lot of

4

innate talent and power as well as a desire to learn. We'd been teaching her how to call forth the naturally occurring magic in the herbs and spices we added to our baked goods. A sprinkle of abundance here, a dash of love there, and a dollop of happiness whenever possible. Whether they knew it or not, it was one of the reasons our customers were so loyal, and word-of-mouth had made the Honeybee such a resounding success.

Well, that and the pure deliciousness we served.

"Katie?"

I turned toward where Aunt Lucy was returning the phone to its cradle on the wall behind the register. She met my eye with an apologetic expression.

Leaving Iris to her baking, I made my way through the shining counters and industrial ovens to the front of the Honeybee. Almost all the chrome-and-blue bistro tables were occupied, though in the middle of the afternoon most of our patrons were working away on laptops or engaged in leisurely conversation over iced drinks and crumb-scattered plates.

In the front corner, my friend Steve Dawes hunched over his computer, pecking away at what I presumed was an article for the *Savannah Morning News*. His honey-colored hair was pulled back in a short ponytail, and his lower lip was clamped between his teeth as he typed. He'd started coming in most afternoons, saying the office was too loud to work in. I figured he was just lonely since he and his latest girlfriend had broken up. However, Steve knew my uncle Ben wasn't all that fond of him, so I was a little surprised at the reporter's insistence on working in the bakery.

No one waited by the gleaming display case full of

pastries, and the espresso maker was uncharacteristically quiet behind the coffee counter. I checked the bookshelf-lined reading area and saw Uncle Ben had settled onto the brocade sofa to catch up with one of our regulars. A few gray hairs glinted from the tidy ginger beard he'd grown after retiring as Savannah's fire chief, and the corners of his brown eyes crinkled behind his rimless glasses as he laughed at something the other man said. Behind him, Honeybee, my aunt's tabby-striped familiar who had inspired the name of the bakery, sat regally on the windowsill and watched the passersby on Broughton Street out front with typical feline disinterest.

Returning my attention to my aunt, I asked, "What's up?"

Her lips twisted ruefully. "I'm sorry, honey."

My heart sank as I connected her expression with the call that had come in while I'd been on my cell phone with the event rental company.

"Please. Tell me that wasn't bad news."

Her fingertips seemed to move of their own accord as she tucked a stray strand of gray-blond hair into the messy bun at the nape of her neck. She shoved her other hand into the pocket of her vintage linen apron. "Now, Katie. There's a solution to every problem."

"No." I shook my head. "No, no, no."

She offered a gentle smile and waited.

Finally, I sighed. "Okay, what is it?"

"Judge Matthews' father had a heart attack and is in the hospital." She held up her hand. "Don't worry. The doctors say he'll be okay, but the judge is on his way to Chicago, and he doesn't think he's going to be back in time for your wedding."

I gaped. Blinked. And wailed, "What are we going to do?"

From the corner of my eye, I saw a few customers look up. My face grew warm.

"Stop being so dramatic." Lucy's quiet voice was still kind, but the words were harsher than she was inclined toward, and she wasn't smiling. "His father is looking at a lengthy recovery. That poor man." Her forehead creased with sympathy. My aunt had one of the softest hearts I'd ever encountered.

I took a deep breath. "Of course Judge Matthews needs to be with his father now."

"That's more like the Katie I know. I'm sure we'll find a way to adjust for his absence." She suddenly grinned. "You could have a traditional Wiccan handfasting after all."

She was teasing me. I knew that, but this latest complication didn't leave me in a mood that was very receptive to teasing.

"Well." I sighed. "I guess that's what I get for feeling sanctimonious about everything going so smoothly. I should know better than to be smug."

Lucy raised her eyebrows in amused agreement.

The door opened and two men walked in. They wore Savannah Fire uniforms, and the tall, dark, and oh-so-handsome one happened to be my fiancé. His sky blue eyes met mine as he smiled, and he ran one hand through his wavy hair. With him was Randy Post, his coworker who was dating my friend Bianca Devereaux. I hurried to meet them at their favorite table, giving Declan a quick hug and a peck on the cheek even though he was technically on duty until the next morning.

"I have bad news," I announced.

His lips twitched. "Hello to you, too."

"I'm sorry. Hello, love of my life. I still have bad news." And I told him what I'd learned about Judge Matthews.

He sighed. "Dang it. Well, we'll figure it out. There has to be someone who can do the job on such short notice."

"You seem awfully calm." I obviously wasn't.

"I'll ask around," he said. "You do the same."

I took a deep breath. "Yeah. Okay. I'll be asking Google, though. Wedding officiants must have websites, right? Or maybe there's some kind of guild or something." It had been a no-brainer to ask Judge Matthews to marry us because he was a friend of Uncle Ben's. We hadn't considered anyone else.

Randy laughed and spoke for the first time. "I don't think there's a guild, but you never can tell. I'll pass the word, too."

"Thanks," I said. "Deck, do you have time to taste a couple more cupcake flavors? I'm thinking of adding strawberry and vanilla. Made up some samples this morning." For months I'd been unable to choose the kind of wedding cake I wanted. My mother had come up with the genius answer: five tiers of different-flavored cupcakes.

He grinned. "Well, if you insist. Randy?"

"Not my wedding, but I'm happy to sample anything Katie makes."

"Excellent," I said. "I'll get your usual drinks started and bring them out."

A few minutes later, I joined them at their table, plate of cupcakes in hand. Lucy brought their drinks over, then patted Declan on the shoulder. "This should be the last of them. Katie's running out of flavors to try."

"Never," I said.

She laughed and went back into the kitchen.

After careful tasting, which included Declan and Randy having two each of the strawberry and vanilla cupcakes, sans frosting, the verdict was that they were both delicious, but since it was our special day, perhaps we could skip the simple vanilla version.

"Vanilla is mistaken as a plain-Jane flavor, but it's really quite exotic," I said. "It comes from the seed pod of an orchid, after all."

Declan tipped his head to the side. "If you want vanilla cupcakes, too, I'm not going to stop you."

"Nah. You're right. We'll stick with the seven kinds we already have."

Randy went to select some pastries from the display case to take back to the firehouse, and I leaned toward Declan. "Everything going okay at work?"

He frowned. "Fine." The response was mildly curt, and I changed the subject.

I wasn't the only one who had a connection to the paranormal. Declan wasn't a witch, mind you, but a spirit had attached himself to my fiancé at the moment of his birth. Most of his life he'd been unaware of how Connell had guided him, essentially serving as a strong sense of intuition and the occasional kick in the pants. When Connell had made himself known, Declan had a hard time with it for a while but eventually came to accept that Connell was a part of him.

A few weeks before, Connell had saved me from a

powerful hex, but had become disconnected from Declan in the process. I'd had my issues with Connell, who was loud and brash but also kind and protective. It wasn't until he'd vowed not to take over Declan's body at inopportune times—like in the bedroom—that we'd finally set the wedding date. Now Connell was gone. I missed him. However much Declan tended to keep those kinds of feelings to himself, I knew he missed Connell exponentially more. Worse yet, he'd had a close call during a house fire on his last shift, a dangerous situation that I firmly believed his guardian spirit would have guided him away from.

I couldn't help but worry.

Loaded with enough baked goods to feed an army, Randy and Declan left. I returned to the kitchen to let Lucy know what we'd decided.

"That sounds good, dear. The strawberry will make a nice addition, and I agree that eight flavors might be a bit much."

My cell phone buzzed in my pocket, and I drew it out. "Great." I shook my head and held the phone out to my aunt. "Eliza just texted me."

Her bemused expression turned to one of alarm as she read the text out loud. "'I need to speak with you. Can you come to the house?' Oh, dear. What on earth can that be about?"

"Don't worry. She's probably fretting about yet another aspect of the wedding where we're breaking with tradition." Declan's oldest sister was not shy about sharing her opinions, of which she had an abundance. "So far, she's unhappy that we're getting married so late in the evening, that the party will start before the actual wedding, then pause for the ceremony, and that Mungo will be my ring bearer. Oh, and she hates that we're renting all those mismatched antique chairs instead of tidy folding chairs for people to sit on. Who knows what else she's taken issue with?"

Lucy made a face. "Sisters can be difficult."

I snorted. "Well, I know exactly who you mean." Lucy and my mother had gone through some strained times over the years. "But as an only child, I'm new to the whole sister, or rather sister-in-law, dynamic."

"Better figure it out, niece o' mine." She grinned. "Since your beloved comes complete with four of them."

"At least Aggie's been great." Declan's mother preferred *Aggie* to Agnes, and the nickname suited her. She was a strong though easygoing woman, and I'd been afraid she might try to muscle in on the wedding plans at the last minute. However, she'd merely offered her help when needed and timely words of encouragement when I'd thought I might lose my mind before actually saying *I do*.

My aunt made a shooing motion. "You've been summoned. Better go before the afternoon rush kicks in."

I wrinkled my nose and untied my apron. "I'll get online when I get back. There's got to be someone who can marry us on such short notice."

"That's the spirit," my aunt said.

Barely managing not to roll my eyes, I said, "I won't be long. The house the McCarthys are renting for the week is over by Chippewa Square."

I added my apron to those that hung from the row of pegs on the back wall of the kitchen and continued to the office. Mungo raised his head and watched with

11

bright interest as I slid my cell phone into the side pocket of my tote bag.

What the heck. Why not? Never mind that Eliza didn't appear to care for dogs.

"You want to come with? Declan's sister wants to 'speak with me.'"

Mungo's nose wrinkled much in the same way mine had. However, he sat up and wagged his short tail, game to accompany me.

"Thanks, buddy. I could use the support."

Yip!

On the way out, I grabbed a pastry bag stamped with our logo of an orange-striped cat and filled it with cookies and glazed fritters. Uncle Ben looked up as I moved toward the front door of the bakery, a question in his eyes. I smiled and sketched a wave. Lucy would tell him where I'd gone. I ignored the feeling that Steve was watching from the other side of the room as I opened the door and stepped out to Broughton Street.

Chapter 2

With the air conditioning blasting, I guided my Volkswagen Beetle through the famous squares of the Savannah Historic District and a few minutes later turned onto the block where Declan's mother had rented a house for the week. These days Aggie lived in Boston, but she'd raised her family in Savannah, and she, along with Eliza and Declan's youngest sister, Rori, had arrived a week early to spend extra time on their old stomping grounds.

Declan had landed smack in the middle of his sisters, birth-order-wise. On either side of him were Camille and Lauren, both of whom were married and would be arriving in a couple of day with their families, so only his oldest and youngest siblings were already in residence. Aggie might be a gem of a future mother-in-law, but I was still deciding what kind of sister-in-law Eliza would be.

Try to give her the benefit of the doubt. Maybe she'll be less judgmental after the wedding.

Maybe.

"Wonder what she'd have to say if she knew I'm a witch, and you're my familiar," I murmured to Mungo, who was sitting in my tote bag, strapped into the passenger seat beside me.

Yip!

Smiling, I adjusted the sprigs of holy basil and lemon balm that I'd arranged in the tiny bud vase attached to the dash of the Bug. Each was excellent for promoting calm, and together they made a pretty little nosegay as well. Lately I would take as much calm and pretty as I could get.

A car pulled out of a parking space across the street from the McCarthy family rental. Thanking my parking karma, I quickly guided my little car into it. Killing the engine, I sat in the cool metal bubble of the Bug for a few moments to gather my thoughts—and my resolve.

No matter what complaint Eliza has this time, I'm going to be pleasant yet firm.

Taking a deep breath, I opened my door and stepped onto the street. Going around to the other side, I retrieved my tote with Mungo inside and marched toward the two-story, wrought-iron-embellished property where I'd been summoned.

A sign that read WISTERIA HOUSE was affixed to the brick exterior by the paneled wooden door. The sidewalk in front was also made of bricks, arranged in a neat herringbone pattern. Six red cement steps led up to the ornate entrance. I passed beneath the live oaks dripping with Spanish moss and began climbing them. A movement to my right drew my attention. A bearded man was using handheld shears to trim the boxwood that separated the yard from the one next to it. He wore a white jumpsuit in the stifling heat, but he looked so cool and serene as he evened out the top of the hedge that I pegged him as a native Savannahian. He looked up, and I nodded to him. He nodded back and returned to his task.

Large pots filled with annuals flanked the door. Admiring the petunias, verbena, and variegated sweet potato vine, I rang the bell and waited. The sun blazed down on my shoulders, and I welcomed the warmth after a morning spent inside. I closed my eyes and turned my face up to soak in more.

A soft whirring sound reached my ears. I opened my eyes and saw dozens of delicate dragonflies descend around me. There were tiny ones the size of my thumbnail ranging to larger ones nearly three inches across. Their multicolored, iridescent hues glinted and flashed in the sunlight. They perched on the edges of petals, leaves, unopened buds, and along the rims of planters. They lined up along the wrought-iron railing and clung to the brick wall. One even landed on my tote bag until Mungo nosed it, and it launched off, only to land on the sign by the door.

Dragonflies. So many dragonflies.

Uh-oh.

Dragonflies were my totem. I'd come to learn that often when I saw a dragonfly, it was a kind of metaphysical tap on the shoulder. A reminder to pay attention. Now, to be sure, I often noticed the ubiquitous little creatures, also known as mosquito hawks, here and there. They certainly zinged around the backyard of the carriage house in droves when mosquito season was in full swing—a piece of luck that enabled evenings on the patio to be quite pleasant without having to use chemicals to keep the biting insects at bay. However, sometimes dragonflies meant something more.

Like when they showed up out of nowhere in large numbers.

My hand crept up, and I rubbed my eyes. When I opened them, the beautiful insects were still there. In the tote, Mungo made a *rawr* sound. I reached down and ran my thumb along the fur between his ears.

"I know. I see them," I said, and suppressed a sigh.

Footsteps sounded, and the door swung open to reveal a petite woman dressed in a gauzy white sundress. With her dark wavy hair and ice blue eyes, this sister resembled Declan the most. However, she had a delicate, heart-shaped face rather than his square jawline and was about a foot shorter than my fiancé.

"Hi, Rori." I held the bag out to her.

Her face lit up. "Oh, yay! Goodies!" She waved me inside with an urgent gesture. "Hurry. We just got it decently cool in here." Her words were rounded with a gentle Southern accent.

I stepped over the threshold, and she quickly shut the door behind me. The chilled air inside the house was a marked contrast to the sun-drenched front step, and Mungo huffed his approval. I set my tote down on the floor. He hopped out but didn't venture more than a few steps.

Aggie had obviously chosen the place for comfort

and elegance. The walls of the rooms I could partially see from the foyer were painted in dark rich tones—indigo in the living room, forest green in the dining room, burnt sienna in the kitchen—while the high ceilings were lighter colored. The furniture was a mix of periods, but all in dark wood and with an abundance of cushions. A gardenia plant on the entry table filled the air with its strong perfume, reminding me of my grandmother. The mirror on the wall above the table reflected the light from the windows on either side of the door, giving the space a bright, welcoming atmosphere.

After a quick hug, Rori stepped back and blew the bangs off her forehead. "Mother wants to shop this afternoon, but I'm trying to convince her to go out on the river. You want to come?"

I made a moue of regret. "I can't. There's too much to do at the bakery." I couldn't remember the last time I'd taken an afternoon to go out on the Savannah River.

"Oh, bummer. I get it, though. We're on vacation, but you're busy, busy, busy. And you made time to bring these over? That's so nice!" She opened the bag and peered inside. "Black-and-white cookies! Only my favorite."

"Oh, please. Any cookie is your favorite." The sardonic words came from behind us.

I turned to find Eliza coming down the stairs. She had Declan's height and square jaw, but her hair and eyes were light brown. She wore little makeup and sported a blunt-cut, chin-length bob. Today she wore butter yellow capris with a sleeveless blouse and ballet flats. When she saw Mungo, she slightly raised one eyebrow but didn't comment.

Aggie followed behind her. Declan's mother had red hair that looked so much like my mother's, I had to wonder if they used the same brand of hair coloring. Hers was cropped into short layers with highlights galore, which suited her pale complexion and brown eyes perfectly. She wore long shorts with a linen T-shirt in a floral pattern and sensible sandals.

Rori rolled her eyes at her sister. "At least I enjoy a little sweetness, Lizzie."

"Don't call me Lizzie. You know I hate it."

Her sister grinned at me.

"Oh, my darling daughters," Aggie said mildly as they reached the bottom of the staircase. "A week with you two simply won't be enough." She bent to pet Mungo, then straightened and smiled at me. "You brought us cookies?"

"And apple fritters. Actually, though, I'm here because Eliza asked me to drop by."

"Really?" Rori asked. "And why is that, Lizzie?"

Eliza's nostrils flared, but she didn't comment on the nickname. "I wanted to have a little chat with Katie."

Rori and Aggie exchanged a look.

"And a phone call simply wouldn't do, I suppose," Aggie said. "Or even stopping by the bakery?"

Drawing herself up, Declan's older sister set her jaw. "Mother, this is important. It is traditional for bridesmaids to be young, single women, and Katie isn't—"

Rori broke in. "I'll tell you what 'Katie isn't.' Katie isn't obligated to listen to your nonsense, Eliza. Good heavens. Who died and made you the boss of everyone?

Just leave her alone. Her friends are going to stand up with her at the wedding, and it doesn't matter if they're married or, um, of a certain age, or preggers or anything else."

Eliza's face reddened. "Aurora, I'll thank you to—"

"No." Rori took a step forward and raised her index finger. "Just no. Mother, will you *please* say something?"

Aggie sighed. "Eliza, your sister might be a bit overly enthusiastic about making her point, but she does have one."

I let out the breath I'd been holding.

Eliza huffed, then turned her attention back to me. "Even though I'm trying to help, I'm obviously in the wrong. I'm very sorry you came all the way over here, Katie."

I ventured a smile. "No worries."

"Yikes," Rori muttered.

Eliza lifted her nose into the air. "I said I was sorry."

I groped for the right words. Eliza wasn't a bad sort, just a little high-handed. Still, I barely knew Declan's sisters, and it had never seemed right to have them in my wedding party. The ladies of the spellbook club, on the other hand, felt just right. All of them, from pregnant Cookie Rios to octogenarian Mimsey Carmichael. *Wedding party* rather than *bridesmaids*. Still, what could I say to smooth things over with my soon-to-be in-laws?

"Eliza," I said. "Would you mind terribly if I asked you to organize a family dinner on Thursday night? Since my parents won't be here until the end of the week, it would give us all a chance to get to know each other a bit more before the wedding. We can even call it a rehearsal dinner. It would be such a big help." I frowned. "Though I'm not sure where we could get reservations for so many people this late . . ."

She was already nodding, though, and a hint of a smile played on her lips. "A rehearsal dinner? Of course I'll do it. I'm sure I'll be able to find an appropriate venue."

Aggie shot me a grin and a small nod of approval.

The doorbell rang, and relief whooshed through me as everyone turned toward the entrance with puzzled expressions.

"Declan's working today, isn't he?" Aggie asked.

"Yes. He gets off his forty-eight-hour shift tomorrow morning," I said.

"I wonder who that could be, then."

"Well, I know how we can find out," Rori teased, striding to the door and pulling it open. Her lips parted in surprise, and the blood drained from her face.

"Tucker?"

I should know that name. Wait . . . Rori's ex-husband? Oh, dear.

From what Declan had mentioned, their divorce hadn't exactly been amicable. There'd been some kind of scandal. The whole family had been relieved when Rori dumped the guy, even though she'd had to move back in with her mother until she got back on her feet.

Eliza quickly moved to her sister's side. "What are you doing here?" Rori asked. "How did you find me?"

Eliza didn't wait for an answer. "Listen, buster. I don't know how you found out she was in town, but you're not welcome here."

Aggie sighed and crossed her arms but remained at

the bottom of the staircase. After glancing down at Mungo, I sidled to one side so I could see their visitor.

One of the most beautiful men I'd ever seen stood on the front step. He wore chinos and a white oxford shirt with leather loafers. His golden hair was slightly wavy and casually tousled in a way that made me want to reach out and touch it. My fingers actually twitched before I clenched them into fists. His smooth skin was tanned, his bright green eyes flashed behind long lashes, and his aquiline nose sat above lips that looked sweet enough to . . .

Wait a minute. Sweet lips? What—?

Those emerald eyes shifted to meet mine, and I felt a tingle along the nape of my neck. He exuded a heady combination of sex appeal, safety, and the sense that he instantly understood everything important about me. Add in his almost painfully handsome appearance, and he was, in a word, perfect.

Too perfect. Waaaay too perfect.

I narrowed my eyes, concentrating, and felt a flash of something beneath my initial perception. It felt . . . bad. *Wrong.* Not wrong as in serial-killer wrong, not quite that. But slimy, for sure. The longer I focused on him, the more it seemed as if I was seeing a slightly off double image.

Tucker was employing a glamour—a magical manipulation of how other people perceived him. Whether he realized he was doing it or not, I couldn't be sure. Everyone has some magic in them, after all, and certain people, politicians and those with a great deal of natural charisma, for example, have a native and instinctive talent for projecting an appealing façade. Still, this glamour was over the top.

Whether or not he was aware of what he was doing, the man sensed I wasn't seeing him the same way anymore. His eyes flashed, and he directed his attention back to Rori. His lips parted in a white-toothed smile, and affection poured from his gaze.

Mungo leaned against my leg, and I felt the subtle vibration of a growl too low to hear.

"Now, sweetheart," Tucker said. "I heard through the grapevine that your brother is getting married, so I knew you'd come to Savannah. I checked with my friend in the vacation rental business, and she told me your family was staying here for the week. I had to pop by and see how my girl's been doing. I've been thinking about you."

Eliza snorted.

Tucker turned and looked at her full on. She blinked and seemed to falter for a few seconds, but then her jaw set, and she glared at him. My assessment of Declan's older sister ramped up a few notches.

"Now, Lizzie," he said in a teasing tone. "You know you love me."

She visibly bristled. "I most certainly do not love you. I don't even remotely like you. And neither does Aurora. Leave her alone."

He shook his head. "I think Rori can speak for herself." Suddenly, he looked over his shoulder at a car going by on the street. He frowned and turned back. "Rori? What do you say? Are you going to show some of that lovely Southern charm and invite me in for a chat? I came to apologize for what happened in DC. You never gave me a chance to really do that, you know."

Rori stared at him with a dazed expression. "Well, I suppose—"

Eliza put her hand on Rori's shoulder. Her sister looked up at her, and I saw her eyes clear.

She met Tucker's gaze. "Um, no. I don't think so. Sorry. I don't have anything to say to you. It's too late for apologies. I've moved on."

Another car went by. Tucker didn't turn around this time, but I saw him hunch his shoulders and rub the back of his neck. A tingle went down my own spine, and I looked out in time to see a dark, nondescript vehicle drive past on the street. It didn't even slow, yet it struck me that Tucker was acting as if someone might be following him. I felt my eyes narrow in suspicion, but he wasn't paying any attention to me.

He trained another thousand-watt smile on Rori. "You sure about that? I have a present for you."

Rori looked intrigued, and her lips began to curve up. Then Eliza's fingers squeezed her shoulder again. Rori blinked and gave a quick shake of her head. "No thanks, Tucker. I don't want anything from you."

"Oh, now. Don't be like that, honey."

Yuck. Just . . . yuck.

His hand dipped into his pocket and came out with a small ceramic birdhouse. About five inches high and four inches around, it was too small to house anything but a hummingbird—and not even that because the opening was painted on. The whole thing was covered with depictions of swirling yellow ribbons, tiny blue-glazed birds, and bas-relief daisies, the edges of their protruding petals gilded with gold paint.

It was kitschier than kitsch.

"I tracked this down just for you, Rori. I've been waiting months for a chance to give it to you. I hope it can make up for some of the difficulty between us."

Eliza tried the shoulder squeeze again, but Rori shrugged her off and took a couple steps toward him. After a few seconds of hesitation, she took the birdhouse from his hand. As she did, I noticed he was wearing a totally over-the-top signet ring. A large ruby glinted in the center of it.

Rory turned the birdhouse in her hand. "What is it?"

"It's a music box. See, you wind the base, and then it plays 'When You Wish Upon a Star.'" He took it from her to demonstrate, then handed it back to her. A few bars of the classic Disney song plinked weakly from inside. "I know it doesn't look like much, but it's quite valuable, and I remember how much you love that song . . . what's wrong?"

Rori's face had suddenly flushed. She stepped forward, and he backed down the steps. "You want to give me a music box?" she growled. "A *music box*? To make up for what you did?" Her eyes filled with tears, but she blinked them away. "How dare you."

For the first time, the beautiful man looked unsure. "Now, honey, you know that whole thing with your boss wasn't my fault."

The sliminess beneath his smooth surface ratcheted up.

Rori faltered, then shook her head as if to get the impression of him out of it. "No? Then whose was it? I couldn't even get a letter of reference after I was fired, and you . . ." She shook her head again, harder. "Why am I even trying to talk to you? It's impossible." Her jaw clenched, and I saw more of a similarity between the sisters. "Go," she said. "Just go. And don't come back. Not ever." She was shaking. "If I ever see you again, I'll be forced to do something I'll regret."

"Oh, now, Rori. You know you don't mean that." But uncertainty flickered in his eyes.

"I swear, Tucker. I'll do whatever it takes to get you to leave me alone. *Whatever it takes.*"

My lips parted in surprise at the same time Aggie pushed by me to stand by her daughters.

"I think you'd better move along, son." Her tone was firm, but when her eyes met his, she swayed a little.

Mungo moved to stand beside Rori, his feet planted foursquare and his shoulders hunched. This time his growl was quite audible.

Tucker stared at my dog, taken aback. Looked up at me. Then at Eliza. "Ah. I see. Right. I'll just be on my way then. If you change your mind, I'm at the Spotlight Motel." He paused. "My apartment is being, er, exterminated. You know, termites." He turned and started toward the street. On the sidewalk, he stopped and peered left and right, then looked at Rori over his shoulder. His hand came up, and he made the universal phone gesture with his thumb by his ear and his little finger by his lips.

I'll call you, he mouthed, then turned and, dodging a mail carrier who had paused on the sidewalk to watch the exchange, scurried in the direction of the river.

The gardener who'd been trimming the hedge stood looking between the departing man and the cluster of women in the doorway.

When we stepped back, Eliza didn't quite slam the door, but it was close. To my surprise, she reached down and gave Mungo a quick scritch behind his ears. "Good dog."

I looked around at the other three women standing in the foyer. "Was that who I think it was?"

"Tucker Abbott." Aggie appeared to have regained her equilibrium.

"My ex-husband." Rori's face was blotchy with emotion.

Eliza shook her head. "Thank God you didn't have any children with that man."

A strangled sound rose in Rori's throat. Clutching the music box, she turned and fled up the stairs.

"Eliza, really. Was that necessary?" Aggie asked.

She pressed her lips together. "You must agree, Mother. It's a blessing they didn't. Rori would have had to deal with that troglodyte for the rest of her life if they had a child. As it was, their marriage, short as it was, never should have happened. I'll never forgive Declan for introducing them." Eliza looked at me. "I'm sorry you had to witness that."

"I, uh. Well. Tucker is certainly . . . interesting."

"He's a wolf in sheep's clothing. Don't be fooled, Katie."

"Oh, I wasn't."

She quirked an eyebrow at me, perhaps reassessing me as I had her.

Then the moment was gone. Eliza turned away and

put her hand on the banister. "I'd better go make nice with Rori." She sighed and trudged up the stairs. "Thank you for the goodies, Katie."

"You're welcome," I called to her retreating back. It had been a small price to pay for not having to argue with her about my wedding party. The floor show had been a bit intense, though.

"Well, my dear." Aggie half smiled. "Welcome to the McCarthy clan."

I gave her a wry look and bent to pick up Mungo. "Thanks, *Mom*."

She looked surprised, and I couldn't help grinning as I turned to leave.

Then I saw something that I hadn't noticed before and paused. The mirror on the wall over the entry table had a frame constructed of stained glass.

And the designs in that glass were of dragonflies in every conceivable color.

Oh, for Pete's sake. Enough already. I got it.

Whatever I was supposed to be on the lookout for, it had something to do with Tucker Abbott. Or maybe, Tucker Abbott himself was what I was supposed to be on the lookout for. I certainly hadn't cared for the way he talked to Rori. Still, he hadn't seemed dangerous. Just . . . icky—and maybe a little paranoid.

"Katie? Are you all right?" Aggie asked.

I forced a smile and began walking to the door. "Fine and dandy. A little tired." I opened the door and stepped outside. "See you soon."

"Okay . . ." her voice trailed behind me as I hurried to my car.

Halfway across the street, I realized my shoulders

were bent forward. I straightened and lifted my chin, immediately feeling better. Dragonflies or no, whatever they portended this time was going to have to wait. It was too soon since the last time the appearance of my totem had preceded a tragedy.

Simply too darn soon.

And nothing was going to ruin my wedding.

Chapter 3

On the way back to the bakery, I shoved all thought of dragonflies out of my mind and tried to wrap my mind around what had just happened with my future in-laws. I'd known Rori was divorced but didn't know many of the details. I still didn't, despite having met her ex.

Well, not exactly met. The image of his face as he'd realized that I could see through his glamour flicked onto my mental movie screen.

"You know," I said to Mungo, who was buckled back into the passenger seat. "The more I think about it, the more I have to wonder if this Tucker fellow realizes what he's doing. Could he simply think he's that naturally attractive and persuasive?"

Yip!

"He has to know he's fooling people, that he's a different guy inside than what he projects." I stopped at a red light and glanced over at Mungo. He was watching me with bright, intelligent eyes. "Which begs the question of what he is inside, really. I mean, he's obviously a jerk, but there was a pretty unpleasant undercurrent to his vibe. And what's up with that music box? I have a lot of questions for Declan."

However, they'd have to wait. My familiar yawned, then settled farther into the seat as the light turned green. I accelerated toward the parking garage near the Honeybee.

The bakery was packed, and the afternoon passed in a busy blur. I managed to break away to research possible wedding officiants who could step in for Judge Matthews and left two of them voice mails checking on availability. I didn't feel great about either of them, since I didn't know them. Still, we needed someone to marry us, and I was hoping I'd at least have some options by the time Declan got off work.

By closing time, I was tired and hungry. Uncle Ben must have been, too, because he offered to pick up some takeout from Rancho Alegre and bring it to the carriage house. He and Lucy were coming over to help get the last things in order, including unpacking boxes I'd been ferrying from Declan's apartment for more than a week.

"Oh, yum. That would be awesome." I turned off the music and reached for the light switches.

"What can I get you?" He had a pen in his hand, waiting to take my order.

"Hmm. How about a Cuban bowl. No, the ropa vieja." Shredded beef in creole sauce. *Yum.* "No, wait." I held up my hand. "The pabellón criollo." My stomach audibly growled at the very thought of the shredded beef in creole sauce with the additions of fried egg, rice, black beans, plantains, and queso fresco.

My uncle grinned.

I let my hand drop. "Go ahead and laugh. I'm hungry, and I love that place."

"You skipped lunch again, didn't you?" Lucy asked.

I shrugged. "No time."

She made a face but didn't admonish me. "We'll see you at your house, then."

"Sounds good. And thanks for spending your evening doing this."

"Oh, it won't take long."

"I don't know." I picked up Mungo so he wouldn't have to walk on the hot pavement outside. "There are a lot of boxes."

"And we'll have a lot of help. I called in the cavalry."

"The spellbook club?"

"Sounds like they can all make it. Honeybee? We're ready to go," Lucy called.

In response, the orange-and-yellow-striped feline strolled languidly out from the library section of the bakery and stepped delicately into her fancy leather carrier.

Bending to kiss my aunt on the cheek, I said, "You are a gem. And they're gems, too."

"I'll get enough food for everyone." Ben reached into his pocket for his keys.

I gave him a kiss on the cheek for good measure and grabbed my tote bag.

Cookie Rios was already there when my familiar and I arrived at the carriage house. She was standing on the sidewalk by the street, chatting with my neighbor and good friend, Margie Coopersmith. Cookie's baby bump had become pronounced beneath her lime green sundress, and her jade-colored eyes sparkled as she laughed at something my neighbor said. The bright sunshine brought out hints of natural red in her black hair, and her golden-brown skin glowed with health and happiness. A silver pendant in the shape of a stylized heart hung around her neck. It was an intricate piece of jewelry, but I knew it also happened to be a voodoo talisman of love her husband, Oscar, had given her.

Margie wore khaki shorts and a sleeveless button-front shirt. Her white-blond hair was swept into a practical ponytail, and her broad Scandinavian face was tanned from a summer spent with her kids at the community swimming pool. She kept a practiced eye on Baby Bart, her three-year-old who would probably still be "Baby Bart" when he was fifteen. The older Coopersmith twins, Jonathan and Julia, could be heard playing in their backyard.

My friends turned when Mungo barreled out of my car and headed straight for Bart. The little boy greeted the dog with outstretched arms. Moments later they were both sprawled on the lawn, and Bart was shrieking with laughter.

Margie motioned me over. "Thank heavens you're going to be back home in another week. Us married ladies are going to have to get together for a glass of wine so I can regale you with advice on wifedom."

Experience told me the wine would be pink, it would be sweet, and it would come in a jug almost too big to lift.

Cookie rolled her eyes. "Just like she's been offering

me advice on momdom." Though she'd moved to the United States with her mother and brother when she was a child, a slight Haitian accent still lilted beneath her words.

Margie wagged her finger and grinned. "I've had both those boxes checked for years. You might as well take advantage of my experience."

"It's true she makes the mom thing look effortless," I told Cookie. "And she does a lot of it by herself, too, since Redding's on the road so much." Margie's husband was a long-haul truck driver. "Come to think of it, they make the marriage thing look pretty easy, too, even with his job taking him away. Maybe we should listen to her."

"Ha!" Margie said. "Maybe our marriage works so well exactly because that man of mine is gone so much!" Her tone was bantering, and she was laughing, but I could tell she missed him.

"How long this time?" I asked.

"Another few days. Don't worry. He'll be back in time for the wedding."

I nodded. "Good. Are the flower kids still excited?" I'd asked the JJs, which was Jonathan and Julia's collective moniker, to be my flower kids at the wedding.

"Over the moon." Margie pulled out her phone to check the time. "Speaking of those two, I suppose I should wrestle up some grub for them. I'm trying one of those meal services. You know, the ones that send you all the ingredients and you simply put it all together?" Margie was the first to admit she was a consummate disaster in the kitchen.

"How's that going?" Cookie asked.

"I've only tried two of them. Burned the first one, and the second one was too raw to eat. Threw it away and nuked some mac and cheese. But if we go with the Goldilocks principle, tonight's dinner should be just right. At least I hope so. It's chicken tacos, and those kids love themselves a taco."

"Third time's a charm," I agreed. "Good luck!"

She gave us a thumbs-up, leaned down, and took Bart's hand. Together they walked toward her house. Mungo looked up at me from where he'd been playing with Bart.

Yip?

"Come on, little guy. Let's get to work."

Jaida's SUV pulled up behind the Lexus that Cookie had purchased when she started selling real estate. The back door of the vehicle lifted, and Jaida's familiar bounded out. Anubis was a Great Dane with gorgeous brindle markings. The huge dog reached Mungo in three leaps, and the two touched noses in greeting. Jaida exited her vehicle, briefcase in one hand, bottle of wine in the other.

"You've come prepared," I said.

"I thought we might want provisions. Sorry, Cookie."

"There's sweet tea in the fridge," I said.

"That'll be fine," the younger witch said. "I never drank much before the pregnancy, so I don't exactly miss it."

"I would," Jaida said with feeling. "Especially wine with dinner." She held up her briefcase. "I need to change my clothes. Came straight from court."

Her silky blue suit gave testimony to that. She'd cut her hair quite short for the summer and had switched out contact lenses for tortoiseshell-framed glasses that suited her strong features and mahogany skin. She was one of the best defense attorneys in Savannah, a kick-ass witch who specialized in tarot, and a wonderful friend.

"You brought clothes in your briefcase?" I asked.

"Well, sure. All my work stuff is in my computer bag."

"Right." We walked to the tiny porch of the carriage house, and I opened the door for them. "I'll join you in a sec. I'm going to let the dogs into the backyard."

Anubis and Mungo happily gamboled through the gate as soon as I opened it. It was shady back there, and a small stream cut diagonally across one corner with cold, clear water for them to drink.

As I came back around toward the front door, Lucy pulled up in her 1964 convertible Thunderbird. Mimsey Carmichael was in the passenger seat and popped out the door as soon as Lucy put the car in Park. She bustled toward me, blue eyes twinkling, and her mouth curved up in a delighted smile. The bright pink of her gauze tunic and slacks made her look like a spring camellia bloom, and the bow perched on the side of her white pageboy haircut matched perfectly in tone. Pink was the color of both calm and energy, as well as youth and childlike joy. Mimsey loved color magic and wore pink a lot. Perhaps that accounted for her youthful appearance and demeanor though she was over eighty.

"Lucille offered me a ride, and I took her up on it

faster than green grass through a goose. I do love a convertible."

"You should get one, then."

"Don't think I haven't thought about it. Especially one like Bianca's." She pointed.

I looked over to see the last member of the spellbook club parking across the street. I agreed with Mimsey. I loved Lucy's big ol' boat of a soft top, but Bianca Devereaux drove a cherry red Jaguar.

She turned off the rumbling engine and got out. Her cropped slacks and a lacy cold-shoulder top looked cool and comfy and probably cost more than my new refrigerator. Bianca had made a ton of money in the stock market after her husband discovered her newfound interest in Wicca and moon magic. The jerk had left her high and dry. That was bad enough, but he'd also unforgivably abandoned their daughter, Colette. However, Bianca had found she had a talent with numbers and investments—and the occasional spell didn't hurt, either. With some of her investment proceeds, she'd opened Moon Grapes, a wine store on Factors Walk overlooking the river. She, too, carried a wine bottle.

Of all of us, Bianca looked the most like a stereotypical witch. Her long black hair was piled high atop her head this evening, her skin remained almost translucently pale despite the fact we were well into summer, and her green eyes were so bright they would have been alarming if they didn't contain so much kindness.

Lucy had gotten out of her car with Honeybee's carrier, and now waited for Bianca. As they approached, a white ferret with a black Zorro mask peeked out of Bianca's bag. Puck was an unconventional familiar, but at least he didn't give me the heebie-jeebies like Cookie's did. Which reminded me that I hadn't seen Rafe, Cookie's king snake. He was probably lounging at the bottom of her bag, content to stay hidden and not frighten Margie. Rafe was a nice enough snake, as snakes go, but I'd be fine if he remained hidden. I wasn't unhappy that Heckle, Mimsey's obnoxious parrot, had apparently elected to remain on his perch in her flower shop, either. He was a loyal and brave companion to her, but he wasn't above offering the occasional mean-spirited comment.

"Looks like the gang's all here," Lucy announced with a smile. "Show us where to start, and we'll see what we can get done before Ben shows up with our supper."

I went to hold the door for them. "You all are the best friends. Thank you for coming to help get this place in order."

"You'd do the same for any of us," Mimsey said as she stepped across the threshold.

That was true but didn't make me any less grateful.

"Oh . . ." Bianca trailed off as she came inside. She hadn't seen the place since it had been gutted after the fire. "I love it."

"Nice fireplace," Jaida said, trailing her fingers along the gray stone mantel as she passed it on her way to the bedroom to change her clothes.

I gazed around in satisfaction. The hand-scraped teak floor gleamed, and the formerly peach walls were now painted a gentle sage green. We'd replaced the purple fainting couch and wingback chairs I'd found on Craigslist right after I'd moved to Savannah with a contemporary sofa and matching chair in a dark eggplant shade. Declan's red rocking chair, repainted a deep maroon and softened with pillows, joined the seating area around a low coffee table. That filled up most of the postage stamp living room, and we'd painted the built-in bookcases by the short hall to the bedroom and bathroom a darker shade of the green on the walls. They would soon be filled from the boxes stacked in front of them.

The wooden shutters that covered the windows had also suffered from the flames and smoke, but I'd loved how they'd looked. The replacements were lighter and had adjustable louvers. Opposite the front entrance, French doors still opened out to the back patio, a poured cement affair that was next on my list to spruce up when our budget allowed.

Which wasn't going to be for a while. Between the wedding—even though we'd kept costs down with the help of our friends—and the renovations, we'd gone through the insurance proceeds and tapped our savings. Even our honeymoon would have to wait.

I didn't care, though. Being back in the home I'd adored since the very first time I'd laid eyes on it, new and improved and with my new husband, was all I could wish for.

"Most of the changes are in the other rooms," I said, sparing a glance up at the loft. It was our television room as well as the guest room, but with the expansion of the bathroom and the addition of a laundry room and a walk-in closet on the main floor, the space above had grown as well. There was room in the loft for a queen-sized foldout sofa now, rather than the futon I'd had before, and we'd added an office area by the window that looked over the backyard.

Jaida returned from the bedroom wearing white shorts and a black tank top. She strode to the entrance of the kitchen, now twice as wide as it had been so the space between the kitchen and the living room felt more open, and the rest of us joined her.

"You guys can really cook in here," she said with an overblown wink. "If you know what I mean."

"Jaida!" Lucy said.

I shook my head.

Bianca rolled her eyes. "Where are your wineglasses?"

"In one of those boxes." I waved at the stack on the floor.

"Never mind," Lucy said, leaning down. Her cat was out of the carrier and batting at a half-open carton. "Honeybee found some juice glasses. We'll use those."

I stifled a sneeze and rubbed my eyes. Bianca had brewed a moon potion that had largely cured my allergy to cats, but now my sniffles seemed to be kicking back in.

Lucy straightened with a glass in each hand and noticed my distress. "Oh, dear. Honeybee, I think you need to join the boys in the backyard."

The cat arched a skeptical eyebrow before agreeably sauntering to the French doors. Mimsey opened one side, and Honeybee went out to join Mungo and Anubis, who were collapsed in the shade of the gazebo.

"Now." Lucy rubbed her hands together and looked around. "Let's dive in."

And dive in we did, juice glasses of wine at hand, and managed to empty several boxes before Ben showed up. Once he did, we set up the unbelievably fragrant Cuban food buffet style on the counter and loaded my newly unpacked Fiestaware plates to take into the living room to eat. It was a tight fit for everyone, even though the familiars willingly partook of their share al fresco and left the indoors to us.

I was so hungry by then that I ate like a ranch hand. Soon, I was back in the kitchen for seconds. My phone rang on the counter as I was returning to the living room, and I doubled back to grab it. My heart did a little happy dance when I saw it was Declan. The image of my handsome fiancé flashed through my mind as I put my plate down and answered his call. I always missed him during his weekly forty-eight-hour stint at the firehouse.

"Hi there!" I greeted him. "Guess what? The spell-book club is all here, helping to unpack. I thought it would take me all night, but we'll probably be done in a couple of hours."

"Hey, darlin'. Glad to hear it." There was something in his voice.

I took a deep breath. I didn't want Declan to know how much I worried now that his guardian spirit wasn't watching and guiding him. On one hand, I never wanted him to doubt that I had the utmost confidence in his ability to deal with anything that might come up. On the other, I figured the last thing he needed was to worry about my worrying about him.

Keeping my tone light, I asked, "Is anything wrong?"

He took a deep breath. "You could certainly say that." Another deep breath.

With difficulty, I waited. Whatever it was, Declan wasn't too injured to phone me.

"Rori just called me. She found her ex-husband at the Spotlight Motel."

A deep sense of dread plunked into my solar plexus. "Found? What do you mean, found?"

"He's dead."

Chapter 4

"*Dead?* How? Oh, Declan."

"More than just dead, is my guess. I mean . . . well, you haven't met Tucker. He's . . . he *was* a real piece of . . . anyway, for some reason Rori called me instead of the cops. She told me there's blood, and the room's torn apart, so I'm guessing he didn't die from natural causes." I heard the roar of an engine.

"Are you in your truck?"

"Yeah, I'm on my way over there. I've already called the police. I don't get why she was even there. I have a really bad feeling about this."

The image of dozens of multicolored dragonflies flashed to mind.

"I have a bad feeling, too. See, I met Tucker this afternoon." I told him everything I could remember from my visit to his family's vacation rental, ending with, "Declan, there was something off about the guy."

"I'll say. But he's been out of her life for three years. Why would she go to that motel when she loathes the guy?"

"I'm guessing he still had some sway over her."

He swore quietly.

"Where's Rori now?" I asked.

"I told her to go to the motel office and wait. Then I notified the police and called you."

"I'll be there as soon as I can," I said. "I'll bring Jaida." A glance at my friend elicited a nod of agreement as she rose from her seat on the sofa and grabbed her briefcase. "You know—just in case." I was thinking of Rori's parting words to her ex that afternoon.

I'll do whatever it takes to get you to leave me alone.

Surely, she wouldn't have . . . nah. I knew better than that. Still, having a lawyer around wouldn't be a bad idea.

"Thanks." I could hear his relief in the single word. He might be the big bad emergency responder, but this was his baby sister. "I love you."

"I love you, too," I said.

We ended the call, and I turned to see everyone had stopped eating to listen to my end of the conversation. Ben and Lucy stood at almost the same time.

"What was that all about?" Cookie asked from the rocking chair. "Who's dead?"

"Rori's ex-husband. Tucker Abbott. She found him at the Spotlight Motel."

Jaida wrinkled her nose and moved toward the door. "That's a pretty seedy place. What was she doing there?"

"No idea," I said. "She wouldn't tell Declan anything on the phone. He's on his way over there, and so are the police. Sorry to bolt like this. Lucy, will you take Mungo with you and watch him tonight? I don't know what's going to happen, or when I'll be home."

43

"Of course," she said. "Don't worry about a thing. Shall I take Anubis, too?"

Jaida shook her head. "Gregory's working late at the office." Gregory was her partner in life and law. "I'll drop Noobie on the way and meet you at the Spotlight."

"All right," Lucy said, then looked at her husband. "Ben."

He smiled at her with his eyes. "Of course I'm going with them. How about I drive, Katie?"

My shoulders relaxed a little. "Thanks, Uncle Ben. I'll get my bag."

"One of you call Lucy when you find out what's going on," Mimsey demanded as we were going out the door. "Then she can let the rest of us know."

"Okay," I agreed, and offered a faltering smile to the four women still gathered in my living room.

"It'll be okay," Bianca said with a confidence I didn't feel. Then I remembered not too long ago when I'd said the same thing to her. Turned out, I'd been right.

Jaida called Anubis from the backyard and they hurried to her vehicle. She drove off almost before Ben and I were out the door.

"Did Declan talk directly to Quinn?" Ben asked as we crossed the front yard.

My uncle had been Declan's mentor in the fire department. Their deep, almost father-son relationship had been the reason I'd met Declan in the first place. They'd both known Detective Peter Quinn for years. I'd met the detective after moving to Savannah, but since then I'd ended up involved in eight of his homicide investigations in a little over two years—the last one only a month before.

Quinn was not going to be happy when he saw me again so soon.

"I'm pretty sure he'd have told me if he had." I grabbed my phone out of my tote bag. "I'll call Quinn on the way."

Ben pulled open the passenger door for me. I was about to slide into the seat when two brown eyes blinked at me in the dim light of the cab. My familiar cocked his head at me as if to say, *What took you so long?*

"Dang it, Mungo. How do you *do* that?" When he'd first come into my life, he'd insisted on showing up in the back seat of my car whenever I left for work. Eventually, I'd had to agree to let him come with me to the Honeybee every day.

Now his mouth opened in a wide doggy grin that showed his pink tongue and pearly canines.

"You are one stubborn boy," I said. "Okay, fine. You can come. But you've got to stay in the truck. I'll leave the windows wide open, but you can't jump out and nose your way into things. I have to be able to trust you. Deal?"

Yip!

Ben rolled his eyes and closed the door after I was seated with my dog on my lap. "You gals and your animals. Sheesh." He wasn't a witch, but because of Lucy, he'd known the spellbook club members for years. Thankfully, he accepted our quirks with equanimity and good humor.

For the most part, at least.

Ben headed toward the Southside neighborhood, and I called Lucy to let her know she didn't have to dog-sit my familiar after all. Then I brought up Detective Quinn's direct cell number on my phone. After six rings, my call went to his voice mail.

"Hey, Quinn. I understand a body was found at the Spotlight Motel. There's a—" I stopped myself from saying a personal connection. That could come across entirely wrong. And I didn't want to mention Rori until I knew more. "—a reason I'm interested in this case, and wanted to give you a heads-up that Ben and I are on our way over there." I hung up and looked over at Ben.

"That sounded pretty lame," he said.

I sighed. "Yeah. You'd think I'd know what to say in circumstances like this."

Ben reached over and patted my shoulder before putting his hand back on the wheel to make a turn onto Bull Street. "If memory serves, you've never been in circumstances quite like this before."

"No kidding," I muttered.

Mungo licked my chin, then leaned his head against my chest. I settled back and wrapped my arms around him. Ben stopped at the red light on Derenne Avenue, the intersection where Bull turned into White Bluff Road. My thoughts racing too fast to track, I watched drivers pumping gas under the sterile LED lights of the Chevron station. Ben was quiet, too. Soon we were winding past Bianca's neighborhood of Habersham Woods and then the Oglethorpe Mall.

"You obviously know where we're going," I said.

"Occupational hazard," he said. "You get to know everything about a town when you're its fire chief."

"Do you know anything about the Spotlight? I don't know it."

"It's been around since the fifties. Back then, it was quite something, I guess. The original owners had a café across the street, too. The Dizzy Spoon." He shrugged. "Now the Spotlight is simply a cheap place to stay the night. Or the week."

"The hour?"

He side-eyed a look my way, then returned his attention to the road. "No-tell motel? Not that I'm aware of."

"I was asking because Jaida said it was seedy."

"Hm. Well, yes. There have been a few incidents over the years. Low-level stuff, though. Not murder."

He made a few more turns, and the blur of emergency lights painting the darkening sky guided us the last few blocks to our destination.

The Spotlight was on the edge. It was on the edge between Midtown and Southside. It was on the edge between a residential area and a strip mall that featured a laundromat, a pawn shop, a nail salon, a sub shop, and a low-rent lawyer I'd seen advertise on late-night television.

One final turn revealed the tableau: a single-level series of rooms in an L-shape, each with a parking space directly in front of the door. At the end of the short branch of the L, neon script in the window read OFFICE with V C NCY flashing beneath it. A tall, Sputnik-shaped sign hovered above the empty swimming pool in front of the office. The sign read SPOTLIGHT MOTEL and below that advertised *Wi-fi!* in an excited font above the well-worn offerings of *Free HBO* and *Air Conditioning*.

Declan's king-cab truck was parked on the street in front of the whole shebang, which made sense because the parking lot was crammed with emergency vehicles. I recognized the white van near the motel office and knew Ed Carroll, the Chatham County medical examiner, must have already arrived. An ambulance with a caduceus on the side and a Savannah fire truck took up a chunk of real estate in the middle of the lot. I knew this place didn't fall within the jurisdiction of Five House, where Declan was stationed, so he'd had to take off from work to go to a call another firehouse was responding to.

A call he'd instigated. Oy.

Ah, and there, at the far end of the lot, half hidden by a patrol car: Detective Quinn's nondescript gray Chevy.

Ben parked his truck right behind Declan's. The temperature was still in the eighties, and we rolled the windows all the way down for Mungo. I reminded him to stay inside. I could have sworn he rolled his eyes before he stood on his hind legs and put his front paws on the side of the door to watch us walk toward the fray.

No one had cordoned off the lot yet, but we paused at the edge. None of the bustling police and paramedics seemed to notice us. That wouldn't last long, I was sure.

"Stay here," I whispered to Ben. "I'll be right back."

Luckily, he didn't follow as I quickly strode around the edge of the lot and made my way toward where most of the activity seemed to be centered, at the doorway of Unit 11.

I'd seen more dead bodies than I liked to admit, and it was something I'd be happy never to have to do again. However, there was something in particular I wanted to see in this case. When the officer by the door was called away, I edged to the opening and carefully looked around the jamb.

The room was a mess. Drawers had been pulled out, even in the brightly lit bathroom at the back, and the bed had been stripped. The cushions of the single armchair leaned haphazardly against the wall. There hadn't been time to process the scene, so the room was also empty of people—except the one on the floor. Tucker was sprawled between the foot of the bed and the pressboard dresser that served as a television stand. He wore the same chinos and button-down shirt he had earlier that day. One of his loafers was half off his foot. I was pretty sure the smudge of red at his temple was blood.

Finally, I gathered my courage and looked at his face. His not-exactly-perfect face. Gone with the shimmer of life was the glamour he'd hidden behind. Gone, too, was the slimy feeling I'd sensed from him. He was just a blond man with eyebrows that were bushier than I remembered, a slightly crooked nose, and a rather weak chin. Still, I recognized him as Rori's ex.

There was a buzz in the air of the room, I realized. The feeling of ozone if not the smell itself. Closing my eyes, I reached out with my witchy senses. They confirmed my initial thought that strong magic had taken place here. However, all I sensed now was aftermath. The magic itself had left the building.

Was I feeling the remnants of Tucker's glamour now that he was dead, or was this something else?

"Please, ma'am. You need to move along," a uniformed officer said. "We're asking residents to return to their rooms until we can speak with them." He gestured vaguely.

"All right, Officer. Thank you." I turned and headed down the row of rooms.

Ben waited by the corner of the building where I'd left him. "What did you see?"

"Nothing good," I said. "Whatever happened, I think Declan was right when he said Tucker Abbott didn't die of natural causes."

Another van turned into the parking lot and managed to secure a spot. Two crime-scene techs exited the vehicle and beelined straight to the open door of Unit 11.

The roar of an engine on the street behind us turned out to be Jaida arriving. She swung into an open spot down the street and seconds later was hurrying toward us.

"What's the sitch?" she asked.

"Don't know yet," I said. "You made good time."

"Traffic was light," she said in a distracted tone as her assessing gaze flicked over the scene. "Let's go see what's up."

We started toward the office. As we neared, I saw movement behind the glass door, and a moment later, it swung open. Declan came out with Rori. He wore his uniform pants and dark blue SAVANNAH FIRE T-shirt but had changed from work boots into running shoes. One hand was clasped protectively around his sister's shoulder as he scanned the area. His blue gaze paused on Ben's truck, then found me.

We met halfway, and I reached out to touch his arm. His hair was limp with perspiration, and worry creased the skin around his eyes.

"Are you okay?" I asked Rori.

"I guess so." Her throat worked, and her eyes were red and swollen.

"Oh, honey." I gave her a big squeeze.

"Hi, Ben," she said when I stepped back. Then she gave Jaida a quick, uncertain half smile before saying, "I'm sorry about all this."

"Hey there, yourself," Ben said in a gentle voice. "Now don't you fret. We're gonna—"

Frowning, I broke in. "What do you mean? Why would you be sorry?"

Her wave indicated the whole fracas in the parking lot. "All this. You having to come here. The timing so close to the wedding." Her eyes teared up. "Everything."

Alarmed, I looked at Declan, then back at her. "You can't possibly think this is your fault."

She sniffed.

Declan squeezed her shoulder and sighed. I could tell he was frustrated. "My little sis here takes on a lot of burdens. Tucker was especially good at triggering her guilt. I keep telling you, Rori—you didn't do anything wrong."

"I know," she said in a small voice.

Jaida stepped forward and introduced herself. "Jaida

French, attorney at law. I'm a friend of Declan and Katie's."

"Oh, okay. Um, nice to meet you." Rori looked between Declan and me uncertainly. "Do I need a lawyer?"

"I hope not," Declan muttered.

"What happened?" I asked.

Rori took a deep breath, and it seemed to re-center her. "Tucker called me."

Just like he said he would.

She went on. "He told me he needed me to come here tonight."

Declan's face flushed, but he didn't say anything.

"Go on," I prompted.

She made a face. "He said he wanted me to bring the music box he'd given me."

"Wait," Jaida said. "What music box?"

"Her ex-husband gave it to her this afternoon," I said.

Rori nodded. "He said he was sorry but he owed someone some money and needed to sell it. He wouldn't let up. Finally, I told him I'd bring it."

"Rori!" Declan's face had turned bright red. "What were you thinking?"

Beside me, Jaida sighed. I hadn't had a chance to tell her about Tucker's glamour. However, he'd convinced Rori over the phone to come to the motel. Could he have used his Voice—a magical augmentation of words that made them irresistible? Because that took conscious, focused effort. I also happened to know from experience that using one's Voice could be quite effective even over the phone.

Not knowledge I was proud of, by the way.

"What did Eliza and Mother have to say about you coming here?" Declan didn't mask his distaste.

"I didn't exactly, you know . . . tell them. I took an Uber."

"That's what I thought," he said.

"I'm sorry," she almost wailed. "I had to come, or he'd just keep bugging me. I don't know what nonsense he was up to—and yes, I did know he was up to something, because Tucker was *always* up to something—but I wanted to give him the music box back—along with a piece of my mind—and get closure. Final and forever closure."

He opened his mouth to say something else but then closed it with what appeared to be great effort.

"Okay," Jaida said. "So what happened when you got here?"

"I knocked on the door. No one answered, but it wasn't quite closed, so I pushed it open." She shuddered.

"And then?" I asked, as gently as I could.

"I'd like to know that, too," came a voice behind me.

We all turned to see who'd spoken. Detective Peter Quinn looked cool and collected as usual. Tan and always smartly dressed, he managed the Savannah summer like a pro in his sports jackets and ties. The silver in his hair reflected the blue and red lights, and his gray eyes betrayed absolutely nothing he was thinking.

"Hello, Quinn," I said. Then I corrected my informality for Rori. "Detective Quinn, I mean."

"Ms. Lightfoot. I got your message. Very informative."

I half smiled and let his sarcasm pass.

"Ben." He nodded to my uncle. "McCarthy." Another nod, and then he looked at Rori. "And you're Aurora McCarthy?"

She swallowed audibly and nodded. "Yes sir."

He licked his lips. "I see. You're related to Declan here?"

"He's my brother," she answered. "See, he and Katie are getting married. I'm in town for the wedding, along with my mother and sister. All my sisters. And their families. But only Eliza is here now. And my mother . . ."

Quinn waited until she grew quiet, then said, "All right. Now that we have that established, would you like to tell me about the dead body you found?"

"He's my ex-husband. Tucker Abbott. I opened the door to his room when he didn't answer. The light in the bathroom was on, and there he was . . . on the floor." She shuddered.

"He was expecting you?" Quinn asked.

Rori nodded miserably.

He frowned, then looked around at the rest of us. "Ms. McCarthy, I'd like to speak with you someplace a bit more private. The motel manager has agreed to let me use one of the rooms here for interviews. Will you please come with me?"

She looked terrified but said, "Um, I guess."

Jaida stepped forward. "My client will be happy to assist in any way she can."

Rori threw her a grateful look and visibly relaxed.

The barest flash of irritation crossed Quinn's face as he realized Jaida wasn't going to let him talk to Rori alone, but it disappeared so quickly I wasn't sure I'd seen it at all. He nodded and gestured for them to follow him.

"We'll wait here," Declan called.

His sister shot him a weak smile over her shoulder.

"Let's wait in the office," he said to Ben and me. "It's cooler."

Chapter 5

It wasn't just cooler; it was like an icebox inside the office of the Spotlight Motel. I shivered and looked around. There was a wooden counter to my left and a row of three plastic molded chairs on my right. Two vending machines took up most of the opposite wall, a well-stocked hot drink station between them. Behind the counter, there was a tight space that fit a recliner, side table, and small television. An open doorway on the far side of the recliner led to another room, and I glimpsed enough to realize there was a small apartment attached to the office.

Maybe the motel could be considered seedy, but everything I saw in here was as neat as a pin and very clean. The floor was spotless, and the items on the counter were neatly arranged, including the framed nameplate that read DAYLEEN in red and purple counted cross-stitch. Two healthy Boston ferns hung in the corners, and the air smelled faintly of coffee and lavender room spray.

A woman hurried through the doorway from the

apartment. "I'm so sorry, but we're not taking any more guests this . . . oh, it's you again." She said this to Declan. "How's your sister?"

"Talking with the police detective now."

She waved her hand in our direction. "And they're with you?"

"Yes. Ben, Katie, this is Dayleen Stefanos. She takes care of things around here."

We nodded to each other.

"Hey, I'm going to go check in on what's going on," my fiancé said. "I'll be right back." He exited, and I saw him heading toward a group of firefighters who were talking in the parking lot.

I guessed the motel manager to be in her mid-forties. She was tall and lean, with a face that had seen plenty of sunshine over the years and long yellow hair in a braid that fell over one shoulder. The white tank top she wore over cutoff jeans revealed well-muscled arms. Ginormous gold hoop earrings brushed her shoulders whenever she turned her head. Her eyes were red-rimmed, her mascara smudged.

"Nice to meet you, Dayleen," Ben said. "Are you any relation to Nick Stefanos?"

Her brown eyes flashed. "He's my brother. You know him?"

Of course he does. Sometimes it seemed as if my uncle knew everyone in town.

"We've played golf a few times," he said. "Good guy. Terrible putter, though."

"Yeah," she said softly and looked away. I could tell she wasn't thinking about her brother or his golf skills.

Ben took a step forward and leaned against the counter. "Rough night, huh?"

"I'll say." She frowned and ran her hand over her face. "Rougher for Tucker."

No kidding.

"Terrible having something like this on your property," Ben said. "You own the place?"

She shook her head. "I live here and manage it."

She'd called Rori's ex by his first name, as if he might be more than a guest of her establishment.

I moved to stand by Ben. "Did you know Tucker Abbott well?"

Her eyes filled, and she nodded her head. Finally, she managed, "He'd been living here almost two weeks."

Two weeks? No way would it take that long to exterminate termites, even in an entire apartment building. He lied to Rori about why he was staying at the Spotlight.

"Such a sweetheart. His girlfriend had kicked him out," Dayleen continued. "I think he'd lost his job, too."

Well, that answered that.

"Oh, dear," I said. "Where was that?"

Beside me, Ben cleared his throat, but I ignored him. Asking questions in a situation like this was second nature. Besides, I was honestly curious about what kind of work Tucker had done.

But Dayleen's shoulders came up to her ears and dropped, a gesture I took to mean she didn't know.

I barreled ahead. "So you two became friends?"

"Uh-huh." She sniffed.

"Good friends?" I raised my eyebrows, while at the

same time giving her an encouraging and sympathetic smile.

She understood. "Oh, not like that. I mean, he'd come hang out in here sometimes. You know, when he needed someone to talk to. But that was all. He wanted to get back together with his girlfriend."

Dayleen was a soft shoulder to cry on.

She ducked her head. "Besides, Tucker was a little young for me."

A soft shoulder who had a crush on him.

"Was he close to any of the other residents?"

"Nah. We don't get many guests this time of year." Suddenly, her head came up. "Oh, God. Someone is going to have to tell his girlfriend. Ex-girlfriend."

"Do you know how to get ahold of her?" I asked.

"Huh-uh."

"Do you know her name?"

"Effie."

"No last name?"

She looked stricken. "He never said."

"It's okay. Did she ever come here?"

Ben side-eyed me, but I ignored him.

"She might have, but I don't know what she looks like," Dayleen said. "A couple of women came to see him. A couple that I know of, that is. It's not like I sit around and watch the units all day. I have a life, you know."

"Well, of course you do," Ben said. "I imagine you have security cameras to keep an eye on things."

Bingo.

However, a regretful expression settled on Dayleen's

face. "We have the cameras all right. They haven't worked for almost a year, though. I keep telling the owners, but it hasn't been a priority." She gave a little snort. "I bet they'll fix them now."

I suppressed a sigh and could sense Ben's disappointment as well.

"Were the two women together?" he asked.

"No. Different days. One was this afternoon. A man a couple of days ago, too. Blond guy. Kind of scary. Whenever Tucker had visitors, it always seemed like there was an argument. I don't know why. He was so nice. From the sound of it, I thought he and the guy were going to fight right there in the parking lot. Next thing I knew, though, he was driving off, and Tucker went back into his room." Talking seemed to help distract her from the upset of a dead body in her motel.

"Do you know if anyone else came to see Tucker today?" Ben asked.

She waved her hand. "Mostly I just hear cars and voices from in here." She glanced at the television, and I wondered how many hours a day she was glued to it. Couldn't blame her, of course.

"I imagine you've already told Detective Quinn all this." I turned and looked out the window at the fracas in the parking lot. All the emergency lights had quieted except a patrol car at the far end of the lot. Declan stood in the cluster of firefighters, listening as one of them spoke and gesticulated wildly. He could have been describing the victim, but for all I knew, he was telling a story about his latest fishing trip. I returned my attention to Dayleen.

"Nooo . . . not yet. But I will." Her eyes sharpened

with suspicion. "You sound kind of like a detective yourself."

Ben jumped in. "Occupational hazard, I guess. We're firefighters." He gestured to where Declan was nodding to his chatty colleague. "Something like this, I guess we just start asking questions and solving problems." He reached over and gave my shoulders a one-armed squeeze. "Guess my niece here picked up on the same tendency."

I watched as her suspicion drained away when she learned he and Declan were firefighters. Not that Ben was anymore, and after becoming fire chief, he hadn't actually fought any fires for years. Still, he had a point. Helping and problem solving were in his blood.

Then she squinted at me. "You're a firefighter?"

"Me? Oh, no. I'm a baker. We own the Honeybee Bakery down on Broughton Street."

"Oh, I've heard of that place. My best friend swears you make the best rosemary scones she's ever tasted."

"You should come in." I extended the invitation automatically. "I'll let you try one for free."

Dayleen gave a little sigh. "Thanks. It's hard to think about eating right now, though."

I ducked my head. "That's for sure." My own lovely Cuban dinner felt heavy in my stomach, and I could feel the beginnings of heartburn.

"I wish I could help more," Dayleen said. Then she brightened. "Wait a sec. I bet the cops can track Effie down at her job."

"You know where she works?" Ben asked.

"Tucker told me she's a hostess at Belford's. Say, I don't suppose you'd tell her about Tucker, would you?" She was looking at Ben when she said it. "You seem awfully nice, and I bet you have lots of experience with situations like that."

Slowly, he nodded. "I do indeed. But the police will handle it. I don't want to step on their toes."

"Yeah, I guess. But she should know."

I saw Declan heading back toward the office. Quinn, Rori, and Jaida were coming out of the motel unit where he'd been conducting his interview. Rori called out, and Declan turned and waited for them. Moments later, the four of them were crowded into the office with Ben and me.

"Lightfoot, I want to talk to you next," Quinn said.

I blinked. "Me? Why?"

"Because," he said curtly.

"Katie?" Jaida asked, and took a step toward me. I shook my head. She nodded and stepped back. Quinn and I had had more than a few conversations, some of them confrontational, but I didn't think this one would require the presence of an attorney. More likely, he wanted to know if there was a magical aspect to this crime, for the simple reason that I was present. He'd only recently learned I was a witch and still had mixed feelings about the idea of magic existing at all. If Jaida was part of the conversation, not only would Quinn feel even more uncomfortable than usual talking about such things, but it would be harder for me to get any information from him. Quid pro quo, and all.

Dayleen watched with curiosity as I followed Quinn back out to the parking lot. Without a word, he strode across the asphalt to Unit 4. I had no choice but to trot after him. Once inside, he closed the door except for a five-inch gap. Protocol, I assumed. He gestured toward the battered desk chair and sank into the worn upholstered chair next to the window.

His lips pressed together as he regarded me across the short distance. "Katie, what the hell is going on?"

Chapter 6

The chair creaked as I shifted my weight. The weak light from the environmentally friendly bulb in the desk lamp cast a circular pall on the industrial carpet in the motel room, and I wondered for a moment how often that carpet was cleaned.

"You know as much as I do, Quinn. More, I should think."

"Is there a . . . paranormal aspect to this homicide? I mean, you *are* Janey-on-the-spot. And when that happens, there always seems to be another layer—or two—to the situation."

I hesitated. Eventually, I'd learned that my supposed "calling" as a lightwitch might account for how often I ended up smack-dab in the middle of police investigations that somehow featured the paranormal. It happened a lot, and I couldn't say I was happy about it in the least. But Savannah was one of the most magical cities in the US, in addition to having bragging rights as the most haunted. If a lightwitch was going to be called, it would be here.

The murder victim's use of a glamour may not have

been intentional, though I couldn't see how it would be so strong otherwise. I only knew the basics about glamours and needed to find out more from an experienced witch in the spellbook club. However, there was the cluster of dragonflies on the potted plants outside Aggie's vacation house, along with the stained-glass dragonflies around the mirror, not to mention the feeling of magic in the air of Tucker's motel room.

Finally, I answered, "I'm not sure. There are some reasons I think there might be. I met the victim this afternoon, and he was using a glamour."

"A what?" Quinn asked.

"A glamour is a kind of magical illusion. I could tell that Tucker was making himself more appealing than he really was."

"Uh-huh." His skepticism was palpable. I was pretty used to it by then, though. "How would something like that get you murdered?"

I shrugged. "Maybe it didn't. I'm just telling you what I know. For all I know, my involvement in this one might only be personal."

He frowned.

"Remember Mavis Templeton?" As if he wouldn't. "The only reason I got involved then was because you wanted to put Uncle Ben in jail."

He had the good manners to blush.

I'd neglected to mention the theory the spellbook club had come up with that Mavis Templeton may have been practicing a bit of black magic on the side before she'd been killed. We'd never really know, but she was one mean old lady, that was for sure.

"It's possible the only reason I'm here is because of

the family connection. Not"—I held my hand up, as if in warning—"that there is a connection per se, other than Rori McCarthy's bad luck in stumbling on her ex-husband's body."

"You're saying it was a coincidence?" He sounded skeptical.

My hand dropped. "Could be. Could also be . . . that whole lightwitch thing I told you about. Or both. Wait. How exactly did Tucker die?"

He shook his head and didn't answer.

I tried again. "Was there anything that made you think there was a paranormal aspect to his death?"

"Nothing struck me like that."

"Okay. From what I understand about Tucker, he was the kind of guy who might have made some enemies." Too late, I realized I didn't know what Rori had or hadn't told Quinn. Maybe I should have had Jaida tag along with me after all.

When Quinn nodded, I was relieved. "Let's just say this isn't the first time Mr. Abbott has crossed our path."

I straightened in my chair. "Oh?"

He gave me a look. "That's not how this works."

"Come on, Quinn. Did he have a record? He must have. I bet there are a half dozen suspects right off the bat."

He rubbed the bridge of his nose. "His name has been linked to a couple cases of fraud, but his legal record is clean. I'll do some more digging, of course. There could be civil suits. And you might be right. Declan's little sis might have been in the wrong place at the wrong time. Problem is, I still don't quite understand why she was here at all." His eyebrows rose a fraction.

I gave him a wide-eyed look. "I'm sorry to hear that. Perhaps it was the way you asked the question?"

He snorted. "Why don't you just tell me, and then we'll be able to cross her off our list and move along."

"Seriously? I have no idea what you all talked about in here, but I'm pretty sure Jaida wouldn't appreciate me weighing in on that interview." I stood. "Tell you what. You check up on the leads related to the fraud cases, and if I find out anything regarding some magical aspect to this murder, I'll let you know."

Glaring, Quinn rose. "Katie, if you know something, you need to come clean."

"I *don't*! But I feel like you're trying to do some kind of end run, for whatever reason, and I'm not going to be part of it. She's my sister-in-law, Quinn, and if you have any intention of focusing on her as a suspect, remember that you don't have the best record in that department." As soon as the words left my mouth, I wanted to take them back. He had a great knack for narrowing suspects, actually, just not in cases having to do with magic. His record was the best in the department, though. No matter that it was partly due to yours truly.

This case might involve magic, or it might not. Either way, getting on Detective Quinn's bad side right now wasn't going to help anyone.

"I see," he said stiffly. "Well, thank goodness you've been there to set me straight. You may go."

"Quinn," I said.

He opened the door.

"Sorry. I'm getting married on Saturday. I'm a little frayed."

Slowly, he turned and gave me a long look. "How well do you know your sister-in-law?"

"I know her . . . well, we haven't spent much time together," I admitted. "A few days around the holidays when we were visiting Declan's mom in Boston. But I like her, and I have good intuition when it comes to judging people."

He continued looking at me.

"You don't think she actually killed Tucker, do you? I mean, seriously. She's a tiny thing." However, Quinn hadn't said how he'd died. For all I knew, someone had shot him.

He gestured to the open door. "After you. I'll be in touch if I have any more questions."

Worry warred with guilt as I slipped past him to the motel parking lot, but I didn't know how to smooth things over. A glance over my shoulder showed him standing in the door frame, watching as I walked away.

It'll be okay. Quinn and I have been through worse, and we always end up friends. Sort of friends. On good terms, at least.

As I crossed the asphalt to the office, I saw that Aggie and Eliza had arrived and were ushering Rori toward their rental car. Worry creased their mother's forehead. Anger clouded Eliza's face, and her jaw was set. I could only guess the talking-to Rori was in for.

Ben was engrossed in a conversation with a paramedic by one of the ambulances. I could tell from his body language he was deep in his role of counselor. Declan and Jaida were by the office and met me halfway.

I gestured toward my uncle. "What's he up to?"

"Catching up with an old protégé," Declan said.

"Ah." Ben had a lot of those in the community.

"How'd it go?" Jaida asked.

I made a face. "I'm not sure. Quinn tried to get me to tell him why Rori was here in the first place. He said she didn't have an explanation."

Jaida pressed her lips together.

"Don't worry, I didn't say anything," I said. "Was he just trying to confirm her story?"

She sighed. "I wouldn't normally tell you—attorney-client privilege and all—but you already know. She told Quinn the same thing she told us, that Tucker wanted her to give him the music box back and she wanted closure on her marriage—and on her divorce. He looked at the music box but said he didn't see how Tucker could get any real money for something like that. Gave it back to her. As for the rest, I could tell it sounded like girly mumbo jumbo to Quinn." Her mouth gave a wry twist. "He asked why she didn't try to get closure over coffee rather than coming to a motel at night."

"Coffee shop sounds a lot better to me, too," Declan grumbled. "Or telling the jerk to get lost on the phone, tossing that birdhouse thing in the garbage, and calling it good. It wasn't like she was breaking up with him or anything. They were already divorced."

I put my hand on his arm. "They were. Then he showed up in her life again. You're a guy, so maybe it would be different for you. Rori wanted to feel in control, wanted to say her piece, and cut all ties."

After a moment, he blew out a breath and nodded. "Yeah, okay. But you can't say she doesn't have closure now."

Jaida and I looked at each other and sighed. I changed

the subject. "What did you find out from them?" I gestured to the paramedics, who were getting ready to leave the scene.

"Apparently the room was a real mess," he said.

"I saw. A fight?"

"Maybe. Probably. But the drawers were all pulled out, his luggage had been dumped. Someone was looking for something."

"Money?"

"If Tucker had money, he wouldn't be staying in a place like this," Declan said.

"But he told Rori he owed someone. Did she tell Quinn that?" I asked.

Jaida nodded. "How did he die?" she asked. "Quinn wouldn't tell us."

"Me, either," I said.

"They said it looked like he'd suffered a severe blow to the temple. Looks like he hit the corner of the dresser. He might have been struck first, or he was pushed and fell and hit his head on the way down." He looked at his watch. "Listen, I've got to get back to Five House."

Jaida turned to me. "I need to get going, too. Full day tomorrow."

I gave her a hug and inhaled her cinnamon scent. "Thanks for stepping in like you did."

"Oh, honey, of course." She stepped back. "I'll check in with you tomorrow, okay?"

I nodded, and she walked to her vehicle.

"You're going back to work?" I asked Declan.

"Might as well," he said. "My mother has Rori in hand, and there's nothing I can do right now." He peered at my face. "Unless there's something I don't know about."

I shook my head. "No. I just miss you."

"You want me to come home?" he asked.

He was serious. If I asked him to, he'd call in and get the rest of his shift off. I loved him for it, but he was already taking time off around the wedding. Besides, he was right. There wasn't anything either of us could do tonight. Quinn had his suspects to question, and we could only hope one of them turned out to be the killer.

I managed a smile. "No. You go on back to work."

"You sure?"

"Of course." I brightened the smile.

He hesitated before finally saying, "This feels really off. Not just the murder. Not just Rori. It's because Connell is gone. I can feel his absence like an ache, Katie. And sometimes when I'd normally know exactly what to say or do without thinking about it, I don't. It's really disconcerting."

"I'm so sorry," I said, putting my arms around him. "I haven't had a chance to talk to the spellbook club about how to get Connell back. I'm hoping they'll have some ideas. We'll dive in right after the wedding."

"Thanks. I never knew how much a part of me he was." He gave me a quick kiss. "Gotta go." And he headed back to his truck.

Ben saw him go and glanced back to where I waited. He quickly finished up his conversation and met me at his pickup. When I climbed inside, Mungo greeted me as if I'd been gone for days, jumping onto my lap and licking my face. The enthusiastic welcome calmed my nerves, which were more jangled than I'd admitted to myself. After he'd settled down, I buckled in, and Ben took off.

"I'd better call Lucy," I said. "So she can at least let Mimsey know what's going on."

"I'll tell her," Ben said. "Let's get you back to your car so you can go home and get some rest."

I looked at my watch. It was after nine thirty. I rarely slept for more than two or three hours a night, a condition that I'd always thought was a sleep disorder, but it turned out had something to do with my magic. Tonight, I felt far too jittery to fall into an easy sleep.

We pulled away from the curb, and a familiar Audi turned onto the street and drove slowly toward the motel. Its left turn signal came on, and it stopped, waiting for us to go by. I sat up in my seat to see if the driver was who I thought it was. Sure enough, Steve Dawes peered through the windshield. I shouldn't have been surprised, but even though he came into the Honeybee nearly every day, it was disconcerting to see him in this environment. Steve tended to cover more high-profile cases, or at least cases that involved the moneyed and powerful. His eyes widened when he realized who was in the truck, and his head turned to watch as we drove by.

No doubt he'd quiz me tomorrow at the bakery, especially if he found out the woman who'd discovered the body was the sister of his old nemesis. Declan and Steve had had a difficult history before I came into the picture, but once I did—and had sort of been seeing them both for a short time—the enmity between them had only increased.

I sat back and sighed.

"Was that Dawes?" Ben asked. He didn't sound happy. My uncle had been Team Declan from the get-go.

"He's probably on call tonight."

"Hmph," was the only response.

Refraining from comment, I hugged Mungo to my chest. Anticipating Steve's questions ramped up my anxiety another notch. A few deep breaths helped, but I was still a little shaky when Ben dropped me at the carriage house and drove away. I went inside, thinking I might unpack a few more boxes before calling it a night. When I flipped on the light, I sucked in a surprised breath.

The spellbook club hadn't left after supper as I'd expected them to. They'd stayed and unpacked every box, arranging books on the shelves and items in the kitchen. It was stunning how they'd known just where everything should go. Mungo followed me into the bedroom, his nails clicking on the floor behind me. In the walk-in closet—a far cry from the armoires I'd been using to house my wardrobe up until now and the bags stuffed under the bed that Declan had kept his things in—I stood with my mouth open.

"Ohmygod," I breathed. "Mungo, will you look at this?"

In the brief time I'd been gone, the spellbook club had not only unpacked the moving boxes but also organized our brand-new closet. Four double-hung rods expanded the space for clothes and freed up the middle of the back wall for a full-length mirror. On one side, my clothes were hung, and on the other, Declan's. A single high rod on the left held longer items like coats and dresses, separated into his and hers. On the shelves to my right were cubbies for shoes; baskets for unmentionables, scarves, and the like; lidded boxes with blank labels; and larger cubbies for hats and sweaters. A ladderback chair with a plush cushion sat in one corner.

And there, hanging on a valet hook that swung out of the wall, was my wedding dress. A smile spread across my face, and I moved to run my fingertips over it. Eliza would hate it, since I'd ditched the idea of a fancy white gown. The white dress I'd bought for my first wedding to Andrew-the-jerk, the wedding that never happened (thank goddess), had been rather well recycled, I thought, into a zombie bride costume for Halloween. Instead, I would be married in a simple, sleeveless sheath of plum-colored lace that fell to mid-knee and widened at the top to barely fall off my shoulders. Matching lace covered the custom pumps on the floor beneath it, and the slip and fancy undergarments, no garter belt, thank you very much, hung behind the dress, all ready for the big day.

Then I saw the card taped to the mirror.

Congratulations on your new chapter, Katie!
Wishing you and Declan all happiness and love—
and the most organized closet on the block!

> *Blessed Be ~ Lucy, Mimsey, Bianca,*
> *Cookie, and Jaida.*

P.S. look in the cupboard above your scarves.

My heart full from this show of love, I found my neatly arranged scarves and opened the cupboard above them. The scents of herbs and spices drifted into the rest of the closet, and I reached in to draw out the silken bag there. It was tied with a silver cord in a complicated series of knots. A sachet—an enchanted one. I held it to my nose and inhaled the fragrance of dried apples, cinnamon, ginger, jasmine, rosemary, and lavender. It was a heady mix, and all herbs and spices that invoked different aspects of love—adoration, fidelity, loyalty, respect, and desire. I could feel that Lucy and the others had triggered those qualities with a spell. I left the sachet on a shelf, so its magical essence could touch everything we wore.

Stooping, I picked Mungo up and gazed around at the beautiful and tidy space one last time.

"We have the best friends," I whispered, then flipped off the light and went back out to the living room.

Outside the French doors, the backyard was bathed in silvery light. The moon would be full the night before the wedding, but even in its waxing gibbous state, it cast a bold illumination that seemed to call to me. The closet had distracted me, but now I felt quivery all over again. There was something about Tucker Abbott's death that was gnawing at me. My intuition hadn't flared in the way it usually did when I encountered evil.

But something was off.

I needed to ground myself, to dispel the extra energy sparking under my skin and in my brain. I glanced over and noticed the corked bottle of red wine the ladies had left on the kitchen counter. Wine was great for grounding buzzing energy. However, I wanted my first night in the carriage house after the renovations to be with Declan, as husband and wife, so I'd be driving to his apartment still that night. Plus, it was late. Probably a good idea to forgo the wine.

I stepped out to the back patio and stood there for a long moment. The fence that ran around the yard cast angled shadows onto the gardens Declan had helped me cut out of the sod when I'd first moved to Savannah. One patch was for vegetables, another for herbs, culinary and magical, and I'd recently added a small cutting garden. The bed by the back corner was devoted to magical plants—the yellow-flowered witch hazel I'd made my wand out of, hellebore, comfrey, angelica, wormwood, and more. In the center, a rowan sapling reached moonward, gracing the ground with the dark, lacy patterns of its leaf-strewn branches. Behind it, a small stream burbled its way across the corner of the property.

A laugh drifted through the air from the Coopersmiths' house, and I craned my head to look around the corner. The curtains at the back of the house were open, and I could see Margie sitting at her kitchen table, her phone in one hand and a Twinkie in the other. Ducking back, I decided against going out to the gazebo to cast the grounding spell I had been contemplating to calm my nerves. Instead, I went back inside, locked the double doors, turned off the light, and climbed the stairs to the loft.

Mungo watched from below, then turned and trotted over to the front door. Flopping down in front of it, he put his head on his front paws and gazed up at me. My familiar had seen this movie before and was setting himself up as my sentry.

Chapter 7

There hadn't been any boxes to unpack in the loft of the carriage house. The television was still at Declan's, but on one of his days off he'd brought over his collection of DVDs and vinyl records, files, and other office-centric items. The new desk was already set up by the window, and the comfy sofa sat facing the empty space on the wall where the television would be mounted, a combination coffee table and ottoman in front of it.

Smoke from the fire downstairs had stunk up this second level, but my insurance had paid for most of the furnishing to be replaced. The one thing I'd refused to replace was the wooden secretary's desk tucked into an alcove near the top of the stairs. It wasn't a working desk, at least not in the traditional way of thinking of one. Lucy had given it to me shortly after telling me about my gift, and my altar sat behind the drop-down lid, close at hand but hidden from everyday view. I'd had to move the desk into storage during the remodel construction, but I'd moved it back into the loft as soon as I'd been able and set up my altar again.

It might have been my imagination, but I could have sworn the wood still smelled faintly of smoke as I unhooked the hasp and lowered the dropleaf to rest horizontally. Then I lit three white candles and put them in a row along the top of the desk.

I ran my fingertips over the lacy shawl that served as my altar cloth. My nonna, also a hedgewitch, had knitted it from fine cotton thread. Her love and magic were woven into the tiny, meticulous stitches, making it a touchstone for my own intentions when I was casting. Then I gently touched the items arranged on the lace in turn. A witch's altar is very personal, and I'd gathered examples of the classic tools of magic that resonated with my particular sensibilities. The chalice, representing water, was a small hand-blown glass bowl I'd stumbled onto at a flea market on one of my rare days off from the Honeybee. Air was represented by an antique kitchen knife that served as my ritual athame, which rested gently on a collection of small feathers. Next to it, an Indian arrowhead perched on a cairn of smooth pebbles, representing the element of earth. And for fire, my witch hazel wand rested next to a two-inch figurine of a phoenix carved from red tourmaline. This last was a new acquisition, in honor of the carriage house metaphorically rising from the ashes.

Once I'd connected with the items on my altar, I slowly closed my eyes. A soft doggy snore from my sentry downstairs made me smile. A few deep breaths helped to center me. This wasn't a spell per se, not in the sense that I needed to cast a protective circle, invoke the elements, and the like. This was simply a way to get rid of the excess jittery energy I still felt after the evening's events. It had been one of the first things Lucy had taught me, and though grounding energy was generally more effective on the actual *ground*, this was an alternative that would work.

And hopefully, I might understand the feeling of *wrongness* in Tucker's motel room. Of course, the whole situation had been wrong. A man was dead, after all. Although this wasn't my first experience with such things, I hadn't encountered that sense of magical ozone before.

Standing in front of the altar, I reached out mentally and slowed my breathing.

In. Out. In. Out.

Eyes still closed, I raised my hands in front of my waist, palms facing one another. Drawing them toward each other, and then apart, I concentrated on the energy flowing between them. After a few times, I felt the resistance when I pushed my hands together. Breathing my intention into that space, I gathered my nervous tension there, molding it with my hands into an invisible but palpable ball of energy.

My eyes popped open, and I focused on the swirly glass bowl, the chalice on my altar. With care, I moved my hands over the chalice and *pushed* my excess energy into the vessel, willing it to stay when I released it. I stepped away. The candles sputtered, then burned bright again.

The ritual worked. I felt lighter, more at ease, and the tight muscles in my neck had loosened. Rolling my shoulders, I thanked the elements. I touched the lace of the altar cloth and thanked Nonna as well. Whether her spirit was nearby or not, I was grateful. So many times, she'd shown up to help me when I needed it, so I had the feeling she was never too far away.

After extinguishing the candles, I reached for the chalice. Holding it carefully from the bottom, I carried it down the stairs and out the front door. Mungo padding behind me, I crossed the small porch to the rosemary topiary Lucy had planted by the front walk and kneeled beside it. Gently, I placed the bowl on the ground next to the rosemary and tipped it toward the plant.

I could sense the energy flowing to the plant, neither good nor bad, simply an excess that I didn't need or want. It seeped into the earth and into the resinous roots of the herb, from there dispersing through the leaves into the air and through the roots into the earth and the water it held. Some of it merged with the fiery verve of the herb itself, and I knew I'd added to its protective and feminine power.

Standing again, I inhaled the warm, humid air and gave a nod to the waxing moon. The smell of night-blooming jasmine filled my nose, and in the distance, a train whistle faintly moaned. I smiled down at Mungo, and we went back inside. I returned the chalice to my altar and closed the secretary's desk. I took one last look at the fabulous closet the spellbook club had organized, closed the shutters on the front windows, turned off the light, and locked the door. Soon, Mungo and I were on our way back to Declan's apartment.

The grounding ritual had removed the static that had been clouding my mind, and as I drove, I felt a new clarity of thought about the evening. At a light, I reached over and scratched Mungo behind the ear. He panted his appreciation.

"You know what?" I asked. "There were remnants left over from a powerful spell in Tucker's motel room. I thought maybe it was something Tucker did himself, but I'm not so sure now. I don't know enough to tell Quinn, but I'm pretty sure it's somehow related to his death."

Mungo made a noise in the back of this throat.

I glanced down. "Yeah. I sure would like to ask Connell what he thinks about that."

Yip!

Ah, Connell. Not just your run-of-the-mill spirit, but a leprechaun spirit, Connell had long been connected to the males of the McCarthy clan. He'd stayed in the background of Declan's psyche until he'd inadvertently been brought out during a séance a couple of years before.

It had sometimes been a difficult relationship between Declan and his resident spirit. Then last month a horrific thing had happened. In the course of returning my stolen magic back to me, Connell had sacrificed himself and been drawn far, far away.

We'd thought he was gone altogether, but then he'd contacted me in a dream. Not my dream, but Declan's. Apparently when I'd got my magic back, I received a little bonus—the ability to eavesdrop on others' dreams within a certain proximity. Pretty cool in theory, but more of a pain in practice.

With everything going on in the last month, I hadn't had time to really explore my new ability. All I knew was that, because of it, I'd been in fleeting contact with Connell. We knew he was lost but had no idea how to find him.

I arrived at the apartment and took Mungo around the block for a final walk before heading inside. As we ambled and Mungo stopped to check out the smells every six feet, I reviewed the evening at the Spotlight. I wondered whether Rori had really decided to go to the motel herself, or if Tucker had convinced her without her realizing it.

"So say Tucker cast his glamour spell intentionally and also used his Voice on Rori. Would someone with that kind of talent need to sell a kitschy music box for money and live in a seedy motel when his girlfriend kicked him out?" I murmured out loud. "Seems like a stretch. There was magic in that room all right, but maybe it wasn't his. I wonder if it's possible to cast a glamour spell on someone else. But why would anyone do that?"

A woman on the evening's last walkies with her Yorkie glanced my way, and I pressed my lips together. But Mungo had heard and stopped to look up at me. His brown-eyed gaze didn't hold any answers, though.

We finished our perambulation and climbed the stairs to the apartment. Once inside, I raided the refrigerator for a snack. A piece of leftover baked Brie and a fresh peach for me, and a bit of leftover chicken stir-fry on jasmine rice for Mungo. I changed into a pair of soft shorts and a spaghetti tank in preparation for bed, then settled onto the couch with my laptop and a cup of chamomile tea.

I was still hoping Quinn would find the killer among his suspects, but I couldn't resist seeing what I could find out about Tucker Abbott online. Though I'd met him only the one time, he had definitely piqued my interest. Not in the way he probably piqued a lot of women's interest, but because of the façade he seemed to so successfully employ. Eliza had called him a wolf in sheep's clothing, and Quinn had said he was involved in some kind of fraud.

First, I e-mailed the members of the spellbook club, thanking them for their work at the carriage house, the surprise closet arrangement, and the magical touch they'd added at the end. I'd thank them all in person, of course, but I wanted them to know right away how touched I was by all they'd done for Declan and me.

A quick Internet search for Tucker Abbott brought up the usual ads for background checks. It was tempting, but they wanted me to pay for a subscription. Money was tight enough, and it wasn't like I was going to use a subscription.

I scrolled down, getting hits for other people with the name "Tucker." I went back and enclosed the name in the search box in quotation marks so any results that didn't have "Tucker Abbott" together would be eliminated.

Bingo.

Well, not so much bingo, I realized as I read. It was a business announcement from a few years back. A new vacation rental business, specific to Savannah and the surrounding area, had opened its doors in competition with the national vacation rental companies. Tucker was listed as an employee, and he was in the picture of the new staff in the article. Then I noticed the byline was one Steve Dawes. Back then, he'd taken a break from crime reporting to write a column on local businesses. It was how I'd met him in the first place, when he covered the grand opening of the Honeybee.

What had Tucker said about how he'd found out Rori was in Savannah?

I checked with my friend in the vacation rental business, and she told me your family was staying here for the week.

I felt certain I was looking at his "friend" online right then. Was his job at the vacation rental place the same one he'd told Dayleen that he'd lost? But if he'd been fired, then why would anyone there tell him where to find Rori?

Oh, Rori. What were you thinking, marrying this guy?

At least she'd gotten out quickly. Then I remembered Eliza saying she'd never forgive Declan for introducing them.

There's a story there, I bet.

I didn't see any other results for Tucker Abbott. For someone who appeared to dabble on the edge of legality, perhaps on the other side as well, he had virtually no online presence. On the other hand, maybe that was part of living in his shadow world, namely staying in the shadows.

I closed the laptop, put it on the coffee table, and beckoned to Mungo.

"Come on, buddy. Let's hit the sack."

It was midnight when we went to bed. My thoughts were still circling Tucker's murder, but lazily. The grounding ritual was still working. I was nudging the softness of sleep when I had the strange sensation of something in my eye. Something huge. I tried to ignore it. Sometimes that helped, and it went away on its own. I knew there was nothing in my eye. The woman in the apartment next door had a recurring dream that she had a piece of popcorn stuck in her eye, and thanks to my newfound dream-sensing ability, I'd had the pleasure of having the sensation more than once. She was an avid dreamer, especially about food. At least I was able to tap into the sensations of her dreams only as I was drifting off, not all the time. But still, I was looking forward to not having anyone close enough to read except Declan and Mungo. Their dreams I had tapped into enough times that I was learning to manage it. Other people, not so much.

The sensation got worse, until I came fully awake and it went away. I threw back the covers and padded out to the kitchen to retrieve my phone. One of the advantages of having a firefighter boyfriend was he didn't mind when you texted him in the middle of the night at work.

I e-mailed two possible alternatives to Judge Matthews, but haven't heard back. Strangers, though. Any ideas?

I waited. It was possible he was taking a nap. After all, the men and women at the firehouse grabbed a bit of sleep whenever they could on a forty-eight-hour shift.

However, about a minute later, he texted back.

I do have an idea! Will follow up. In the middle of a call right now. Can't chat.

I sent him a thumbs-up and went back to join Mungo, who was still sprawled on the bed. It was nearly one when I drifted off again, but there was blessedly no sensation from the woman next door. I selfishly wished her a long, dreamless sleep for the rest of the night.

Chapter 8

Four a.m. saw me donning my running clothes and filling a water bottle. Mungo hadn't budged from his spot at the foot of the bed. I left him to his slumber, well aware that he had no interest whatsoever in going on a run with me. Outside, the air was delightfully crisp and free from exhaust. The eastern sky was a bruise of purple and blue with a few strands of peachy tendrils reaching to the west. The scents of brugmansia and night phlox teased at my nose as I stretched, and then I set off. Farther from the landscaped gardens around the apartment building, the telltale scent of the local paper mills cut through the clear air. Ignoring it, I ducked my head and plowed along the four-mile route that had become my habit while living at Declan's apartment complex.

Back home, I showered and left for the bakery. Mungo looked sleepily out the car window as we drove. He wasn't a morning dog, but he'd still managed to eat his scrambled egg breakfast. I'd passed on the eggs, figuring I'd grab something at the bakery.

Inside the Honeybee, I flipped on the lights, started up the music, and set the ovens to preheat. The sourdough loaves that had been slowly rising overnight went in first. By the time they were sitting on the counter, their crisp crusts audibly crackling as they cooled, I had buttermilk rusks and pecan toffee cookies ready to pop in the ovens.

Next, I removed some cookie dough Iris had mixed up the day before from the refrigerator. Flecks of cloves, rosemary, anise, and cinnamon flecked it, becoming more apparent as I rolled it out on the counter. Humming under my breath as I worked, I invoked the protective powers of that unique and tasty combination of herbs and spices. Whatever a customer might need protection from, these cookies would help. Using cookie cutters in the shapes of suns, crescent moons, and stars, I filled three baking sheets and popped the delectable bites in the oven as soon as the other cookies were done.

I was filling the pastry case with still-warm goodies when Lucy showed up at six thirty. Iris came in soon after, this time wearing a Honeybee baseball cap over her blue locks.

"Where's Ben?" I asked.

Lucy gave an elaborate shrug. "When I left, he was talking on the phone with Declan."

"Ah. We should start calling Ben 'Counselor.'"

"He does seem to have a talent for it."

"With Connell gone, I'm glad Declan has someone else to talk to."

My aunt shot a look toward Iris, who knew nothing about Connell. However, our helper was wearing earbuds and bopping around the kitchen as she gathered ingredients.

Ben showed up right before we opened at seven. When I asked him about Declan, he waggled his eyebrows mysteriously.

"Whatever," I muttered, and went to open the door.

The customers beelined straight to the glass display case, where Lucy was already waiting with bags ready to fill with baked goods. Ben had taken up his station behind the coffee counter, and the whine of the espresso machine filled the air as he started a couple of drinks for regulars before they'd even ordered.

Steve came in. He was earlier than usual and for once wasn't carrying his laptop bag. It was a safe bet that he had his reporter's notebook tucked in a pocket, though. I gave him a quick nod and hurried behind the register to ring up orders.

As I made the change for six crullers and a mochaccino, I saw him saunter into the reading area of the bakery. He rubbed Honeybee along the back of her neck as he looked out the window. He obviously wasn't here for an early morning treat. As soon as he had an opportunity, he'd be quizzing me about Tucker Abbott's murder. When I glanced over at Ben, he was studying Steve with narrowed eyes, all the while turning the frothing pitcher beneath the steam handle with practiced expertise.

The first rush died down, and I went to the sink to wash my hands. When I came back out, Steve met me at the entrance to the kitchen. He wore hiking shorts, a LIFE IS GOOD T-shirt, and chunky sandals. A few days' worth of beard clouded his narrow jaw. You'd never have guessed he was worth a fortune.

You'd never have guessed he was a member of the oldest druid clan in Savannah, either.

His eyes were serious, but he flashed a white-toothed smile at me. "Can we talk?"

I made a wry face. "Who doesn't love to hear those words?"

He shrugged. "Sorry. But . . . ?"

"I saw you at the motel last night. I'm sorry, but I don't have any information for you."

"Ah, but I might just have some information for you, Katie." His eyes flicked toward Uncle Ben, who was still watching him. "How about we chat back in the alley."

"Um," I began, but he was already pushing past me, toward the back door. Intrigued against my will, I followed.

Closing the door behind me, I breathed in the combined scents of waffles from the breakfast joint down the street and a faint whiff of garbage from the Dumpster that hulked on the far side of the Fox and Hound Bookshop. The alley was surrounded by three-story brick walls, their blank expanse relieved by the occasional cluster of pipes or web of cables and bricked-over windows above. Closer to the ground, power meters and metal access boxes punctuated the utilitarian space. A few doors down, a yellow delivery van was parked behind one of the retail stores.

"Nice choice." I waved at the surroundings before folding my arms across my chest and squinting at Steve. "So you knew Tucker Abbott."

He leaned his shoulders against the wall by the doorway and propped one foot behind him, the picture of confidence and ease. Still, I sensed tension coming off him.

"Not exactly," he said.

"He was in your column."

"Yes, I remember featuring the business he worked for, but our interaction was minimal. I've heard of him, though."

"Oh? What have you heard?" I asked.

"Only that he wasn't a man you'd want to go into business with. He tried to convince Father to invest in some land scheme." Steve's dad was a venture capitalist, though honestly, I'd never figured out what that meant in real-life terms.

I snorted out a laugh at the idea of Tucker trying his glamour on the leader of the Dragoh druid clan. Then I sobered. "Was Tucker a druid, then?"

Steve looked surprised. "Nah. At least not that I know of." He looked thoughtful, then shook his head. "No, we'd know if he was. Why would you ask that?"

I considered for a moment how much to say. What would it hurt to tell Steve what I'd noticed about Tucker in our one brief encounter? Steve had been one of the first people who'd known I was a witch, and we'd been through some intense times together.

"I met him one time, and one time only," I said, leaving out that it had been only hours before he'd been killed. "But the guy was all glamoured up. It was stunning how appealing he came across on the very first impression."

Steve let out a whistle. "Well, what do you know." He grinned. "How long did his first impression last on you?"

"Not long."

"Mm. Of course not. I bet some people never saw through it, though. A handy thing for a con man. Did you sense anything else about him? Magically, I mean?"

I shook my head. "I couldn't even be sure he knew he was using a glamour."

"Yeah. It could have simply developed as a kind of occupational hazard."

"Or benefit." I glanced toward the door. "The second rush is going to be coming in soon. What did you want to tell me?"

"It looks like Aurora McCarthy is a suspect in Tucker's death."

"Oh, please. That's ridiculous." I gave a casual shrug, despite knowing Rori was likely still on Quinn's short list.

Steve's head slowly wagged back and forth. "Not from what I hear." He wasn't smiling, but he didn't seem very upset by the notion, either.

"Oh, really? And from *whom* did you hear it?"

"Sources." He looked smug.

"Sources," I repeated. "What kind of sources?"

"I'm a crime reporter. You think I don't have sources within the police department? Not to mention other agencies. Like, for instance, the office of the medical examiner. Even, believe it or not, the fire department."

A hard knot of worry was beginning to form in my stomach, but I kept my tone light. "And what do these brilliant *departmental* resources have to say about Rori?"

"Rori. That's cute. Well, for one—" He held up a

hand and ticked off a finger. "There was an argument in the parking lot, and the motel manager thought it might have been between Tucker and, er, Rori."

"She didn't know who it was," I said. "Only that it was a woman's voice. One of two who visited Tucker. Oh, and did you know Tucker argued with a man in the parking lot, too? According to the manager, at least."

He grinned, and I realized I'd just given him more information than he'd had. He ticked off another finger. "According to Dayleen, Tucker owed someone some money and was hiding out from them at the Spotlight."

I already knew Tucker owed someone money, but not from Dayleen. She hadn't told us he was hiding at the motel, either. Of course, Steve could be very persuasive. In fact, he wasn't above using the occasional glamour himself.

Not that he usually needed to.

Another finger. "And it turns out that Tucker got his ex-wife fired from her job. Coincidence?"

"Probably," I said in a dry tone. "From the little I know of him, Tucker Abbott did a lot of people wrong. The guy had enemies. Even Quinn told me he knew of some people he thought might be after Tucker. I don't think Rori was on his list." Not that list, at least. But I didn't need Steve speculating about Declan's sister in the paper, either.

"You sure?" Steve asked. "Because she didn't seem to have a very good reason for being there that night, at least not that she shared."

Who had Steve been talking to? Quinn himself?

"She had a perfectly good reason," I said.

"Oh?" He lowered his foot from the wall to the ground and leaned toward me. "What was it?"

I felt like squirming. I could just see Steve saying something in a news article about the victim's ex-wife seeking closure. "It's personal," I said.

"Right." He went back to leaning against the wall. "Does this personal reason explain why Aurora, sorry, *Rori*, doesn't have an alibi for the time frame of Abbott's murder?"

"What was the time frame?" I asked a little too quickly.

He gave me a knowing look. "Between five and six in the evening. Declan's little sister had come back from shopping with her mother at four, but she decided to take their car for a little drive on her own. To visit some of her childhood haunts, she said."

I frowned. How did Steve know all this? "That's all circumstantial. Rori didn't kill anyone."

"Somebody's been watching too much *Law and Order*," he said.

Rolling my eyes, I asked, "Have you seen Rori McCarthy? She's a tiny thing. And why would she search his room?"

"I guess you have your sources, too," he said with a flicker of admiration. "And the answer is because she was looking for something of value. Maybe anything of value, if she felt he owed her after getting her fired. As for how Mr. Abbott died? He hit his head on the corner of the dresser. All he needed was a push with the right leverage. Even a woman of small stature could manage that."

I shook my head. "All that is really weak. And why

are you telling me this in the first place? You make it sound like you're trying to be helpful, but you're not doing it to help Declan's sister."

"No, I'm not." He licked his lips. "Katie, I want you to know what kind of family you're marrying into."

My lips parted in surprise.

"This whole engagement-marriage thing has been kind of rushed, don't you think? Maybe you should find out more about his family. Step back. Maybe it's a sign that Judge Matthews can't marry you."

I stared at him, utterly speechless.

He shrugged. "Sorry. I overheard your conversations with Lucy and Declan about the judge yesterday. Listen, I'm not saying not to marry Declan. I just think you need to take a little time to think. To make sure you're doing the right thing."

After a few beats, I managed to speak in a coherent sentence, albeit a short one. "I'm sure, Steve. Why are you doing this?"

"You never really gave me a chance, you know," he said quietly.

"Steve, I'm sorry," I said in as gentle a voice as I could muster. "I simply don't feel that way about you."

"You did, once. You might again." Hopeful now.

"That was different."

"You know we have a connection."

"We do," I admitted. "Or did. But—"

"But you want to be married. To be a wife."

"No, that's not—"

"No, I get it. I do." He turned and gazed down the alleyway. His jaw set. "I'll see you later, Katie-girl." And he walked away.

"Steve!" I called after him, but he didn't even look back. Sighing, I turned and went back into the bakery.

"There she is!" Lucy said. "Katie, Declan's here."

He stood in the library, flipping through a book. His gaze flicked to the back door, and then to me.

Smiling, I joined him and gave him a quick hug. When the Honeybee had first opened, the idea was to have a small lending library where customers could take any book that appealed to them or leave a book for someone else. The books were originally provided by the members of the spellbook club, who chose the titles using their witchy intuition. We all still brought in books we ran across that felt like they might be helpful to someone, but the small library had grown substantially from our patrons' donations, and now filled all the shelves Ben had gradually added.

Customers weren't the only ones who benefited from the books in the Honeybee library. Cookie had been drawn to a book on parenting, Mimsey had stumbled into a romance that she knew would make her granddaughter feel better after a breakup, and I'd found more than a few volumes that spoke to me. So I wasn't exactly surprised when Declan tilted the book he held so I could see the title. I was, however, surprised when I read it: *Lucid Dreaming for Beginners*.

I blinked, considering the idea for the first time. Then I took the volume from him and scanned the back. I looked up. "A dream in which the dreamer is aware they're dreaming. Connell contacted me from your dream. How did I not think of that before?"

Declan raised his eyebrows. "Do you think it might work? That we can find Connell and bring him back?"

"It's certainly worth a try."

He nodded. "I'm glad to hear you say that. I'll take this with me."

I grinned, feeling hopeful. "By all means. Are you still on shift?"

He shook his head. "Scott told me to leave early." There were dark half-moons under his eyes.

"When was the last time you slept?"

His lips pressed together, and he didn't answer.

"Go home and take a nap," I urged.

"I might, though I don't feel like I'll be able to sleep." He gently snorted. "Rori can, though. I texted her and got no answer, so tried my mother. She says my dear sister hasn't come out of her bedroom yet this morning. Slumbering away like a baby."

I looked at my watch. It was eight twenty. "And why shouldn't she?" I asked. "Last night was traumatic—I mean, she discovered the body of the man she'd once been married to, for heaven's sake. A little rest is probably good for her." And to me, at least, it indicated her conscience was clear.

"Yeah, maybe." Declan tipped his head to the side. "Ben says you were talking to Steve Dawes out in the alley."

Thanks, Uncle Ben.

I led Declan over to a bistro table in the corner by the window, away from other customers. "He stopped by to chat. He covered the murder last night for the paper."

"Is that what he stopped by to 'chat' about?"

I scrabbled for what to tell Declan about what Steve

had had to say. It was definitely a bad idea to tell him Steve thought I should cancel our wedding.

"Pretty much," I said.

"What did he want?"

I hesitated.

Declan gave me a look.

"He was concerned about your sister."

"I bet."

"Well, sort of. Apparently, he has some, you know, sources. They told him Tucker was killed between five and six yesterday evening." I paused.

"And?"

I sighed. "That Tucker was hiding from someone he owed money to, and he argued with some people." I wrinkled my nose. "And Rori doesn't have an alibi for the time of the murder."

The blood drained from Declan's face. "What? Where was she?"

"She said she was driving around Savannah."

My fiancé rubbed his face with both hands.

Lucy bustled over with a big mug of coffee for Declan, along with a cat's head biscuit layered with Tasso ham, sharp cheddar, and a slather of fresh peach jam. "You look a sight." She placed the plate in front of him and handed him a napkin. "Eat."

I couldn't help smiling a little. I knew the jam contained ginger, which was a classic spice for providing strength and healing as well as soothing the soul.

He smiled, too. "Thanks, Lucy."

She waited, hands on her hips, until he'd taken a couple of bites, then gave a sharp nod of approval and went back to the kitchen to get Iris started on the next batch of baking.

I settled my elbows on the table and rested my chin on one hand. "Tell me about Tucker. Eliza said you introduced him to Rori."

Chapter 9

Declan rolled his eyes, swallowed, and took a big swig of coffee. Then he said, "I've always regretted it, but yeah. I did introduce Rori and Tucker."

"So you knew him first?" That was news.

"I'd just met him. Another firefighter put us in touch. He'd joined a real estate investment group here in town, headed by Tucker. The idea was that members could buy real property together, so no one would be investing a ton of money and everyone could reap the benefits. There were four members, and they were looking for a fifth."

"Hang on. You mean you were going to buy property with people you didn't even know?"

"Well, they knew each other. See, Tucker convinced a good friend of his—meaning someone he'd convinced was his friend—and that person had another friend who was interested. That friend then had a friend, and so on. All these people were involved in the fire department or law enforcement, so it didn't feel like we were strangers at all. I was to be the last in the chain. Tucker said five was the perfect number to spread out the costs of the purchase—it was a small apartment building—without diluting the profit too much."

"Sounds great. It was a scam, of course."

"Of course."

"How much did you lose?"

"Me? None. I decided against joining the group."

"You knew?"

He made a face. "The guy was really convincing, so much so that everyone who got involved was then *also* convincing. After a short time, Tucker didn't even have to say anything. They sold themselves."

I felt myself nodding. "Once someone is committed to believing something and is also surrounded by others who think the same way, it's almost impossible to change their minds. But you didn't fall for it."

"Let's just say I had a feeling. A strong feeling." He gave me a you-know-what-I-mean look.

"Connell," I said.

He nodded, chewing on his breakfast again, then swallowed. "I'm pretty sure he saw what was really happening and set off my alarms. Even back then, before I knew anything about him." A haunted glimmer flickered behind his eyes.

I reached over and put my hand on his.

He gave my fingers a squeeze before reaching for the last bite of biscuit. When he was finished eating, he said, "Tucker and the rest of them worked on me for a few weeks before giving up. I didn't have any bad feelings about the people involved, not even Tucker. I just knew I didn't want to be part of their investment group. This was five years ago, and Rori still lived here in

Savannah. One time when Tucker came by to talk to me, she was at my place."

"And the rest is history." I'd known the bare bones, but Declan had been sketchy on the details—probably because he didn't like admitting that if he hadn't introduced them, his little sister wouldn't have married a con man.

"Tucker really seemed to like Rori." There was a note of protest in Declan's words.

I made a noise in the back of my throat.

"Well, you might be right. But he *seemed* to be head over heels. He even told her some of the stuff he was involved in."

"The investment group?"

He shook his head. "Not until later. It would have been harder to convince Rori he'd reformed and was on the straight and narrow because of his great love for her if she knew he was scamming her brother's friends."

"He did scam them, then."

"Oh, yeah. They found a fifth investor, another firefighter, and they all gave Tucker twelve grand to use as a down payment on the apartment building."

"Why didn't he go to jail?"

Declan's smile was sardonic. "He was a con man."

"But . . . fraud."

"The deal fell through. Their money was gone, and Tucker gave them all sorts of reasons for why it happened. And like in a lot of situations like that, no one reported it. They either chose to believe him or were too embarrassed to admit they'd been conned."

My mouth fell open. "You're kidding."

He sighed. "I wish I was. Now, the last member to

join the group, Carolyn Becker, did file a complaint. The district attorney didn't think there was enough to prosecute, however, especially since she was the only one of the investment group who reported Tucker."

"Dang," I said in wonder. "This must be one of the fraud cases Quinn mentioned."

"Carolyn didn't give up, though. She filed a civil suit. Won, too."

"Good. She had the chutzpah to put her ego aside, and she got her twelve thousand dollars back."

Declan shook his head. "Nope. She got a judgment for that much, but to the best of my knowledge, she never saw the money. A judgment is one thing—getting the defendant to pay it is something else."

"Oh, for Pete's sake. And Rori married this guy?"

"Well, all this other stuff came out after. In the meantime, Tucker courted my sister for a few months, and then they eloped." He grinned. "Eliza about lost her mind when she found out."

"I bet."

"They lived here for a little while, and Tucker tried to stay on the straight and narrow. Then Rori was offered a job at a big market research firm in DC. It was her dream job, and there was a lot of opportunity for growth."

I remembered her saying something about her dream job and closed my eyes. "He screwed it up for her, didn't he?"

When I opened my eyes, Declan was nodding. "They moved to DC. She was making good money, using her business degree, but Tucker was having trouble getting a full-time job. He tried another kind of scam. Something about cars. Rori didn't know anything about it, but when it all hit the fan, she lost her job."

"Poor thing. No wonder she's bitter."

"It took her a while to get the job she has now."

"The community center in Dover?" I asked.

"That one. Rori had to move back in with Mother for a while so she could get back on her feet."

"I remember you telling me that. What about Carolyn Becker? Is she still around?"

"Sure. She used to work at Two House, but she transferred to Four House about a year ago. She moonlights as a personal trainer at the River Street Athletic Club." Since firefighters worked a single forty-eight-hour shift each week, many fit other jobs into their time off. Declan tended to work extra hours doing fire inspections and giving safety talks at schools and other organizations.

"I think Bianca belongs to that gym. I wonder if she knows Carolyn."

"It's likely. Randy and Carolyn worked together at Two House and got to be pretty good friends." Randy and Bianca had been dating for several months.

Declan rose. "Listen, I need to get a shower and change. Maybe a nap, if I can manage it. I'll let you know when I get ahold of Rori." He gave me a kiss, then glanced around at the few customers, saw no one looking, and gave me another, lingering one.

The door opened and a half dozen people came in. I gave my fiancé another quick peck on the cheek and hurried to help Lucy take their orders. He was gone when I turned around.

*   *   *

After what Declan had told me, I was surprised to see Rori come into the bakery at about ten o'clock. Lucy and I had frosted the carrot cupcakes and filled in the empty rows of brookies in the display case with fresh warm ones. When I saw Declan's sister, I wiped my hands and came out from the kitchen to give her a hug.

She looked like she needed it and clung to me for a moment longer than I was expecting before letting go. Her face was pale, and the skin around her eyes was puffy.

"How are you doing?" I asked.

Rori lifted her chin. "I'm all right."

Lucy looked up then, spied Rori, and came over to bestow another hug. "Honey, I'm so sorry. What can I get you? Maybe a nice cup of coffee and a vanilla scone?"

I nodded my encouragement, knowing the vanilla would provide a dose of happiness and strength.

She shuddered and shook her head. "No, thanks. I've been awake since five. My stomach is a mess." Her hand ventured to her abdomen.

"And you haven't had a thing to eat, I suppose." I put my hand on her shoulder and guided her toward the library area.

Lucy went behind the coffee counter, and I saw her reach for a mug. She glanced up and nodded to me. She had something herbal in mind. I left her to it.

The coffee table was littered with empty cups and crumpled napkins. I gestured toward one of the poufy chairs, and Rori sank into it as I quickly gathered the detritus and took it back to the kitchen. When I returned, I saw she'd removed her shoes and tucked her legs underneath her. She rubbed her eyes, then looked up at me.

"Declan was by earlier," I said. "He said he's been trying to get in touch with you."

She sighed. "I know. I just couldn't talk to him. Or Eliza. They're both angry at me for going to that motel last night. They don't understand."

I gave her a smile. "About you returning his gift, or wanting to tell him off and never talk to him again?"

A miserable shrug. "Both."

"But Tucker was a strangely irresistible guy, wasn't he?"

Her eyes brightened a little in hope that I understood. "He was. You saw that right away, didn't you?"

"Indeed, I did."

A small smile lightened her features. "He's always been like that, but this last time I saw him, I mean, when he was alive, it was like his charm was on steroids." The smile dropped. "But when I found him at the motel, he seemed so, well, so unattractive." She looked miserable. "That sounds horrible, but I don't mean it that way. It was almost like he was a different man, even though I completely recognized him." She licked her lips. "Tucker was the first person I've ever seen who'd passed on. You've seen lots of bodies, though, haven't you, Katie?"

I winced inwardly.

"Are they all like that? Do people always look that different when they're, you know . . . dead?"

"Not exactly," I said and changed the subject. "So you've been avoiding Eliza, too?"

"And Mother. Even she's angry at me. I snuck out early, and she figured out I wasn't in my bedroom about an hour ago." She lifted her phone. "Totally blew up my cell with texts."

"They both love you. They're concerned."

"Yeah," she said in a small voice. "I know."

"Have you answered?"

She shook her head.

"Rori, they're worried. Let your mother—and Eliza, and Declan—know where you are so they can relax."

Her jaw set, and for the first time I realized Rori wasn't just younger than Declan, she was about two years younger than I was. She would have been twenty-three or twenty-four when she eloped with Tucker. He'd looked to be around thirty to me, but it was hard to tell with the glamour. In the brief time I'd known Rori, she'd seemed capable and sure, but now that seemed stripped away to leave a bewildered waif. My heart went out to her.

"They're worried," I repeated gently.

"Yeah, okay. You're right, of course." Her head bent over her phone as her thumbs tapped around the tiny keyboard. When she was done, she sat back in the chair with an air of relief.

Lucy chose that moment to come over with a steaming cup of tea. "Peppermint green tea with lavender," she said. "Just try it."

"Thank you," Rori said, and took a sip.

"Where have you been all morning?" I asked when Lucy had gone back to the kitchen.

"Just walking. Along the river, through the squares. Places we used to hang out as kids."

"And that's what you were doing yesterday between five and six?" I asked. "Revisiting old haunts?"

She looked toward the window, where Honeybee was in her usual spot on the sill. "Yeah. Remembering stuff. You know—my childhood, high school. My marriage." Her gaze returned to me. "It wasn't all bad, you know. Tucker could be a lot of fun. He was different than anyone I'd ever known."

"Declan told me he introduced you."

"He did. But it wasn't like he was trying to set us up or anything. We hit it off right away, and Tucker could be pretty persistent."

"And persuasive."

She nodded. "He was a born salesman. It's all he ever did. When I met him, he was working for a vacation rental place. You wouldn't think that involves much salesmanship, but he knew exactly how to stage the houses for photos, where to advertise, stuff like that."

"I saw an article about that company, and he was pictured." I left out that I'd seen it the night before when I was trying to find out more about her ex. She didn't seem to notice, though. "Was he still working there? I mean, before he got fired?"

She lifted one shoulder and let it drop. "I have no idea. I'd guess not. He moved from job to job a lot."

"You seemed pretty upset with him at the house," I said.

Her face clouded. "Like I said, he was a born salesman. Unfortunately, he wasn't above selling things that weren't actually, you know, for sale."

I wrinkled my nose. "Declan told me something happened in Washington, DC."

"Tucker was working part-time for a used car dealer." She made a face like she'd suddenly smelled something rotten. "But it turned out he'd sell a car twice, once on the lot, and once on Craigslist as a private citizen— under a different name, of course. Then he'd disappear, and the private buyer was out the money and didn't even know who to go after."

I let out a snort. "Wow. Are you serious?"

"I know, right? He got away with it for a while. Only one person reported it, they were so embarrassed at being taken like that. I think he counted on that, because it had worked before. But then he tried to pull the scam on the wrong person." She blew out an angry breath. "My boss's wife. Can you believe it? She was furious, and she reported him. The police didn't do much about it, but then Tucker attended a Christmas party with me, and I personally introduced her to my husband, the man who had conned her. I tell you, Katie, it was a mess."

I felt sure that if it had been me, I'd have described the situation a bit more colorfully. "I bet it was. Did Tucker go to jail?"

"Naw. He gave the money back, and she let it drop. I lost my job, though. My boss thought I was in on it. They all did. It was awful. I knew Tucker was a little sketchy, but not that bad. I filed for divorce within the week."

I reached over and squeezed her hand. "I'm sorry."

She snagged my gaze. Those intense blue eyes were so much like Declan's that I couldn't look away.

"Katie, my brother told the family a little about the murder cases you've been involved with."

I braced myself. "Oh?"

"Will you help me?"

Frowning, I asked, "Help you with what?"

"I want to find out who killed Tucker. I told you I wanted closure, and I feel like understanding what happened and why he was killed is how I'm going to get it."

"Maybe," I said slowly. "But the police are investigating. Don't you trust them?"

She shrugged.

Never mind that I myself didn't always trust Detective Quinn. He was quite competent, of course, but when there was magic involved, he didn't always know what to look for.

This is Declan's sister, not to mention a victim who used glamour spells. And then there's the heads-up from my dragonfly totems.

I sighed inwardly. The truth was, I was already looking into Tucker's murder. I'd sneaked a look at the crime scene, practically interrogated the manager at the Spotlight Motel, poked around online, and had been gathering background on Tucker most of the morning. Even with the wedding and family in town—and more to come—it was as if I couldn't help myself.

"Okay," I said. "I'll do what I can to help. I'm not sure where to go next with this, though."

Rori studied me for a few seconds, then seemed to make a decision. Swinging her feet to the floor, she leaned over and reached into her bag. Her hand came out holding the music box Tucker had given her. She held it out to me.

"Tucker said he needed to sell this because he owed someone money. That means it has to be worth some real coin, don't you think?"

I took the little ceramic birdhouse and looked at the

bottom. There was a faint maker's mark there, but I knew nothing about how to figure out how much money Rori might be able to get for it.

"Jaida said Detective Quinn didn't think it was worth anything. It's one of the reasons . . ." I trailed off.

"One of the reasons what?" Rori asked.

One of the reasons you're on his suspect list.

"Never mind," I said. "You think it could be valuable?"

"That's really why I was driving around yesterday," Rori said. "Trying to figure out whether to keep it or not. Whether it would be better to have the money from it or better to confront Tucker and close that chapter of my life forever."

"And you decided to close the chapter."

She half shrugged. "Yes. Plus he sounded pretty desperate when he called. But I had to wait until after supper to get away from Mother and Eliza. By that time, well . . ."

"It was too late," I finished.

"Now I'm wondering how much this might be worth. Maybe it was why Tucker was killed."

"The music box?" I asked, surprised. "For the money he owed, maybe, but probably not for this thing. This, um, lovely little thing," I amended.

She laughed. "It's not exactly my style. But if I could sell it . . ."

"Hmm. What did you have in mind?" I asked. "As far as finding out how much it's worth."

She beamed. "Will you come with me?"

"That depends on where you're going." I was starting to get frustrated with Declan's little sis.

"I want to take it to a friend of Tucker's."

I felt my eyes narrowing. "Who's this friend?"

"His name is Hudson Prater. He's an antique dealer here in town. I looked him up, and he's still in business. Will you come? I've never done this kind of thing before, and Declan says you're good at investigations."

"Do you need to leave, Katie?" Lucy asked from behind my left elbow. She'd materialized without my noticing it, and now grabbed our empties to take back to the kitchen. "We can handle things. Go ahead."

I turned and looked at her. She was giving me a you-know-you-want-to look.

"Oh, good!" Rori said and hopped to her feet. "I have the address of Hudson's store right here."

Chapter 10

My aunt was right; I did want to find out more about the music box, but perhaps as important, I wanted to keep an eye on Rori. I went back to the office to grab my tote and explain to Mungo where I was going.

"Do you mind staying here?" I asked. "I don't know what the protocol is for dogs in antique stores."

He grunted and rolled over on his back on the club chair. I gave him a belly scritch, and his eyes drifted closed. I didn't think he'd be mysteriously showing up in my car this time.

Before I left the office, I called Declan. He answered with a mumble.

"Sorry I woke you," I said. "Rori is here."

"Mmph. Yeah. I see I got a text from her. Is she okay?"

"Yes. But she's insisting we take the music box Tucker gave her to some friend of his to see how much it's worth." I told him what she'd said.

"A friend of Tucker's? I don't like that."

"He owns an antique store, so it's not like we're meeting him in some back alley."

"Yeah, okay. Listen, I'm going to make some calls, see if I can find out anything from my friend at the medical examiner's office." I wondered whether he had the same friend that Steve did. "Call me when you find anything out."

"I will. Oh, and Deck? I heard back from the wedding officiants I e-mailed. Neither are available."

"Hmm. Maybe we should have your mother bring her guy down from Fillmore after all." My mother actually had offered to pay for Pastor Freeman to fly down to Savannah to marry us.

"Very funny," I said. "I like the old guy well enough, but it seems so . . . I don't know."

"Like your mother getting her way."

I made a face even though he couldn't see it. "I hate to say it, but yes."

"Don't worry. I'm working on my idea."

"What is it?"

"I have to check into a couple of things first. Then I'll tell you."

"Okay," I said reluctantly. But I trusted him, and when we hung up, I felt better.

Prater's Antiques was near the intersection of Victoria and Bull. We passed a Popeyes fast-food restaurant, and soon turned into a small parking lot. I parked the Bug, and we got out. The only other car in the parking lot was an ancient Buick Riviera.

The door was glass, but so dirty you couldn't really see inside. Rori pushed it open, and we entered a hoarder's paradise. Furniture was wedged into every conceivable space, leaving a maze of narrow aisles for customers to navigate. On top of the breakfronts and dining tables, dressers and buffets, upholstered sofas and well-worn chairs, smaller furnishings were stacked along with everything from tea sets to metal advertising signs, paintings to dishware. In the back, I spied a rack of clothing, and wondered if that was where the smell of mothballs originated. The odor mixed with what I thought of as granny-attic smell—a combination of weathered ink on paper, dust, and mysteriously hidden mildew. The humidity didn't help the smell, and the laboring air conditioner didn't help the humidity. Or the heat, for that matter.

I grabbed a thin book of piano music from the cluttered harpsichord by the door and fanned myself with it as Rori and I ventured farther into the warren. When we reached the middle of the maze, we discovered a man I was pretty sure must be the owner of the Buick in the parking lot. He lounged in a tattered armchair beside a counter that held an old-fashioned cash register, a rack of postcards, and a credit card reader. The light from the cell phone he was looking at illuminated his lined face, pale eyes, bushy white eyebrows, and bald pate.

When he saw us, he struggled to his feet, a smile already playing on his face. "Hello, hello, ladies! Welcome! Are you looking for anything in particular?" His arm swept wide, taking in the contents of the store. "Because, believe it or not, I know where everything is in my little paradise here. Just say the word." His head tipped to the side as he studied me. "Ah, I have just the thing for you, my dear. Come with me." He turned toward the back of the store.

It might have been an effective technique with some customers, but I wasn't in the mood for a hard sell. I didn't budge. "Um, sir?"

He stopped and whirled back to face us.

"Mr. Prater?" Rori asked. "Do you remember me?"

His eyes narrowed in speculation. "Should I?"

"You knew Tucker Abbott, didn't you?"

"Tucker! Well, Lord yes." He squinted harder. "I do remember you! We only met a couple of times, though. I don't remember your name."

"Rori McCarthy. I was Rori Abbott back then."

He smacked his hands together, and I jumped. "Of course." His thumbs went to the waistband of his faded jeans, which were held up by red suspenders. "But hang on there, gal. Did you refer to ol' Tucker in the past tense? Or was that just because he's past tense to you?" He chuckled.

She shook her head. "I'm sorry to have to tell you, but Tucker died."

His mouth opened in surprise, while that hung in the air for a few beats. "Well, I'll be. Saw him not too long ago. Looked healthy as a horse. What happened?"

"He was, um . . ." She trailed off.

"Tucker was killed last night at the Spotlight Motel," I said.

Hudson Prater looked gobsmacked. "You don't say." The words were almost a whisper. "Killed?"

I nodded.

He tsked.

The sound of the door opening and closing reached our ears.

Maybe this isn't the best place to talk.

But Rori either didn't hear the noise or didn't care. She stepped over to Prater and took a ball of white tissue paper out of her large purse. "I remember him telling me that you do appraisals for people. He said you really knew your stuff, that you were so good you could be one of those guys on the *Antiques Roadshow.*"

Prater beamed. "Tucker said that?"

"He did." Her head bobbed to emphasize her point. "And I have something here I was hoping you could tell me about." She finished unwrapping the music box and held it out to him.

He took it in both hands. "Well, well. Let's take a look, then." Holding it up to the meager daylight that somehow reached this far into the store, he turned it this way and that, then carried the music box over to the counter and turned on the green-shaded banker's lamp on the corner. We followed and leaned against the counter as he worked.

"Mm-hm." He pulled a pair of reading glasses out of his shirt pocket and put them on, then turned the box over to examine the maker's mark on the bottom. "Mm-hm," he said again. He wound the base and set it on the counter. A few plaintive notes of "When You Wish Upon a Star" played, and then the music box fell silent.

Rori looked at me with wide, hopeful eyes, then swiveled her head to watch him again.

He returned the glasses to his pocket and turned off the light. I could feel Rori's eagerness as she waited for the verdict.

"Where did you get this?" he asked.

"It was a gift," she said. I silently applauded her discretion.

"Did the person who gave it to you indicate its worth?"

I suppressed a sigh. This guy was taking the whole *Antiques Roadshow* reference a bit too seriously.

"Not specifically," Rori said, bouncing a little on the balls of her feet.

"Well, now, don't get too excited, hon. I'm real sorry to have to tell you this, but it's a piece of junk."

Rori stilled and stared at the antique dealer. "Junk," she repeated weakly.

"Oh, I'm sorry I called it that. It's a nice enough little knickknack, if you like that kind of thing. And you do, am I right?" He beamed at her again and handed the music box back to her. "So you keep that there on your dresser or wherever and just enjoy it."

"It's not worth anything?" she demanded.

"Maybe twenty dollars. In fact . . ." He fell silent as he thought. "A few days ago, someone was in here looking for a ceramic birdhouse music box. He was real specific about what he was looking for. The way he described it, could have been this very one."

Alarm klaxons went off in my head. "Could you put us in touch with him?" I asked.

"Sorry. I didn't get his name. He was blond, in his early fifties." He snapped his fingers. "I'll tell you what, Miss Rori. If you really don't want this little piece, you can leave it here in case he comes back in. I won't even charge my usual forty percent commission on consignments. Let's say twenty-five percent."

Rori was already shaking her head. "Thank you, but I'm going to keep it."

"All righty, then. You enjoy it."

She nodded and offered him a small smile. "I do so

appreciate you taking a look and giving me your honest opinion, Mr. Prater."

"Don't give it another thought. Now." He looked at me. "You sure you don't want to take a look at—"

I made a show of looking at my watch and broke in. "I'm afraid I'm going to have to come back another time, sir. Bit of a time crunch right now."

He wasn't fooled, but he didn't seem to mind. "I understand."

"May I leave you my phone number in case the man who was looking for a music box like this one returns? Even if Rori wants to keep it, I'd like to talk with him."

Suspicion flashed across his face then was gone. "I see. Sure—go ahead and leave your number." He reached over on the counter and tore off the top page from the daily calendar by the register. It was from the week before. He handed it to me along with a pen, and I flipped it over and jotted my cell number on the back.

"Thanks," I said. "We appreciate—"

The sound of a ringing phone echoed back from the front of the store, then was suddenly cut off.

"Oops, I'd better check on that customer. Look forward to seeing you again, ladies." He hurried off toward the front of the store.

We followed behind, heading for the exit. As we rounded a hulking china hutch, I saw Prater walking toward a woman about forty feet away. She wore a sundress, strappy sandals, a wide-brimmed hat, and sunglasses.

The sunglasses made me think she must have just come in, but she still hadn't taken them off by the time we reached the door, even in the dark interior of the shop. Plus, I'd heard someone enter the store earlier. Puzzled, I turned and looked back as we went out the door. She was blatantly watching us. She turned away as Prater approached her.

"Brr," Rori said, rewrapping the music box in its white tissue paper as we crossed the parking lot to the car. "I just got the strangest shiver. I hope I'm not coming down with something."

"I hope not, too," I said, still distracted.

We walked around the crossover SUV that was now parked by the Buick and got in my car.

"Can you believe the nerve of that guy?" Rori said.

"Because . . . ?"

"Saying my little music box isn't worth anything."

"You don't believe him?"

"Why should I? Tucker said he needed to sell it."

I didn't say anything.

"And at Wisteria House, he said it was valuable," she insisted. Then she sighed and sat back in the seat. "I can't believe I said that. Tucker lied to me. Of course he did. Tucker always lied." Suddenly she slapped the dash. "And I fell for it all over again."

"Did Tucker tell you how much it was worth?"

She shook her head.

"Maybe he wasn't talking about money, then. Maybe he was talking about a different kind of value."

She snorted.

"Can I see it?"

Rori handed me the music box and then turned to stare out the window, a look of disgust on her face.

Tentatively, I reached out with my senses, alert for any evidence that the knickknack held some kind of magic. Any kind of power at all. I traced the edges of the little flowers, ran my finger along the painted ribbon, pushing and prodding, hoping to trigger a secret compartment. I turned it over and looked at the bottom again. I wound it up and listened to the notes that tinkled out.

Nothing. Nada. Zilch.

The gift Tucker had given Rori wasn't worth money, and it was as magically dead as a doorknob. But someone had come to Prater's looking for something exactly like it. Could there be another music box like it? One that actually was worth some, as Rori put it, coin?

Sighing, I reached over and lightly rubbed the sprigs of holy basil and lemon balm in the bud vase on the dash, hoping the scent would help my brain cells and Rori's mood. "We'll keep looking into it."

Chapter 11

"You'd better get going," Lucy said.

I looked up in surprise. The pre-lunch rush had died down, and I'd grabbed a towel to give the bistro tables a wipe.

"To Vase Value," she said. "Mimsey's expecting to go over the arrangements for the wedding a final time."

Doing a mental face palm, I put down the towel and reached to untie my chintz half apron. "Thanks for reminding me."

Of course, we'd worked out the flowers a couple of months ago, but part of wedding planning seemed to be going over everything at least twice—catering choices, fittings and refittings of dresses, a preview of hair and makeup, and now, revisiting the flowers.

"Iris, can you take over for Katie?" Lucy called.

She two-stepped over from where she'd been rinsing off muffin tins to put in the dishwasher. "Sure thing. What's up?"

Handing her the towel, I said, "I forgot some wedding stuff I need to tend to. Can you wipe things down?"

"No problem," she said and sashayed out to the front of the bakery.

"Right. And then you can mix up the sourdough if you want. Give me a shout if you have any questions," Lucy said to her. "I'll be in the office."

Our helper waved her agreement and got to work.

"My supposedly low-key wedding sure is taking me away from the Honeybee a lot lately," I said to Lucy. "I'm so sorry that I keep leaving you in the lurch like this."

She waved away my apology. "Please. This is your *wedding*, Katie. Good heavens."

"The wedding didn't take me away this morning."

"It's okay," she said. "You know you always have Ben's and my support, as well as that of the spellbook club. This mess with Declan's little sister is just awful. You do what you have to do."

"You're the best, Aunt Lucy. And again—the unpacking you all did last night? And that closet . . ." I shook my head in wonder. "I'm going to guess you charged the herbal sachet with a little extra spell work, too."

"With a little help from our friends, dear." She gave me a wide, warm smile.

I gave her a smile of my own. "I'll hurry."

Mungo hopped right into the tote as soon as he found out we were going to Vase Value. He adored Mimsey, of course, but for some reason he seemed to enjoy hanging out with Heckle, too. The parrot was often rude, but Mungo didn't seem to care a bit. Probably a familiar thing.

It was a short way and a spate of rain had moved through and cooled things down a bit, so I walked the few blocks to Mimsey's shop. Soon, the canvas awning of Vase Value came into view. Shaded beneath, wooden crates were stacked to showcase a myriad of houseplants and tropicals in full bloom—gardenia, anthurium, hibiscus, and bromeliad among them. Trailing ferns framed the entrance, and on each side, clusters of cut blooms basked in galvanized tubs filled with chilled water.

Pushing the door open, I could see the register, and behind that Mimsey's office and the area where Mimsey and her assistant, Ryan, created their stunning floral arrangements. However, to get there you had to traverse what I had come to think of as the gauntlet of temptation. A single aisle led from the entrance to the counter at the back of the store. Each side was filled with flower and garden-themed gift items jammed onto the shelves and arranged on tables, all interspersed with tiny bonsai trees and herbal topiaries in pots. I steadfastly marched past adorable gardening aprons, unique gardening tools, rubber clogs, gloves, hats, and floral embossed kneeling pads. I managed to ignore the birdhouses made from gourds and old boots and turned away from blown glass hummingbird feeders. Wind chimes and plant markers had no effect. I'd almost made it when I saw something tucked in behind the fairy garden supplies. I had to stop and look.

Now, I don't think of myself as a cutesy kind of woman. Fairy gardens are not my thing. I mean, I get the appeal of the miniature tableaus, the idea of the wee folk visiting my gardens. But I was acquainted with the spirit of an actual leprechaun, albeit a missing one at the moment, and somehow the tiny plastic bridges and wire lawn furniture paled in comparison. No, what had caught my attention was tucked in behind a miniature replica of an Airstream trailer.

It was a sundial, six inches in diameter. When I picked it up, I found it to be much heavier than it looked. The surface was aged copper, and among the lines that indicated the hours, Celtic knots and swirls rose from the surface in subtle bas relief. A green patina graced the edges as if air-brushed on. Even Mungo leaned out of the tote to sniff it, then looked up at me as if to ask why I hadn't already purchased it.

Shaking my head at myself, I carried the sundial back to the counter. Ryan was wrapping green tape around a carnation boutonniere as I approached. His work area was cluttered with wires, different shapes and sizes of vases, decorative ribbons, and cutting tools. My friend's assistant was in his mid-twenties, had a shock of corn-colored hair, brown eyes behind red-framed glasses, and according to Mimsey, possessed an otherworldly talent when it came to flower arranging. She said he was always eager to learn more about his craft, and if the stark Ikebana art piece of cherry blossoms and a single sprout of bamboo on the counter behind him was any indication, his skill was only improving.

He looked up and grinned as I approached, then stuck his half-finished arrangement in a block of floral foam and wiped his hands with a towel.

"Hey, Katie. All ready for your big day?"

"I sure hope so."

He rang up my purchase, and I slid it into the side pocket of my tote.

"Say, aren't you guys worried that someone might take off with one of those plants out front?" I asked.

He offered a facial shrug. "Right? But oddly, that's never happened. Mimsey says not to worry. She's got it handled."

Protection spells galore, I bet.

"And she's the boss. I just do what I'm told."

"Speaking of the boss lady, is she available? I think she's expecting me."

He gestured toward her office, where she was standing behind her desk talking on the phone. "Feel free. But be warned. Our supplier tried to overcharge for those white rose petals for your wedding, and she's setting him straight."

Mimsey firmly returned her phone to the cradle then, and I knew I wouldn't want to be the person who'd been on the other end of the line. She looked up and saw me. A smile transformed her face, and she waved me in.

"Katie!" She bustled around the desk and threw her arms around me and at the same time Mungo, still in the tote, as far as they would go.

Which wasn't that far, since her arms were so short. Today, she wore linen slacks the color of lime sherbet and a gauzy top in the same color trimmed with strawberry pink. Green being the color of both money and plant magic, she wore some shade of it to work several days a week.

"Sit down, sit down." She pointed to the guest chair.

I put my tote on the floor and sank onto the seat. Mungo hopped out and went to sit by Heckle's perch in the corner. The huge multicolored parrot had been

Mimsey's familiar since she was a teenager. He still looked as bright-eyed as she did, peering down at his canine visitor and then tipping his head to the side to look at me.

Squaaaawk! Katie's gettin' hitched! Squaaaawk!

"Yes, she is," Mimsey said cheerfully. "Now, let's take a final look to make sure we're on the same page." She pulled a file out of her desk drawer and extracted a series of photographs. "I've already ordered the white rose petals, and plenty of them, to create the carpet for you to walk down to the gazebo."

"Ryan said there was an issue with the price?"

"Not anymore there isn't. Cheeky man thought he could pull one over on me. But we're all set there. And you were very sure about the casual arrangements on the tables, which made it easier to tailor them to add a bit of flower magic here and there. Here's what I had in mind for the small vases of flax and apple blossoms."

"Flax for domesticity and apples because we've chosen each other."

"Right. Apples mean 'you're the one for me' in essence. And I'll add sprigs of fern to augment the magic all around." She beamed, truly in her element.

"Sounds good. What about the sunflowers?"

"For devotion and adoration. Yes, I love them, but really, they'll clash with the fancy roses, don't you think?"

"Yeah, I see what you mean."

"So let's put big ol' bunches of sunflowers all over the inside of the carriage house. They're cheery, and they really pop in a small space. You won't need anything else."

"I like it!"

"Oh, good. Because there's a reason roses are so popular at weddings. With your permission, I'd like to add a few more red roses on the gazebo, for *love*, honey! Love and respect. I mean, the white petals are necessary to show up in the twilight of evening against the lawn, but you simply must have plenty of red roses at your wedding."

I grinned. "Well, if you say so."

"I do. Now, your wedding bouquet. That has to be perfect."

"I think the one we already designed is perfect," I said with a frown.

She shuffled some pictures around and found the one she wanted. Brightening, she said, "Why yes. This is just right. I'd forgotten Ryan made a sample after we talked last time. Here's the photo."

It was a simple arrangement of two kinds of lavender and baby's breath with a single giant red rose smack dab in the middle. The whole of it was twined with the tiniest possible leaves of bird's foot ivy. Just looking at the picture made me happy.

Mimsey replaced the photos in their folder and sat back, clearly satisfied. "Good. Now that that's taken care of, tell me about the murder." Her bright blue eyes glittered with interest.

"Didn't Lucy fill you in?"

"Yes, last night after Ben told her. I'm sure some information was lost as it traveled down the grapevine. It always is."

"Oh, gosh, Mims. Rori is Declan's sister, and—"

She held up her hand. "Yes, I know all that. What I

really want to know is what you're doing about finding this killer."

I gave her a wry look. "So far I've asked a bunch of questions. You know I'm kind of busy right now, don't you?"

"Busy schmizzy. You have a calling, Katie. You must follow it."

Mimsey, who was truly the leader of the spellbook club even if no one actually said it out loud, deeply believed that I could not outrun my calling to right wrongs in the magical world. I'd thought the same thing when I was first told I was a lightwitch but, as a result, felt more trapped than "called." Then I'd learned I did have a choice. Of course I did. We all have choices. So far, I'd chosen to follow the calling, even though it was touch-and-go sometimes. Knowing I could say no made saying yes feel better.

And like it or not, this time I'd committed again.

Rather than rehash all that with Mimsey, I leaned forward and asked, "What can you tell me about glamours?"

Her perfectly shaped eyebrow raised a fraction. "Why do you think I know anything about such things?"

It took me a couple of moments to catch on, and when I did, I laughed. "Oh, you think I'm asking because that's why you look about fifteen years younger than you actually are?"

"You know I don't . . . I would never . . ." she spluttered.

"Relax. I'm asking because Tucker Abbott used one. I figured it out the first time I met him. Well, okay, that was also the only time I met him. But it was strong. Over the top, really. He was way too perfect in every way. That's what alerted me that something was wrong right away. If he'd been a bit more subtle, I might not have noticed as quickly."

Maybe that was why Eliza had seen through the façade as well.

Mimsey's eyes sparkled. "Ooh, a glamour. Well, isn't that interesting. And strong, so probably not accidental."

"I wondered that, too. I remember you remarking one time after seeing some politician at work that a lot of people in that profession use glamours as part of their personality."

"Indeed. See, a lot of people, witches included, think that glamours are all about appearance. That's part of it, but not all of it. In the end, it's about charisma. How someone is perceived physically is generally a large part of charisma, but beauty is in the eye of the beholder, and *that* is what glamours are about."

"Putting beauty in the eye of the beholder?"

She half shrugged. "That's as good a way to put it as anything."

"Then that would have to depend on the beholder, at least to a degree. Some people make better marks than others?"

"Absolutely. And certain people use a glamour instinctively."

"And if it's not instinctive? How do you create a glamour?"

Laughing, she wagged her finger. "First off, I don't."

Squaaaaaaaaaawk!

"You hush, mister," she said to Heckle, then turned her attention back to me.

My eyes were narrowed, as if by squinting I would be

able to see if she had added a little extra something to how I perceived her.

"Stop that." She rolled her eyes. "Now listen, if, *if* I were to do such a thing, there are a couple of ways to go about it. First, I could cast a circle as we do with so many spells, and then work with a mirror to invoke change in whatever area I thought needed improvement."

I made a face. "I hate to put it like this, but that sounds like—forgive me—magical thinking. If it worked, the diet industry would be out of a job."

"In most cases, you'd be right. With enough power, a witch could effect change in how she was seen by others using that method. Usually, however, casting a glamour that way affects the spell caster more than anything—changing how they see themselves, boosting confidence, that kind of thing." She sighed. "True self-acceptance is so much better, and it lasts a lot longer."

"I'm having a hard time imagining Tucker pointing to his face and intoning a spell to make it better looking."

"There are other kinds of glamour spells. You can confer magical power to scent, perfume or cologne for example. But probably the most common is to use a sigil."

My forehead knitted. "You mean a magical symbol?"

"Right. A written sign, worked into everyday routines like applying makeup or using shaving cream or lotion."

"What kind of sigil? Are there specific ones for making yourself appealing?"

"Not really. The best kind of sigil is created by the witch, male or female, as a personal symbol representing the desired alteration. So the sigil could look like anything. As with any spell, it's the intent that counts."

"I wonder if Tucker did that? Traced some sign on his face in shaving cream every morning or some such."

"Declan's sister was married to him. She might be able to answer that."

"I'll ask her. This morning she said he'd always been handsome and larger than life, but when he came to see her yesterday, he was downright mesmerizing. That makes me wonder if he's always had a natural glamour and only recently figured out how to up his game."

"Was he dating anyone?" Mimsey asked.

"The motel manager said his girlfriend just broke up with him, and he was trying to get back together with her."

Her eyebrows rose, and she grinned. "There you go, Katie. I might be making assumptions, but I bet a recent girlfriend would know a bit about Tucker's morning rituals."

"I only know her first name." I began to frown, then brightened. "And where she works. She's a hostess at Belford's."

Mimsey looked at her watch and then waggled her eyebrows at me. "That sounds like the perfect place to have lunch today, don't you think?"

Shaking my head, I said, "I can't take a lunch."

"Then you've eaten?"

"No, but I've already dumped too much on the others at the bakery lately."

"Nonsense." She stood and picked up her cell phone from the desk. "I'm texting Lucy right now that you're going to lunch with me at my insistence."

"Mims . . ."

"Hush. Let me do this." She finished typing on her phone, which she was surprisingly fast at, and bent to grab her purse from under the desk. "Mungo, you stay here with Heckle, and I'll bring Katie back in an hour or so."

Yip!

Chapter 12

Mimsey drove, and on the way, I sent Rori a text to ask if Tucker had ever traced designs on his face when he shaved or applied cologne. Her response was immediate.

WTH? I don't get it. He just shaved like men shave and then left the stubble in the sink.

I texted back.

Never mind.

By then Mimsey had located a parking space near the southwest corner of City Market. Two stories high and made of brick, the Belford's building had been built around 1900 to house Savannah's Hebrew Congregation. Two decades later, the Belford family purchased it for their wholesale foods business, and in the 1990s it became one of Savannah's fine dining restaurants. Declan and I had eaten supper there a few times. Though they were considered a steak and seafood place, the Southern fried chicken with Gouda mac and cheese and collard greens was to die for.

I'd never been to Belford's for lunch. As Mimsey and

I strolled by the arched windows that marched down the front of the building, I felt like a teenager playing hooky. Inside, the walls were also brick, and the expanse of wood floor glowed umber beneath dark, linen-covered tables.

"You know, it's unlikely Effie will even be here," I said to Mimsey as we waited to be seated. "Given what happened to Tucker last night. The manager of the Spotlight Motel wanted to make sure someone told Effie about Tucker's death, so she would have told the police about her. Knowing Quinn, he'd interview the victim's recent girlfriend the first chance he got."

"Oh, I expect you're right, dear." Her eyes twinkled up at me. "I was hoping we might be able to find out her last name, though. At the same time, we can indulge in a lovely lunch. I hardly ever get to spend time with you anymore, and rarely alone."

"We're so busy at the bakery—" I started.

"Which is wonderful, of course," she broke in. "But also, a very poor excuse for how hard you work. Iris is working more than half-time, isn't she?"

"She is, but—"

"You're not indispensable, dear. Working twelve hours a day six or seven days a week is not good for you."

Before I could protest, a goateed man appeared to seat us. Definitely not Effie.

He pulled out a chair for Mimsey, who settled into it with a murmured thanks. Then she looked up at him. "The other night my husband and I ate here, and there was a lovely young woman hostessing."

"I expect that would be Nadine, ma'am. Or perhaps Effie."

"Yes! Effie. And what is her last name again? My husband thinks he might know her family."

"It's Glass, ma'am."

Well, that was easy.

"But I believe all of her family is in Tennessee."

"Ah, I see. I'll let him know." She flashed him a charming smile.

He smiled back. "She's over there behind the bar, if you want to ask her yourself."

My head turned so fast, my neck cramped.

"Oh!" Mimsey looked around in a much more lady-like manner. "I didn't realize she tended bar as well."

"The regular guy called in sick, so she's covering his shift. Makes a mean bourbon and grapefruit, if you're interested. Fresh squeezed juice."

"Thank you so very much, but delicious as that libation sounds, I think I'll pass. We'll stop by to chat on our way out, though. She looks terribly busy right now."

It was true. The big-haired blonde mixing drinks behind the bar was working alone, though she appeared unflustered as she shook and poured for the lunch crowd.

He nodded and stepped back as a waiter brought us water and asked us if we had any questions.

I eyed the shrimp and clam linguine, but Declan had said something about making pasta for dinner. Instead, I opted for a cup of she-crab soup and a grilled pimiento cheese sandwich. Mimsey delicately sipped her way through a bowl of watermelon gazpacho, and we let talk of murder and weddings go long enough to catch up on our lives. As we chatted, I did my best not to watch Tucker's ex-girlfriend working behind the bar. For the most part, I was successful.

When we were finished eating, I looked at my watch. My companion frowned and shook her head. She insisted on paying the check. Taking her time, she counted out cash and a generous tip. I thanked her for lunch, but by then, I was fortified with considerably more calories than I needed and was practically twitching in anticipation of talking to Effie Glass.

"Come along, Katie. We've been handed the perfect opportunity to find the next clue in the case."

Amused, I followed her across the restaurant to the bar. "You sound like Miss Marple," I murmured.

"I'll take that as a compliment."

We'd arrived toward the end of the lunch hour, and the crowd had thinned out as we'd eaten. Now only two people sat at one end of the bar, and the drink orders from the tables had dried up. Tucker's ex-girlfriend stood at the opposite end of the expanse of dark walnut, cutting up limes. When we approached, she put the knife down and looked at us expectantly.

As I'd seen from the other side of the room, Effie had blond hair—but not just blond. Every color of blond, with highlights on top of highlights on top of more highlights. It was curled and fluffed and sprayed to the point where it barely moved when she turned her head. Her eyebrows were shaped and painted, her eyelashes were longer than nature could ever have managed, and there was no way those fingernails were real. The thing was, she pulled it all off with confident aplomb, and I had to admit she looked fantastic. Her black shirt and slacks were the perfect canvas for all the glitz and glamour.

Glamour. Is that what I'm seeing?

I looked closer. No, her skin wasn't perfect, and her

features were a little irregular. She wasn't employing magic; she was employing expert beauty tips.

"Hello, ladies. What can I get you?" she asked.

Mimsey hitched herself up on a bar chair, which increased her height considerably. I followed her lead, wondering what she had in mind.

"Honey, you don't need to get us a thing," she said, her voice infused with sympathy. "I only wanted to stop by and extend my condolences."

I leaned forward slightly, trying not to be too obvious as I gauged Effie Glass' reaction.

She blinked, then gave a faltering smile. "Um . . . ?"

"Regarding Tucker Abbott," Mimsey said. "Tragic. Just tragic."

"I'm sorry, I'm sure we've met, but . . ."

My friend nodded wisely. "Mimsey Carmichael. You remember now, don't you?" There was something in her voice.

Then I realized with a shock that it wasn't something *in* her voice, it *was* her Voice. In all the time I'd known her, I hadn't known she possessed that talent and had certainly never witnessed her using it. Her Voice was markedly different from mine and Cookie's, the only other member of the spellbook club who had that skill. It was like a scalpel versus a butcher's knife. I watched in awe as Mimsey's few words slid subtly through Effie's resistance, grateful the older witch was on the side of good.

Effie's face cleared. "Mimsey."

"And this is my friend, Katie Lightfoot."

She didn't even look at me. "Of course. How are you?"

"I'm fine, dear. The question is, how are you?"

The other woman looked blank for a moment, and I suddenly had the horrible thought that she didn't know Tucker was dead. Then her face cleared, and she looked down.

"Well, it was quite a shock when the police told me this morning. It had been weeks since I'd seen Tucker, though. We weren't, you know, together anymore."

Mimsey reached over the bar and patted her hand. "Still, it must be difficult."

Effie began to nod, then her lips pressed together, and she shook her head instead. "I would never wish him dead. I wouldn't wish anyone dead. But that man lied to me like you wouldn't believe."

I believed her—on both counts.

"Oh, dear." Mimsey gave a sympathetic shake of her head.

"Over-the-top lies. Like when we were first dating? He told me his uncle had left him a million dollars but that he could only have access to the trust if he could prove he was truly happy. He said maybe I could make him truly happy."

Mimsey's eyes had grown round. "Oh, dear!"

"Can you believe that load of guacamole? I didn't exactly fall for it, you know. I mean, it was too cheesy, like something out of a movie." She paused. "But there was something so romantic about it, too."

"Like out of a movie," Mimsey said.

I stayed quiet as a mouse, not wanting to break the spell. So to speak.

"He lied about quitting his job at the vacation rental place—he was fired—and about where he was sometimes." Her nostrils flared. "*And* who he was seeing.

Oh, and his latest whopper? He said he'd won the lottery. The *lottery*. Told me if I came back to him, we'd run away to live on some beach someplace. Just another movie script. Can you believe it?" Her face was a mix of emotion.

Mimsey opened her mouth to speak, but Effie barreled on. "Well, I sure didn't. Money doesn't grow on trees, my mother has always said. And I didn't believe Tucker when he said he wasn't seeing another woman, either. Because I think he was, no matter how much he denied it."

"Oh?" my friend prompted.

"All of a sudden, he seemed different. Like, somehow more appealing. If he hadn't lied to me so much, I might have been fooled. But right about then, he started wearing this big ol' ring, and he wouldn't take it off, ever."

"A ring?" Mimsey leaned forward. Though her demeanor didn't change, I could tell she was excited. "Where did he get it?"

"Exactly! I know someone gave it to him, someone he didn't want me to know about, because he wouldn't tell me. *He* said he bought it at one of those stupid estate sales he was always working at. All week setting up, and then all weekend selling other people's old crap to people who didn't need it. No time for me at all. Like it would take that much time to put a bunch of price tags on stuff." Shaking her head, she mused. "But Lordy, that man could sell, I'll give him that." Then she exhaled an angry huff of air. "He sold me a bill of goods, that's for sure."

"I'm so sorry, Effie," Mimsey said with genuine sincerity. "I'm glad you're going to be able to move on now. And the police have already spoken with you?"

"They came by my apartment this morning. Apparently Tucker still had me in his phone contacts. I felt like I was really getting over him, and then that detective got me all riled up again. When work called to see if I could bartend for a shift, I leaped at the chance." Suddenly, her eyes welled up, and she choked out, "To keep busy, you know."

Mimsey nodded. "Of course, honey. You don't know whether to feel sad or mad or glad, do you?"

Speechless, Effie shook her head.

The older witch patted her hand again. "Well, don't you worry. It sounds like things were quite complicated between you two. There's no right way to handle all this, and nothing you feel is wrong. Understand?" I thought I heard her Voice again but couldn't be sure.

Either way, Effie seemed to relax. "Thank you. It's helped to talk about it."

"I'm so glad." Mimsey slid off the chair.

Apparently, we were leaving. I desperately tried to figure out how on earth I could ask Tucker's ex if he traced designs on his face with shaving cream on a regular basis without her thinking I had totally lost my mind when Mimsey turned and spoke again.

"Effie, honey?"

"Yes, Mimsey?"

"Which estate sale company did Tucker work for?"

"Gibson Estate Sales. It's a husband and wife team."

"And darlin', what did that ring of Tucker's look like?"

"Oh. Well, it was big, like I said. Gold, with these weird squiggles carved into the sides, you know? And there was a big ruby in the middle. One time, I noticed more squiggles under the ruby itself, like it was set over a, what do you call it? A signet."

"Yes, a signet ring," Mimsey said, arching an eyebrow at me. "Now I want you to take good care of yourself, Effie. And you'll be just fine." Again, a thread of her Voice rode the words. It wasn't a command; more like permission.

"Thank you." Tucker's ex-girlfriend's voice held true relief.

As we stepped onto the sidewalk, I said, "You never cease to surprise me."

"Oh?"

"First off, the way you use your Voice. Can you teach me how to do that?" Even though it was strong, I was extremely reluctant to use my Voice. Actually, because it was so strong. After all, I'd nearly killed Declan with it one time. Believe me, there's nothing like stopping the heart of the man you love with a single word to test a relationship. We'd survived that test, but I'd kept my Voice under wraps since then.

Well, mostly.

"Over time, you'll become more adept," Mimsey said.

I sighed. "Maybe. You're so good, though. Such a light touch. I bet you could hire out to the police. Get the bad guys to confess right away."

"Pfft. I try to do what I can when I can. As you know, one must be judicious in the use of any power that manipulates others." She stopped by her car and gave me a broad smile. "But sometimes using that power can help a confused young woman and at the same time net you a clue in a murder investigation."

Frowning, I waited while Mimsey unlocked the car from her side, and we got in. After she started the engine, I asked, "The ring? Because I noticed he was wearing a big ruby ring when he visited Rori."

"Indeed, the ring. I'll bet anything that ring contained a sigil—or two—that invoked Tucker Abbott's glamour."

"Wow."

"Especially the one hidden by the ruby. My guess is that Tucker had a natural glamour as a part of his charismatic personality. Effie said after he started wearing the ring, he seemed to have even more appeal."

"And Rori said she didn't remember him being so mesmerizing back when they were married. I put it down to familiarity."

Mimsey's eyes twinkled. "That might be part of it, but I think that ring gave his glamour an extra *oomph*, as it were. Another layer."

As she pulled onto the street, I considered. "You wouldn't just find a cool ring and put it on and, boom, you're even more glamorous than before, right?"

Mimsey tipped her head. "Not likely. The power of the ring would have to be focused."

"So Tucker must have had some training in magic, right?"

"Perhaps. Or he found someone else to invoke the power for him. It could be done."

"Oh. I hadn't thought of that. Who would do that?"

Mimsey shook her head. "Someone he knew. Someone he hired. Who knows?"

She parked near Vase Value. We got out and started walking. Suddenly, I stopped dead in my tracks. Closed my eyes. Tried to envision the motel room. Tucker prone on the floor. When my eyes popped open, Mimsey was watching me with an expectant expression.

"What is it?"

"I was trying to remember if I'd seen that ring on Tucker's hand at the motel."

Her eyes widened. "You saw him?"

"Yeah, I sneaked a look when no one was watching."

She grinned, a reaction that should have surprised me, but by now didn't. "And the ring?" she asked.

"No, I don't remember it. But I don't think his hands were in view. And I could have easily missed seeing it, even if I'd been looking right at it. The scene was pretty unpleasant."

She sobered. "Of course it was. Perhaps Peter Quinn can tell you if Tucker was wearing his ring."

"Good idea," I said. "And Mims? Thanks for lunch. Even if we had an ulterior motive for going to Belford's, it was such a nice respite."

Beaming, she said, "You're so welcome, dear. We should do it more often."

Chapter 13

Back at the bakery, Mungo settled in for a nap in his bed on a bottom shelf in the reading area. I texted Detective Quinn to ask if Tucker had been wearing a ruby ring when he died, then I quickly donned an apron. Iris had finished mixing up the sourdough for the next day's baking and was cleaning up the kitchen. Lucy chatted with a customer at the register. Ben was nowhere to be seen. I looked around for whatever might need doing and spied the half-empty pastry case.

When Lucy's customer left, I said, "It must have been a busy lunch rush. I'm sorry I wasn't here. Mimsey insisted I go to lunch with her. I mean, there was someone I wanted to talk to at the restaurant, but still—"

"Katie, we were fine," Lucy broke in with an easy smile. "Relax."

Maybe I wasn't indispensable, as Mimsey had said. I had to admit, I felt a bit ambivalent about that. Nice to think I might be able to take a day off now and again, but also, it was nice to be needed.

"Where's Ben?" I looked around as if he might have suddenly materialized without my noticing.

"He had an errand to run. It shouldn't take long."

"Okay. Well, at least I can restock the case," I said, starting back to the kitchen.

"M'kay," Lucy said in a distracted tone. She was looking at her phone.

"Everything okay?"

"What?" She looked up. "Oh. Of course." She slipped her phone into her pocket.

I filled the trays with chocolate peanut butter muffins, sour cream donuts, and the cheddar sage scones that had been on the menu since the day we opened. I'd bent over to arrange slices of caramel apple coffee cake on the tray on the bottom shelf when a loud voice floated through the air.

"Yoo-hoo! Katie!"

"Hello, Mrs. Standish," I said without looking up. I'd know that voice anywhere. She'd been one of our first customers and continued to be one of our best, frequenting the Honeybee nearly every day.

"Oooh, look at that," she said, sounding like a Southern Julia Child with a bullhorn. "Itty-bitty key lime hand pies. I just love key lime pie!"

I stood and gave her a wide smile. Today, Edna Standish wore a zebra-print caftan with several strands of shiny onyx beads looped around her neck and a white scarf artfully tied over her iron gray hair in lieu of her usual turban. Her nails glittered vermilion, as did her lips, but lipstick was her only makeup. Her astute gaze raked the pastries I'd restocked before rising to meet mine.

"We're thinking of putting those pies on the regular menu," I said. "Perhaps full-sized versions. That flavor is so nice in the heat, you know." Though we had a list of popular items not on the regular menu, which we mined for the daily specials, sometimes we tried out new recipes we wanted feedback on. If they were a hit, they often went into rotation on the regular menu. The key lime mini pies were new, and obviously a big hit since there were only ten left.

"I'll take all of those, honey."

Make that none left.

"And throw in a half dozen of those brookies. And a chocolate croissant. Wait, is that chocolate?"

"Hazelnut spread, actually."

"Oooh! I'll take two, then."

"Deal," I said.

"And what's that?" She pointed.

"I was making samples for my tiered cupcake wedding cake," I said. "Those are hummingbird muffins."

"With pineapple on top? Oh, honey, I'm going to love that wedding cake! What an excellent idea! I'll take three. And how are the wedding plans going?" she asked as I unfolded a box and began loading her order into it.

"Everything seems to be fine. Though there is one hitch."

"Uh-oh!"

"Judge Matthews had to go to Chicago for a family emergency and can't perform the ceremony."

"Oh, no! Do you want me to make some inquiries?"

"Do you have anyone in mind? I don't suppose Skipper Dean might be able to do it? Since, you know, he's the captain of a boat." Skipper Dean was Mrs. Standish's patient paramour and also a frequent customer.

She brayed out a laugh. "Oh, no, honey. I don't think that would be a good idea. Even if it was legal, and I don't think it is in the state of Georgia—you really need to be a judge or magistrate or some kind of clergy before they'll let you marry anyone—he's terribly shy in a crowd. Any kind of public speaking, and he freezes like a deer in the proverbial headlights."

"Really? He seems so confident."

"Well, he is, of course. It's just more of a one-on-one confidence."

I sighed. "It was a long shot anyway." Then something occurred to me. "Say, you know a little something about how estate sales work, don't you? I seem to remember you were in a service group that organized them."

"Oh, Lordy." She rolled her eyes. "I was younger then. It's so much work! You have to inventory everything, and then do all sorts of research to determine value. You have to clean things up, then arrange it all nicely and tag everything. Then there's the sale itself, with scads of people coming through the house to see what kind of bargains they can finagle. And that's only half of it." She started to shake her head, then paused and leaned forward to peer at me. "Why do you ask? Do you know someone who requires that kind of service? Because there are at least two professional companies in town that can take care of all the details."

"Is one of them Gibson Estate Sales?"

She nodded. "Jake and Serena Gibson are quite reputable. Whose estate are we talking about?"

I hesitated. "Well, no one's really. You see . . ." I trailed off, unsure how to explain why I wanted to know.

Mrs. Standish's face suddenly lit up. "You're on the hunt again, aren't you?" she cried with such obvious delight, I had to suppress a smile. "Who died?"

Quickly, I glanced around the bakery. Sure enough, her booming enthusiasm had drawn the attention of half the customers sitting at the bistro tables. I flicked a look at the reading area and debated whether it would be a good place to talk. Almost immediately, I decided against it.

"Mrs. Standish, perhaps you'd like to come back to the office?"

"Pshaw." She stepped around the register and marched into the kitchen with alacrity. Surprised, I trailed behind, gesturing weakly toward the open office door. Inside, she started to sit in the club chair.

"No! Wait. Sorry. Let me move the blanket. Mungo sleeps here a lot, and I'm sure his fur is all over."

"All right," she said placidly, then sank into the chair once I'd removed its protective covering. "Now, dish." She looked at me expectantly.

"You're right," I said. "There is a case. It's Declan's sister's ex-husband."

"Oh, dear. He's not the one who was killed at the Spotlight Motel, is he?"

"How did you know?"

She tsked. "I saw Mr. Dawes' story in the *News*. Such a shame. The Spotlight used to be such an adorable place, back in the day when motels provided welcome respite to car travelers. Motor hotels, or motor courts, they called them. Wholesome, family friendly, reasonable. But now the Spotlight has a rather unsavory reputation, you know." Her eyes sparkled with curiosity. "Tell me more."

"I don't know a lot more than what was in the paper," I said. "Except I learned that the victim worked for Gibson Estate Sales, and I'm wondering about a ring he may have bought at one of the sales."

"Sounds delightfully mysterious. Would you like for me to make an appointment to talk with the Gibsons?"

"You know them?"

"My service group has worked with Jake before. I'd be happy to call and arrange a meeting."

I did some mental calculations regarding the next day's schedule. "Thank you so much, but I think Rori and I will drop in on them tomorrow morning before the rest of Declan's family arrives."

Mrs. Standish was shaking her head. "Oh, no, dear. Dropping in won't do. The chances of catching either of the Gibsons in their office are infinitesimal. They spend most of their time organizing the contents of the houses they're liquidating, assessing the value of items, working with dealers and thrift stores, and even putting things on eBay if they don't sell. It can be an enormous job, clearing out someone's house. Often, you're finding homes for the pieces and parts of an entire lifetime."

"Oh, gosh. That sounds heartbreaking," I said.

"Sometimes it is. Sometimes it's a fresh start. Either way, hiring it out is often the most painless way to proceed. The problem is, sometimes a company like that will work several weeks out. How soon do you need to talk with them?"

"The sooner the better," I said.

"I'm sure they'll meet you if I call them. You know where their office is?"

"I can look it up."

"Of course you can. Is there a good time?"

"In the morning, I guess."

"Excellent." She stood. "I'll call as soon as I arrive home and let you know the time." Her eyes glinted. "In exchange, you must have tea with me after all the wedding festivities and fill me in on all the wonderfully sordid details."

I had to laugh. "I don't know how sordid they'll be, but I'll do my best."

"All righty then!" She sailed out of the office and through the kitchen, startling Iris, who was getting ready to leave for the day. "Goodbye, dears!" she trilled, then grabbed her box of pastries and strode out the door.

"Good heavens," Lucy said. "What was that all about?"

"Mrs. Standish is helping me find out a few things about Tucker Abbott."

My aunt shook her head, but she was grinning. "I adore that woman."

"Me, too," I agreed, looking after the whirlwind that was Mrs. Standish.

My cell buzzed in my pocket, and I saw it was a text from Quinn.

No ring. Why?

I texted back.

Possible paranormal connection. Will let you know when I find out more.

My phone rang. It was Quinn.

"What's going on, Katie?"

Ducking into the back of the kitchen, I lowered my

voice. "I'm not sure. The murder victim may have been using a ring with a magical spell on it. Magically enhanced, see? To make that glamour I told you about even stronger. And I saw him wearing a giant gold and ruby ring earlier in the afternoon, before he was killed. I actually saw it, Quinn. It looked like it might have been worth a pretty penny. Not a fortune, but a few thousand dollars at least. He wasn't wearing it?"

"Nooo." Quinn drew the word out. "And we didn't find it in the room. This is good information, Katie. Not the spell thing. I mean, I know you're a, well, you know."

He can't even say the word witch.

"But I still don't see how, um, magic, got Abbott killed. However, a ring like that could be valuable enough to kill a man over."

"It might." That wasn't what I'd been thinking, but he wasn't wrong. "He supposedly owed someone money."

"I'll look into it. And Katie?"

"Yes?" I waited for him to thank me.

"You can stop looking into Abbott's murder. Okay?"

"But—"

"I need to go now. I'll see you at the wedding on Saturday." And he hung up.

"Well, I never!"

Lucy peered around the edge of the refrigerator. "Everything okay?"

"Sure, if you think Detective Quinn putting me in my place is okay."

"Now why would he do that?"

Why indeed?

Though I hadn't decided whether Tucker using a glamour had any bearing on the case, I had at least been going to tell Quinn about the estate sale Tucker supposedly bought the ring from. Now I'd have to fill him in after I talked to the Gibsons the next day.

The rest of the afternoon passed quickly. Declan called to say he was making his mother and sisters a big spaghetti feed at their house. Aggie had gone out to pick up ingredients for a salad, and I agreed to bring garlic bread from the bakery.

"And dessert, of course. What sounds good?" I asked.

"Surprise us," he said.

I hung up and took stock.

Something cool and light and fruity to offset the heaviness of a big Italian supper. Ah . . . of course: pavlova.

Egg whites whipped with a bit of sugar, cooked in a low oven until the top became a bit crisp and chewy and the inside was the decadent texture of marshmallows. As I whipped the eggs, I conjured up a topping of fresh peaches macerated with cinnamon, topped with a puff of whipped cream, and drizzled with a tiny bit of balsamic glaze.

Perfect, I thought. *Just perfect.*

Chapter 14

We locked the door after the last customer had been served and flipped the sign in the window to CLOSED. Lucy mopped the floor, while I vacuumed the furniture in the reading area. Ben wiped down the blue-and-chrome bistro tables and chairs with disinfectant. Iris had already shined the kitchen to gleaming and left to get ready for a date. I'd finished vacuuming and was about to start tidying the bookshelves when a knock sounded at the door.

Expecting Ben to let whoever was at the door know we were closed, I was surprised when I heard the sound of the door unlocking and then noise from the street as it opened. Peeking my head around, I saw Bianca come in. She wore designer athletic leggings, and a soft yoga top hugged her slim figure. Her hair was pulled up in a ponytail, which swished every time she moved her head. When she saw me, a smile lit up her face.

"Katie! I was on my way by and wanted to drop this off, so you'll have it on Saturday." Puck's masked face popped out of her Coach bag as she rummaged through it. Seconds later, she drew out a velvet jewelry box and held it out to me. "Your something borrowed."

"Oh, Bianca. The earrings?"

She nodded, the smile still dancing on her lips. "I'm so happy you're going to wear them with that gorgeous dress."

I opened the box and gazed down at the pendant earrings inside. Two inches long and set in intricately worked platinum, each sparkled with a large amethyst in the middle and . . .

"Are those brown amethyst?" I asked, pointing to the rows of the jewels that surrounded the semiprecious purple stone. "I've heard of it but never seen it."

"Nope. Those are cognac diamonds," she said. "The lighter ones are champagne diamonds."

"Oh. Wow. That's a lot of diamonds."

When I'd been searching high and low to find the right piece of jewelry to go with my off-the-shoulder wedding dress, Bianca had announced that she had the perfect thing.

And she was right. They were perfect. Also, probably worth more than my car.

"I love them. I really do." Then I managed to tear my gaze away and look up at her. "But I don't feel comfortable having something this expensive just, you know, *around*. Can't you keep them in your safe until the time comes?"

She laughed and waved her hand. "You keep them. Put them in the freezer or something if that makes you feel better. But they're insured."

Shaking my head, I closed the box. "How can you be so cavalier about something like this?" I asked.

"If it really makes you nervous, I'll take them back," she said. "But I think you should keep them until the wedding."

"You sure?" I asked.

"Absolutely." She looked at her fitness watch. "Listen, I have to go. I'm going to slot in a workout at the gym before I'm due to pick up Colette from her friend's house."

My head came up. "The River Street Athletic Club?" She nodded.

"Do you know someone there named Carolyn Becker?"

"The personal trainer? Sure. She's a friend of Randy's."

"That's her. Say, does the management at your gym let you bring guests in?"

"Of course." Her head tipped to the side. "Why? You thinking of joining?"

"Not exactly. I'll stick with running. I really want to talk to Carolyn. Do you know when she might be there?"

Bianca shrugged. "She'll be there now, I expect. When she's not on shift at the firehouse, she usually comes in to train her clients after they get off work."

I did a few calculations. I could go with Bianca to her gym, talk to Carolyn, then buzz by the apartment to change out of my work clothes, swing by the Honeybee to grab the bread and pavlova, and make it in time for spaghetti dinner at Wisteria House with my soon-to-be in-laws.

"Can I come with you?" I asked Bianca, already untying my apron. "I'll drive my own car. But if you could introduce me to Carolyn . . ."

"No problem," she said easily. "I take it you're not looking to engage her professionally, though."

"Nope. Tucker Abbott tried to hook Declan into a real estate scheme. Declan passed, but Carolyn got involved. She lost some money and ended up suing Tucker for it. She won, but apparently, he never paid the judgment. From what I hear, she wasn't very happy."

My friend's eyes widened. "You think Carolyn is a murder suspect?"

One shoulder lifted and then dropped. "I don't know. But it couldn't hurt to talk to her. If nothing else, maybe she can tell me something about Tucker I don't know."

Bianca made a face. "Sounds to me like there's a lot about this Tucker guy you wouldn't want to know." She sighed. "Go grab your things. I'll wait."

I hurried into the office to tell Mungo I'd pick him up on my way to Wisteria House. He responded with a doggy frown and a glare.

"I'm sorry," I said. "Unless you think you might want to try out the treadmill?"

He did not look amused.

"We're having spaghetti for dinner," I said.

He sniffed.

"With bread. I made some for you without garlic. Just butter. Lots of butter. I'll let you have an extra bite."

He huffed.

I kneeled in front of his chair. "Please don't be mad at me. I've got a lot on my plate right now. I'm doing the best I can. And I promise to make it up to you after the wedding."

My familiar studied me, then his eyes softened. He leaned forward and licked my nose, then settled back into his chair.

"Thanks, buddy." I stood. "I'll be back in a little bit."

Yip!

Before I left with Bianca, I stowed her earrings in the Honeybee freezer. I felt kind of silly doing it, but it did make me feel better. We parked down the block from each other and met at the door of the River Street Athletic Club. Inside, I was surprised at the warm atmosphere. I always thought of gyms as being lit with fluorescent lights and boasting lots of shiny surfaces and too many mirrors.

This place had warm wood floors, gentle ambient lighting, and walls painted in soft orange and yellow tones that reminded me of the colors we'd chosen for the interior of the Honeybee. A small juice bar was right inside the door, and through doorways that led from the main gym, I could see a small daycare area and several people dancing to Zumba music.

Bianca greeted the ponytailed man behind the counter. "Mind if I show my friend around a bit?"

He was feeding vegetables into the juicer for a waiting customer. The smell of cucumbers filled the air.

"Of course! Let me know if you have any questions." This last he directed at me. "We have a special right now. Sign up for a year and get three months free."

"Good to know," I said over my shoulder as I followed Bianca between the row of weight machines on the right and elliptical machines, stair steppers, and treadmills on the left. A sign on the wall at the back of the room indicated the entrances to the locker rooms.

Bianca stopped to peer into another room that opened off the main workout area. I joined her in the doorway. A series of straps hung from the ceiling, looking like so many devices of torture. No one was in the room, though.

"What the heck are those?" I asked.

"TRX suspension training. Uses your own body weight. Works on strength, balance, flexibility, and core, all at the same time."

"You do that?"

She laughed. "Sometimes. It's hard. It's also kind of amazing."

"No wonder you look so good," I murmured.

"Doesn't look like Carolyn's here," Bianca said. "This is where she usually works with her clients."

"What about the Zumba class?" I asked.

"Not Carolyn's thing. You can look, though."

"What's not my thing?" a voice behind us asked. "Unless you're looking for a different Carolyn."

I turned to find a tall African American woman grinning at us. She wore electric blue yoga pants and a racerback tank top. A wide floral headband held her braids off her face, and she wore a flame pendant around her neck. I nodded to the necklace.

"Firefighter, right?"

She looked surprised but nodded.

I stuck out my hand. "I'm Katie Lightfoot. I'm engaged to Declan McCarthy."

Her grin widened. "Declan! Good guy."

"I sure think so." I stopped, not sure how to proceed.

"Are you looking for a personal trainer? At least I assume Bianca here told you that's my moonlight gig. I have a few openings in my schedule."

"Actually, no. I'm good. But I did want to talk to you."

"Sounds serious." She pointed inside the room with all the crazy straps hanging from the ceiling. "I have a few minutes while my client gets changed. Let's go in here."

Bianca looked toward the locker room, then seemed to change her mind and came along with us. Carolyn closed the door and went over to a rack of large rubber exercise balls. She bounced three of them to the floor and took a seat on one. Bianca and I exchanged a look, then perched on the other two.

"What did you want to talk to me about, Katie?"

"Tucker Abbott," I said.

Her demeanor instantly altered, her expression hardening. "I must say, that's a surprising answer."

"Declan told me you knew him."

"That little pipsqueak? Tucker, not Declan. Yeah. Why? Did he pull something over on you, too?"

"He, um, didn't get the chance. But Declan told me what happened with the real estate investment group."

One eyebrow lifted. "And?"

"Declan said you sued to get your money back and won, but Tucker never paid the judgment."

"Well, Declan was right," Carolyn said. "Tucker Abbott screwed me over, not once but twice. First by fooling me, and then by refusing to pay what the judge ordered him to." She bounced a couple of times on the ball, then stretched her arms over her head. The movement seemed to ease her irritation a bit. "Now, if Tucker didn't pull the wool over your eyes, what's your interest in him?"

"Did you know Declan's sister married him?"

She gave a wry half smile. "I'd heard something along those lines."

"They eloped. Declan told me they met back when Tucker was trying to rope Declan into the real estate scam. They divorced not long after they were married."

Carolyn swayed her hips side to side on the exercise ball. "Well, at least it didn't last. Hope he didn't take her for too much. I'm determined to get that SOB to pay me. He thinks I'm going to forget about it, let it go." She grinned again. "But that is so not my style. I'll wear him down if it's the last thing I do."

Bianca and I exchanged a look.

Carolyn noticed. "What's going on? Because"—she waved her hand—"something obviously is."

"Tucker Abbott was murdered," I said.

Her jaw slackened, and she leaned toward us, staring first at me, then at Bianca, then back at me. "Murdered? You have got to be kidding."

"Not so much," Bianca said. "Last night. He was killed at the Spotlight Motel."

Carolyn bounced up and began pacing back and forth across the open space. "The Spotlight! That was him? Crud. I guess I'd better give up on getting my . . ." She trailed off. Turned and looked at us. "I wasn't on shift today, so I haven't heard. Do they have the killer in custody?"

I shook my head.

She came over and stood, looming above me. I scrambled to my feet.

"Why are you asking me about Tucker Abbott, Katie?"

"I, uh. Well, you had a history with him, and I was wondering what you could tell me about him . . ." I trailed off.

Her eyes narrowed. "I've heard about how you get involved in Peter Quinn's cases sometimes. This is one of his, isn't it?" She tipped her head toward me. "You think I'm a murder suspect, Katie? Is that what's going on?"

Taking a deep breath, I said, "Tucker hurt a lot of people. One of those people probably killed him."

"Hmm." Nodding to herself, she dropped back to sit on the exercise ball. "And you're probably right. That guy made enemies left and right. And I was one of them, for sure. But not the kind of enemy that would kill the guy. For one thing, he didn't *hurt* me. He made me mad. And I still wanted my money."

"Yeah. I get it. I didn't mean—"

"Also, in case Detective Quinn is feeling frisky about suspecting any and all who Tucker wronged, he can take me right off his list. I was filling in at Two House last night. Overtime, baby. And alibi galore."

I felt thoroughly chastened. "I'm sorry."

"Oh, don't be. Though I do find it kind of funny that Quinn has you doing part of his job for him. But whatever. Good for you."

"Thanks for being so understanding."

"Honey, that is not something most people say about

me. And let's be honest. I'm not happy Tucker finally got his comeuppance, but I'm not heartbroken, either."

The door of the room opened, and a middle-aged man in shorts and T-shirt came in. "Carolyn?"

"Come on in, Marty. Ladies, I need to go. It's been . . . interesting talking with you, though." She looked amused.

"No hard feelings?" I murmured.

"God, no. I'm just sorry I'm out my twelve grand."

Chapter 15

Bianca went to fit in part of her intended workout, and I drove to the apartment. Quickly, I showered off the day and changed into a sleeveless linen dress in robin's egg blue. A dab of eyeliner and some blush sufficed for the evening's makeup. I changed out my usual utilitarian tote bag to a large purse. Mungo would have to hoof it tonight. Then out to my car again, and to the Honeybee.

I parked in the alley right behind the back door and let myself inside. It always felt strange to be in the bakery when it wasn't open and I wasn't up to my elbows in flour and sugar. I bundled Mungo, the pavlova and its toppings, and a giant loaf of bread—sliced, slathered with butter and grated garlic, and wrapped in foil so it could go straight into the oven—into the Bug, locked up, and buzzed over to Chippewa Square.

Rori met me at the door of Wisteria House. She motioned me in with an urgent gesture, looking behind her, where laughter was coming from the kitchen. Carefully, I carried the pavlova over the threshold and set it on the hall table. Mungo padded in behind me and went to gaze longingly up at the dessert I'd brought.

"Come into the parlor," she hissed, opening a door off the foyer.

Bewildered, I followed her into a small room that faced the street. She closed the door behind us.

"What's wrong?" I asked.

"Nothing," she said. "But they don't know."

I frowned. "Don't know what?"

"About going to see Hudson Prater today. About the music box being worthless and Tucker lying to me about it. About you helping me find out what Tucker was up to that got him killed."

"You're not going to tell your mother and Eliza?"

She shook her head vehemently. "And I don't want you to, either."

"Rori, I told Declan we were going to the antique store. I'm sorry, but that's that."

"Well . . . okay."

"And I don't feel right keeping secrets from the rest of your family."

"Oh, please? They'll give me a bad time."

"No, they won't. They love you."

"I'm the baby of the family, and they'll always think of me like that." She pressed her lips together. "Just tonight, okay? Don't say anything tonight."

I rubbed my forehead. "I don't like this." My hand dropped. "However, if it doesn't come up, I won't bring it up. But I need to tell you that I talked to Tucker's recent ex-girlfriend today."

Rori's eyes grew wide. "Seriously?"

"The opportunity came up, and I took it." Quickly, I related what Effie had told Mimsey and me.

"Boy, she sure was talkative."

"She was," I agreed, keeping Mimsey's use of her Voice to myself. "And we have an appointment to see the estate sales people that Tucker worked for tomorrow morning before Lauren and Camille get here with their families." Mrs. Standish had called and told me the meeting was set up for nine thirty the next day. "Can you make it?"

Rori's eyes were bright as she nodded. "Yes. Of course."

"Good. I'll pick you up here."

"No. I'll come to the bakery."

"You can't keep what you're doing a secret from everyone forever," I said.

She reached for the door with a grin. "But I'll save myself the grief they'll give me for a while longer, if that's all right with you."

Declan's homemade spaghetti sauce, studded with herb-flecked meatballs and chunks of Italian sausage and dolloped on al dente pasta, was a big hit. The garlic bread, so soft and fragrant it almost melted in your mouth, was the perfect accompaniment. Aggie's "heartfelt salad"—a combination of romaine hearts, artichoke hearts, palm hearts, and celery hearts—provided a crunchy, umami flavor companion. When all the dishes were done, we retired to the spacious living room with dishes of peach pavlova and glasses of Moscato.

Aggie asked if I knew anything about a service for Tucker Abbott, but Declan stepped in and explained that anything like that would have to wait until the medical examiner did his thing. She blanched and changed the subject. Neither Rori nor Eliza mentioned Tucker's name, though I saw Eliza side-eyeing her sister a few times.

Mostly we talked about Declan's childhood antics, and they told stories about his high school years that I'd known nothing about. At the end of the evening, I felt like I knew these members of his family a bit better and hoped they felt the same way about me. Since I was an only child, the idea of inheriting so much family at once was a bit overwhelming, but also welcome.

And Eliza had stepped up, somehow wrangling reservations for supper for both our families not only on short notice, but at the perfect place—Churchill's on Bay Street, a traditional English tavern on the upscale side that served creative pub grub with a coastal twist.

"I love that place. How on earth did you manage to get us all in?" I asked.

A cool smile curved her lips. "I can be rather persuasive." The smile warmed. "Actually, I called several places first. Churchill's had a last-minute cancellation. Still . . ." Her forehead creased. "Even if we call it a rehearsal dinner, there's no real rehearsal, is there?"

"There's no reason to rehearse," Declan assured her. "The ceremony is going to be very simple, and the families will have plenty of time to get to know each other without adding another thing to the wedding week. I promise."

"I hope so," she said. "Lauren and Camille are both coming in tomorrow in the early afternoon. Katie, will you be able to break away to say hello?"

I nodded. "Of course. Everyone else at the Honeybee is willing to cover whenever I have to leave this week."

"And your parents?" Aggie asked.

"They're at a hardware convention in Las Vegas. They'll fly in from there late tomorrow afternoon. You'll meet them tomorrow night at Churchill's. And then you"—I nodded toward Declan's mother—"and Mama are scheduled at the Hair Connection at the same time on Friday, so you can get to know each other better then."

Aggie smiled. "I'm looking forward to it."

"Vera—that's the salon owner—and her assistant, Zoe, reserved the entire afternoon for facials and mani-pedis for the wedding party. Since they can't work on everyone at once, we're staggering appointments. Then on Saturday, the bridal party will go in for makeup and hair in the afternoon before heading over to the carriage house at five thirty to dress. The caterers will be ready for guests arriving at seven, and then the ceremony will start about eight. The photographer will be taking formal and candid pictures in between." I smiled at Declan. "When we're officially married, the party will continue."

Eliza sighed but didn't protest. I considered that progress.

"That is, if Declan's idea for a wedding officiant pans out," I said, and raised my eyebrows.

He grinned. "It's handled, darlin'. Just one little thing to finalize."

My eyes narrowed. "You're actually having fun with this, aren't you? Not telling me until the last minute."

The grin got bigger. "Yep."

"Fine," I grumbled, but a smile was tugging at my

lips. He wouldn't be so flip if he was at all worried about having someone to marry us on Saturday, and even though I was crazy curious, it was also a relief to let my fiancé completely take over that aspect of the ceremony.

Half an hour later, I subtly let Declan know I was ready to leave, and he made our excuses.

"I like your family," I said as we crossed the street to my car.

"Me, too," he said with a smile. "And they love you."

Declan drove my car back to the apartment, and we left his truck at Wisteria House. With the rest of his family arriving the next afternoon, an extra vehicle might come in handy.

On our way back to the apartment, he brought up the idea of lucid dreaming as a way to try to find Connell.

"I've been looking at that book I found in the Honeybee library. I'd like to try it."

I nodded. "It certainly seems like it's worth a try. Have you ever been dreaming and become aware that you're not awake, that you're in the middle of a dream?"

"Doesn't everyone do that?" Declan asked.

Turning in my seat to look at him, I said, "On occasion. Are you telling me you do it a lot?"

He started to answer, then made a face. "I used to all the time. Not so much now that Connell is gone."

"Wow. I wonder if Connell was engineering your dreams?"

He blew out a breath. "Who knows? Believe me, I'd like to ask him." He slowed for a traffic light.

"So what does the book say? Can you force lucid dreaming?" I asked.

"Not force. I'm pretty sure it doesn't work that way.

But according to what I read, there are ways to *encourage* it."

"How?" I shifted, interested. Mungo jumped down from his perch in the back seat and stuck his head between the seats, also listening.

Declan flipped on the turn signal. "It says to make the room hospitable for sleep. Draw the curtains, turn off the television, that kind of stuff."

"Makes sense. What else?"

"Keep a dream journal. Watch for something called dream signs, which I guess are recurring things that you know the meaning of in your dreams."

"All fine and good, I suppose." I was a little surprised Declan was so enthusiastic about the idea of lucid dreaming. It spoke to how much he wanted to rescue his guardian spirit. "But how does that help you know if you're dreaming?"

"Well, there's this other thing in the book." He sounded a bit unsure now. "It says to test reality. Like when you're awake, so you get into the habit of it. It says to check what you're reading to make sure it hasn't changed, or double-check that the time on the clock is the same. It changes in dreams. That way you know if you're awake or not." He pulled the Bug into a parking spot, shut off the engine, and turned to me.

"Seriously?" I asked.

He lifted one shoulder and let it drop. "That's what it says."

"So you're saying I could be dreaming right now?"

Grinning, he opened the door and got out. "We both could be. Come on, Mungo."

He wiggled through the gap, bounded over the seat,

and jumped to the sidewalk. I grabbed my bag and got out, then I stared at Declan over the top of the car.

"You're making my brain hurt."

Inside the apartment, I changed into sleepwear and settled into bed. Mungo sprawled on the rug on the floor, while Declan puttered in the bathroom. I skimmed the book on lucid dreaming. I closed it and put it on the nightstand as he shut off the light and came into the bedroom.

"Apparently the best way to induce lucid dreams is by inviting them in, by intending to have them before you go to sleep," I said.

"Intention, huh. Sounds like the way you talk about your spell work." He climbed into bed.

I nodded. "Similar. Let's try it. As you're falling asleep, repeat to yourself that you know that you're dreaming, you know that you're dreaming, you know that you're dreaming. Over and over. I'll do the same thing."

"It's worth a shot," he said hopefully. "To get through to Connell."

"Excellent." I reached over, turned off the lamp, and scooched down under the covers.

"Um, it's only nine thirty, darlin'." My fiancé sounded amused.

"Yeah, but—"

"But nothing. I've been away from you for two nights, almost-wife of mine. Connell can wait a little longer for us to try and contact him."

"Hmm. I see what you mean," I said, and reached for him in the dark.

*   *   *

Later that night, we'd each tried repeating the mantra that we knew we were dreaming as we slipped into slumber. I'd slept longer than usual and hadn't sensed anyone else's dreams, which was a relief. Even so, I was awake at three, and up by four. When I got back from my run, Declan was uncharacteristically up and about, and the smell of fresh coffee filled the air. He made toast and fed Mungo, while I showered. Finally, we settled in at the kitchen table for a few minutes before I had to leave for the bakery. Declan set a plate in front of me bearing a thick hunk of wheat toast smothered in butter and sprinkled with a generous layer of cinnamon sugar.

"Oh, Lordy. I don't think I've had cinnamon toast since Nonna made it for me when I was a little kid." I took a giant bite and chewed with my eyes closed. I chased it with a swallow of coffee and sighed in appreciation. "Definitely need to have this more often."

He was grinning when I opened my eyes. "Glad you like it." Then his grin faltered. "It didn't work for me. Did it work for you?"

I half frowned and shook my head. "The lucid dreaming? No. We can keep trying, though."

"Yeah." However, his disappointment was palpable.

Chapter 16

Distracted by our lack of success with lucid dreaming, I walked down Broughton toward the Honeybee from my car. Mungo sat up with his paws on the side of my tote, head swiveling to take in the sights. There weren't many to take in, as it was five thirty and only the faintest hint of promised sunrise brightened the sky on the eastern horizon. It was quiet and calm, the air the coolest it would be all day. Streetlights cast reassuring pools of light along the sidewalk at regular intervals. The sound of a boat horn echoed from the direction of the Savannah River, something that during the hubbub of traffic and people during the day wouldn't have reached our ears.

Maybe lucid dreaming takes a lot of practice, I thought. *Perhaps there's another method to try. Or . . .*

My steps slowed as I considered. There were an awful lot of things that could be helped along with a spell or two. Boosted, as it were. Could lucid dreaming be one of them?

Newly hopeful, I picked up my pace. In front of the

Honeybee, I paused to use the flashlight on my key ring, squinting as the keypad next to the door was illuminated. I entered the code, then slid the key into the lock.

Sudden movement to my left startled me. I spun to face it, heart pounding, breath hissing out in surprise and fear. My hand came up, and I felt power instantly coursing through my veins. I pushed my palm forward, a distant part of me sensing that my skin had taken on a faint, blue-tinged luminosity.

"Katie! It's me!"

Yip!

Several pieces of knowledge came together in my brain at the same time: Mungo hadn't growled or otherwise indicated we were in any danger; I'd almost blasted someone with magic even though I'd never known I could muster such power so quickly; and that someone had Steve Dawes' voice.

"Oh, God. I'm so sorry. I didn't mean to scare you." Sure enough, Steve stepped out of the shadows, his face the very picture of contrition.

"What the heck!" My words came out of my tight throat sounding reedy and frightened, but my emotion had already graduated to anger. "You think that's funny, sneaking up on me like that?"

"No!"

"What were you doing? Waiting for me? Out on a late story, and you think, hey, know what would be fun? Go hang out by the Honeybee and scare the living bejesus out of my friend Katie Lightfoot when she comes to work."

"No! I came here just for you!"

"Great." I snorted. "That's even better." I turned back to the door. The keypad entry had expired, so I entered it again. My hands were trembling from the adrenaline surge.

"Let me explain."

"I can't stop you."

"Okay, then, listen." He took a step toward me.

Quickly unlocking the door, I opened it and went inside. Turning in the doorway, I said, "We open at seven." I would have shut the door in his face, but the hydraulic mechanism that made it close slowly stole that small satisfaction.

It also allowed Steve to stick his foot in the door. Then he pushed it open and came inside despite my obvious desire that he go to . . . well, elsewhere. I was still shaking. I put Mungo down, then turned and crossed my arms.

"Oh, for Pete's sake." He rubbed his hands over his face. "This isn't at all what I wanted. I'm so sorry. I would never frighten you on purpose. I thought you saw me there. You have to listen to me, Katie."

"It doesn't look like you're giving me much choice." I was still upset, but now a part of me wondered if perhaps there was something wrong, if Steve needed my help.

It would have to be something big for him to be waiting for me at five thirty in the morning. Could it be—

"This is the only time I knew you'd be alone. You're always around people, it seems like. I wanted to talk to you without Declan interrupting, or Ben giving me the evil eye, or somebody needing something from you."

Mungo took a couple of steps away, then sat and looked between us as if watching a tennis match. I regarded Steve. He looked like he hadn't been getting much sleep. The only light in the bakery was from the empty display case. It was bright but cast strange shadows along the walls and made the high ceiling fans look like giant hands above.

"Come into the kitchen," I said. "You can talk while I get the sourdough into the ovens."

"No. Not in the kitchen. Please. Just give me a minute, okay? Of your attention. All of it."

Puzzled and a little irritated, I said, "You had my attention yesterday in the alley, Steve. Are you going to tell me all over again that the McCarthy clan is bad news, and I'm rushing into marrying Declan? Or is this about something else?"

Steve's lips pressed together. He took a deep breath, then motioned me into the reading area. Curious now, I followed. He turned on a desk lamp that was tucked into one of the bookshelves, and the room was flooded with a gentle yellow light. He motioned again, and I moved a little closer.

He hesitated, then looked down at the floor. "Katie, I love you."

I blinked. "Steve—"

"Shhhhh. Let me finish." He took a deep breath. "I want to apologize. I've done some not-so-great things to try to win you over. I was wrong."

I took another step toward him. "You don't have to—"

He held up his hand. "See, I thought you were falling in love with me once. I thought if I persisted, you'd come back around to me. I kept thinking that I understood you in a way that Declan couldn't. That you needed someone who could understand your magical

175

abilities, to know what it's like to have a gift like we do. I thought we could practice magic together. That our kids would be amazingly talented. That with my money and family connections I could give you everything."

"Steve," I protested.

"But I was wrong. You aren't interested in money or social status. I don't even know if you want kids. I do know you want Declan, though. And even though I'll never be able to like the guy—I'm sorry, I just can't—I do want you to be happy." He gave me a tentative smile. "Congratulations on your upcoming nuptials, Katie-girl. And may your life be filled with all the things you do want."

My eyes felt hot as tears threatened. I finally managed to speak around the lump in my throat. "Thank you."

That tentative smile again, so unlike his usual smooth and cool confidence. "You're not rid of me altogether, though. I'm still around. I just wanted you to know I want the best for you and the man you chose."

I nodded. "That means a lot."

"I only wish it had been me." He took a deep breath. "But it wasn't."

"You'll find the right person," I said. The women he'd dated since I'd become seriously involved with Declan hadn't worked out, but I truly felt there was someone out there who would recognize what Steve had to offer—and would accept the occasionally shady moves his druid clan made to further their interests.

"Sure, I will," he said, but I couldn't tell if he was being sarcastic or actually agreeing with me. I chose to believe the latter.

"Okay, I've done what I came for. I'm going now,

before I say something stupid." He strode over to the door and wrenched it open.

"Steve?"

He turned.

"Are you coming to the wedding?"

He hesitated. "I don't know."

"Oh."

"I'll be there if I can." And he stepped out to the deserted street.

Slowly, I went over and locked the door behind him. Then I turned to Mungo.

"Well. That was intense." I made a face. "He's right that he's crossed the line a few times, though."

His brown eyes gazed up at me.

I was sorry if Steve was hurting. He was right that I'd been attracted to him for a time. Heck, he was an attractive guy. But he was a bad boy druid, and I disliked what his druid clan was willing to do. Steve wasn't the man I wanted to spend the rest of my life with, and I'd known that for a long time. Declan was, and I'd known that, too.

I turned the engagement ring on my finger. It was an antique design of filigree platinum with a low-profile blue sapphire in the middle. No diamond, practical to wear in the kitchen and garden, and slightly retro. Declan had known exactly what to choose.

Because Declan knew me.

I straightened my shoulders and went to start the ovens for the sourdough.

Rori took a ride share to the Honeybee, and at nine fifteen, we were in the Bug heading toward Gibson Estate

Sales on Broad Street. Traffic was light, and we made good time. Beside me, Declan's little sister fidgeted and fussed. Once again, I'd left Mungo behind at the Honeybee, unwilling to leave him in the car during the heat of the day, windows down or not. He hadn't been happy about it at all, though. I'd have to do something extra nice for my familiar when this crazy week was over.

"What else did his girlfriend say about Tucker?" Rori asked.

"Ex-girlfriend," I said. "And I've told you everything."

She sat back and picked at a cuticle. "I noticed that ring the other day. I'd never seen it before. Did you notice it?"

"It was kind of hard to miss," I said. "But Quinn said they didn't find a ring on Tucker, or in his room." I glanced over at her. "You didn't see it at the Spotlight, did you?"

Her shoulders hunched, and she gave a shudder. "No, but I didn't really take a good look."

"Believe me, I get it." After all, I'd made a point to go look at the room but couldn't bring myself to spend more than a millisecond looking at Tucker himself.

"I wonder if I should go talk to this Effie person," Rori said. "I feel like we might have some things in common."

"Hmm. It's up to you, of course. But I think that might not be the best idea."

"Why?"

"Because digging into Tucker's other relationship sounds like the opposite of closure. And honestly? I think she wants to leave it all behind her."

She looked out the window, then nodded. "You're right."

"Do you still believe finding Tucker's killer is going to give you peace?" I asked carefully.

A few seconds passed before she answered. "You know, I do, Katie. His death is so open-ended at this point. There are so many questions. Once those are answered, I have a feeling some of the other questions I have about him will be answered, too."

"Okay, then." I pulled my car into a space in the office park and checked the number on the side of the building. "Let's go talk to his latest employer."

We located the suite on the second floor and walked in. I stopped inside the threshold, surprised at the lushness of the office furnishings compared to the spare industrial feel of the rest of the building. The small reception area boasted a Queen Anne desk and chair, while large potted plants and framed watercolors provided ambience. Two upholstered chairs offered a place to sit, the delicately carved end table between them bare save for an old copy of *People* magazine.

Beyond was another office, where a man sat behind a large, dark wood desk. He was on the phone when we came in but saw us and held up a finger to let us know he'd be with us in a minute.

The receptionist desk had a bowl of designer chocolate truffles on one corner, as well as a box of tissues with a vintage silver cover, and two copies of an estate sales trade journal. Despite the opulence of the waiting area, I got the impression that all the real business was conducted in the back office.

The man hung up and came out front. Tall and tan, he wore shorts and a polo shirt with boat shoes. His blond hair was graying, and crow's feet radiated from the corners of his eyes. He seemed like the kind of guy who spent as much time as possible on the water or the golf course or both.

"I'm Jake Gibson. You must be Katie Lightfoot."

"I am." I stepped forward and shook his hand. "And this is Rori McCarthy."

He shook her hand as well. "Come on back."

We skirted the front desk and went into his office. The guest chairs there were similar to the ones in the waiting area. The air smelled of expensive cologne and something I had a hard time pinning down. Wet dog? The window behind the desk looked out on the parking lot. Two pictures were perched on the corner of his desk. One was a professional portrait of a beautiful woman I assumed was his wife. The other was of a dog in a canine camo vest, standing in tall, yellow grass.

Jake noticed me looking at the pictures. "Beautiful, no?"

"She's lovely," I said.

"What? Oh, well yes, my wife is gorgeous. I enjoy beauty in all forms, you see." His arm swept the air. "But I was talking about that beautiful hound of mine. Beauregard's his name. Best hunter I've ever had."

I offered a smile.

"Have a seat." He made a vague gesture toward the chairs and then sat down behind the desk. "Usually I meet people at the home where they're thinking of having their sale. Don't get many people who come to the office, but Edna Standish said that's what you wanted. What can I do for you?"

Rori and I exchanged a look. We'd already decided that a straightforward approach would be best, with a focus on where Tucker might have acquired his ruby signet ring.

I said, "Thank you for meeting us with so little notice. I'm sure you're very busy."

He looked puzzled. "Is this about an estate sale?"

"Not exactly. It's about an employee of yours. Tucker Abbott."

Jake's jaw set, and his eyes narrowed. "Former employee. He's no longer with the company."

"I'm not sure if you've heard what happened to him."

"I don't care what happened to him." His voice was flat, his eyes hard.

"He was killed," I said, watching his reaction carefully.

First, he looked blank, then after a few moments he swore. His palm slammed down on the desk, and I jumped. His nostrils flared as he took a deep breath and looked out the window for several seconds. Then he looked back at us. "I'm sorry, ladies. This is terrible news." His lips twisted in a wry smile.

"But you fired him," Rori said. "Right?"

Jake studied her. "Who are you again? And why are you asking me about Tucker?"

"I'm his ex-wife." Rori leaned forward. "See, Tucker had a ruby ring. Huge thing. He told someone he got it at an estate sale, and we know he used to work for you. I thought you might be able to tell me the value of the ring." She gave him a tentative smile. "It's missing, you see."

"Ex-wife, huh. He mentioned that he'd been married. And I know the ring you're talking about. Looking for some insurance money, I take it?"

"Maybe," Rori said noncommittally.

"Well, I can't help you because I don't know where he got it. Unless . . ." He swore again.

"Unless?" I prompted, suddenly knowing where he was going.

He started to say something, then seemed to think better of it and shook his head.

"You think he stole it," Rori said.

Jake pressed his lips together.

"You can go ahead and say it. I was married to the man, for heaven's sake. I know what kind of a person he was. You think he stole the ring."

"It wouldn't be the only time he'd done something like that," Jake muttered.

"Is that why you fired him?" I was feeling my way, but his face told me I'd guessed right.

"Yeah. Turns out he took something from an estate sale about a month ago. It was very valuable to the son and daughter of the deceased homeowner. They specifically called and said not to include it in the sale. Tucker insisted it wasn't anywhere in the house, but I'm pretty sure he took it."

Rori leaned forward. "What was the item? Was it the ruby ring?"

But Jake Gibson must have decided he'd said too much. He stood. "I'm sorry I couldn't help you ladies. Good luck."

As we rose from our chairs, the main door opened, and a woman came in. She had dark hair tucked into a baseball cap and wore dark glasses. Something about her seemed familiar. Perhaps I'd seen her at the Honeybee?

"Jake! You'll never believe that house. They're hoarders of the best kind," she said. Then she reached the doorway to the office and noticed us. She slid off her glasses to reveal big blue eyes. It was the woman in the picture on Jake's desk. "Oops. Sorry. Hi, I'm Serena Gibson."

I stuck my hand out and introduced myself and Rori. Her handshake was firm and short, and she exuded a happy, fun vibe.

"We were asking your husband here about Tucker Abbott."

"Tucker! Well, good heavens. He hasn't worked for us for a few weeks."

"So we heard," I said. "How did he come to work for you in the first place?"

She looked surprised and glanced at her husband before saying, "He came to one of our estate sales about a year back. He was looking for items to furnish a vacation rental. It wasn't his rental—that was his job. We found a few choice items he could use, and we got to talking. I started letting him know when there was something he might be interested in at a sale, and eventually he chose to leave his old job and come work for us."

Chose to leave, huh.

She smiled and shook her head ruefully. "That man could sell sweaters in hell. It was a real loss when he left."

Her husband slammed his fist down on the desk. The sudden noise made Rori and me jump, but Serena just rolled her eyes.

"Please, Jake. Not everyone is as used to your histrionics as I am."

He glowered at her. "That one is Tucker's ex-wife. She knows what a son of a—"

She broke in. "Tucker's ex-wife? Really." She tipped her head and gazed at Rori with interest. "And you're here because . . . ?"

Her husband answered. "They're trying to find out how much that ruby ring Tucker wore was worth. Apparently, he told her he got it at an estate sale. Well, nothing like that ever came through on any of our inventories. I would have remembered it, especially after he started wearing that thing. You know what I think? I think he stole it from one of our sales before the inventory was taken. Just like he stole from the Wiggins estate."

That made it sound like he'd stolen something *other* than the ring from the Wigginses.

"Oh, for Pete's sake, Jake, stop it. Tucker didn't steal anything. The Wigginses thought something was in their daddy's house that wasn't. End of story. I still can't believe you fired Tucker without talking to me about it first." She rolled her eyes at him and turned back to us. "Ladies, I'm sorry we can't help you. I don't know where Tucker got that ring. You should try asking him."

"He's dead," Jake said. "Are you happy now? The guy's dead." He pushed past his wife and went through to the main door, slamming it shut behind him so hard, the floor shook.

Chapter 17

Serena Gibson's eyes grew round as she looked between us. "Dead?"

"He was murdered," I said.

Her hand moved to cover her throat. "Oh, no. That's horrible. What happened?"

"The police are looking into it," I said.

Rori said, "Your husband said Tucker stole—"

"Oh, my husband." Serena frowned then moved to stand behind the desk. "He always thought the worst of Tucker. I'm not sure why. Jealousy, probably. Tucker was younger and better looking than Jake. Plus, he flirted. Not that I'd ever . . . you know. But men can be funny that way." She sighed. "You'd think Jake would stop running the poor man down now that he knows he's passed on." A moue of regret crossed her features.

Tucker must have thoroughly fooled her with his glamour.

It sure hadn't seemed to sucker her husband, though.

"But what does Jake think Tucker stole?" I persisted. "From the, what was the name? The Wiggins estate?"

Serena Gibson waved her hand. "I don't even know, honey. Waverly Wiggins said there was some old curio her daddy left her and her brother and to put it aside when we had the sale. But Tucker went through the whole house and never saw it." Her ponytail swished as she shook her head. "False accusations aside, there's no reason why he'd steal something like that." She shrugged and held her palms up toward the ceiling. "Honestly, Jake handled all the communication with Waverly and her brother. I was working another sale at the time. After the sale, they more or less let us go." She wrinkled her nose. "Okay, fired us. See, once the official estate sale is over, we usually try to find places for the items that are left—online auctions, consignment shops, donating to thrift stores, things like that. Part of the package. They decided to take that over themselves while they got their daddy's place ready to sell." She squinted her baby blues. "Or do you already know all that? Do you have a connection with the Wiggins family?"

Rori shook her head.

"Never heard of them before today," I said.

"Well, you sure seem to have a lot of questions about them if you're only here about some ring of Tucker's. I mean, I know you're his ex, and there's probably bad blood between you, but good heavens. The man just died. That seems awfully cold." She smiled to soften the harshness of the words.

Still, Declan's sister started to protest.

I cut her off. "We needed to follow up on some questions the insurance company had. Come on, Rori. We have to get going. Thanks for your time," I said to Serena and turned to leave.

"Sure thing. Again, sorry we couldn't help," she said, sinking into the office chair and taking out her cell phone.

That was when I noticed a crack in the drywall plaster by the door frame. It was out of place amid the casual luxury, most of which I felt sure had been purchased from the estate sales the Gibsons organized. I could only imagine what their house looked like. I walked past it and out to the exit.

Rori trotted after me. When we were outside, she said, "Why did we have to leave so quickly? Didn't you hear? Tucker stole that ring, and he stole a curio from those Wiggins people. Do you think it's my music box?"

"Maybe," I said. "But I think we need to talk to the Wiggins family. Because something is off."

She frowned and got in the car. "What do you mean?"

I started the engine. "First off, Jake said Tucker stole something valuable from the Wigginses. We're pretty sure that music box isn't worth more than twenty bucks. Secondly, he seems to have a bit of an anger problem. Did you notice the dimple in the wall board in his office? Right by the door?"

Wide-eyed, she said, "No."

"Just about the size and shape a fist would make if someone punched a wall in a temper tantrum."

"Ohmagod. Jake hated Tucker. Do you think he could have killed Tucker because he stole from their clients? Or maybe Tucker stole from Jake!"

My eyebrows knit. "I don't know. Maybe. He didn't seem to know Tucker was dead, but if there was an altercation where Jake pushed him and he fell, Jake might not have realized he'd killed him."

I looked over and saw Rori had grown pale. "Why do you think Tucker gave you that music box?"

"He said he wanted to apologize."

I thought of Steve's apology to me in the dark of the predawn bakery. It had been genuine, heartfelt, even poignant. However, thinking back to Tucker's apology to Rori, his had been anything but. He'd seemed much more concerned with the cars that were passing on the street behind him.

Almost as if someone was following him.

The music box had been in his pocket, sure. But what if he hadn't planned to give it to Rori? What if he'd foisted it on her for the afternoon, perhaps for safekeeping, always intending to get it back? Could he have counted on her not throwing it away or breaking it? Maybe not for long, not the way she felt about him. But if my line of thinking was correct, he *had* counted on being able to convince her to give it back that very night. And he'd been right.

His timing was just off.

"Maybe Tucker took the music box because he thought I'd like it."

I finished buckling my seat belt and turned to look at her. "You make thievery sound like some big romantic gesture."

She shrugged. "Maybe it was. For him."

"Where's the music box now?"

"In my room at home."

"I don't know what the deal is with that thing, but I want you to hide it as soon as you get back." I wracked my brain. "Put it in the freezer, at the back. It may be worthless as Hudson Prater said, but someone was looking for something like it in his store." A blond man, he'd said. Jake Gibson? "I want to talk to Quinn and see if he's found out anything on his end."

She sighed and leaned against the headrest. "Okay."

I dropped Rori off at Wisteria House and started back to the Honeybee. Then I changed my mind and pulled the car over to call Cookie. When she answered, I asked, "Do you think you could find out if a house is for sale?" She'd been selling residential real estate for months now.

"Probably. What's the address?"

"Um, I don't know. That's why I'm calling you. There was an estate sale there a month or so ago, and the family is getting it ready for the market. The family name is Wiggins."

Cookie laughed. "You're hilarious."

"Why?"

"Because you know the family's name. Katie, just look up the address online."

I rubbed my face. "Duh. My brain is full of too many things."

"I'm supposed to be the one with brain fog, honey. It's eight-eleven Toro Street."

"You found it that fast?"

"I'm at my computer. You want me to give you directions?" I could tell she was teasing.

"Thanks. I think I still know how to use a GPS. I'll see you later." I hung up and fed the address into my phone.

My intention had been to drive by, but when I saw the man mowing the lawn out front and the woman carting a cardboard box out the front door, I pulled to the curb. As I did so, I realized I was probably about to lie to these nice people.

Like, a lot.

Maybe they're not that nice. Maybe they killed Tucker because he stole their worthless music box.

The thought didn't provide much comfort, but I got out of the car anyway.

The man shut off the mower as I approached. The woman stowed the box in the back of the small hatchback in the driveway and turned toward me. Her fingers combed through a shock of blond hair that looked like she'd been doing a lot of that today. Her face was drawn, which accented the crow's-feet around her eyes.

"Hi," I said.

"Hi."

"This is the Wiggins place, right?"

"Yes." She sounded tired. "This was our daddy's place. I'm Waverly Wiggins. This is my older brother, Zane."

He'd left the mower sitting in the middle of the yard and walked over. His yellow hair stuck out in all directions from under his baseball hat. "Help you?"

"Well, maybe. You sure look like you're busy. I was a little surprised to find you here. Thought the place might be up for sale already."

"We're getting there," Waverly said. Her voice was breathy. "It's a lot of hard work."

"I thought the estate sales company did the cleanup afterward. At least the cleanup of the stuff in the house." I pointed vaguely toward the box.

Zane glowered. "They're supposed to. We fired them."

"Oh?"

"You interested in buying our daddy's house?" he asked.

"I'm afraid not. I was wondering about that estate sales company. We're thinking of moving my aunt to a senior living apartment complex, and we'll need some help going through all her stuff."

Sorry, Lucy.

"All I have to say is, don't use Gibson. They're crooks. They'll steal your stuff."

I opened my mouth to say more, but Zane wasn't interested. He turned without another word and went back to his mower.

"I'm sorry," I said to Waverly. "Did I hit a nerve?"

"You had no way of knowing. But Zane's right. Daddy left us something we really needed, but we found out what it was after we'd already brought Gibson in. Daddy was in hospice by then. When we came to get it, it was gone."

"Oh, dear. Can you sue for something like that?"

"It's probably too late." Weariness rolled off her as she looked at the house. "Selling our family home will help a little, but Daddy's medical bills were horrible. It's bad enough that I have two kids in college, and Zane has one." She rubbed her face, then seemed to come back to herself.

"Listen to me, going on and on to a perfect stranger. I'm so sorry."

"That's okay," I said gently. "Sometimes it's easier to talk to a stranger."

Her eyes followed her brother as he crisscrossed the yard. "Well, we're sure tired of hearing each other worry about it." Her gaze returned to me. "There's another estate company in town. If only we'd chosen them, everything would have been all right. You should use them for your aunt's treasures."

"What did the Gibsons take, if you don't mind me asking?"

She shook her head. "It was a little music box. Played some Disney song. A silly looking little thing in the shape of a birdhouse, but it would have made all the difference in our lives."

My heart sped up. She was talking about Rori's music box, all right.

"But now it's too late?" I asked.

She sighed. "It might be. We've looked all over town for it, in case the Gibsons took it to a pawn shop or antique store. That kind of thing. No luck, though."

So it had been Zane in Hudson Prater's store.

"Thanks for the advice," I said, thoroughly puzzled on one hand, and determined to help this poor woman on the other. Maybe Quinn could x-ray the music box. There had to be something about it that made it such a treasure. Something that had gotten Tucker Abbott killed?

At some point very soon, Rori needed to give the box back to its rightful owners. I'd talk to Quinn first, and then I'd tell Rori what I'd learned when I went over to Wisteria House in a couple hours.

"Sure. Good luck." Waverly turned and walked back to the house.

I went back to my car, casting a glance over my shoulder. The house was a mid-range ranch. Nice, but nothing that would bring in really big bucks. It sounded like the Wigginses were in severe financial straits. How could the music box help them out of the jam Waverly had just described?

And what would they do to get it back? From the seat of my car, I sent out tendrils of intuition to try and sense any magical power coming from either Wiggins or the house itself. There was a bit, but nothing unusual. Magic was everywhere, after all. I certainly didn't feel anything like the magical signature I'd felt in Tucker's motel room.

But witches could mask their power. Could Waverly be more than she appeared? Or Zane?

Chapter 18

It was a few minutes after noon when I got back, and the Honeybee was hopping. While I'd been out, the caterer had called to confirm the menu for the wedding. I'd considered trying to do it all from the Honeybee kitchen, but Lucy had quite rightfully talked me out of it. It was enough that we were creating the tiered cupcake wedding cake in-house, seven kinds of cupcakes and all. So as soon as the lunch rush settled down, I sequestered myself in the office and returned the call of the woman Bianca had recommended.

Fifteen minutes later we'd run through all the options, and I'd confirmed the menu items we'd chosen when Declan and I had dragged Lucy and Ben to the tasting session. We'd decided on classic pimiento cheese with crudités and crackers, peach Caprese salad, three kinds of sliders—fried chicken and biscuit, pulled pork, and beef brisket—melon ball and mint salad, bite-sized hush puppies, fried green tomatoes with lemony aioli, tons of herbed grilled vegetables, and plenty of lemonade and sweet tea.

My stomach growled after we'd finished talking about all the delectable food choices. "And the wine will be provided by Bianca at Moon Grapes," I finished.

As I hung up, I remembered my self-satisfaction when I'd thought I was done with the wedding planning, and anxiety stabbed through my solar plexus as I once again thought about our lack of wedding officiant. The previous evening, I'd been fine with leaving it all up to Declan, but in the light of day I felt a new urgency to know who was going to marry us in a few days.

I started to text him, then gave up and called.

"Hey, darlin'," he answered. "I'm caravanning with Mother and my sisters to pick everyone up at the airport. Camille and John coordinated their flight to meet Lauren and Evan in Atlanta, and they're all coming in on the same plane. We should be at the house in about an hour or so."

"Oh, good. I'll be over to see everyone this afternoon. In the meantime, I was kind of wondering . . ."

"Yeah?"

"I know you said you're handling it and all, but I'm starting to wonder if I have to wait until the actual wedding to find out who's going to marry us." I took a breath. "*Darlin'.*"

He laughed. "Go talk to Ben. He'll tell you all about it."

"Ben knows?" Relief whooshed through me. "Oh, thank you. I don't know what you did or what strings you pulled, but thank you."

I heard Rori laugh in the background.

"I think you're going to love it," he said. "I know I do. We'll see you later at the house, okay? Gotta run. Love you."

"Love you, too." But he was already gone.

I went out and put on my apron, then tapped my foot impatiently by the coffee counter while Ben took his time creating a fancy leaf in the foam on top of a cappuccino. He looked at me out of the corner of his eye, and a grin tugged at his lips. When he was finally finished, he handed the mug to the waiting customer and turned to me.

"Did you need something, Katie?" The grin was full-fledged now.

"Declan said you'd tell me who he found to marry us on Saturday."

"Did he now?"

"Stop teasing me."

"Okay, I'll tell you. I sure hope you like who we came up with." His eyes twinkled.

"Uncle Ben!"

He held up his palm to me. "Okay, okay." His hand dropped. "It's me."

I blinked. "What?"

"I'm going to marry you and Declan."

It took a few seconds for it to sink in, but then I flung myself at him and wrapped my arms around his neck. "Oh, Ben! That's fantastic. I can't think of anyone I'd want more than you."

"It will be an honor, honey."

I stepped back. "But Mrs. Standish said you have to be a judge or a member of the clergy?"

Still grinning, he said, "In the last two days, I have become an ordained minister in the Church of Life, and then I had to check in with the probate court to make sure I was listed as the officiant on your marriage license. As of this morning, it's all set!"

"So that's what you've been up to." I was smiling so hard, my cheeks were starting to cramp.

"I take it he told you," Lucy said from behind me.

I whirled to find her leaning against the counter with a knowing look on her face. "You knew all along?"

She laughed. "Of course." Then she gave me a hug. "Isn't it wonderful?"

My head bobbed in agreement. "Even better than Judge Matthews." I turned to my uncle. "Thank you, Ben."

His eyes danced with pleasure. "You're most welcome."

I started to text Detective Quinn about what Rori and I had learned from the Gibsons and my visit to Zane and Waverly Wiggins, but then stopped. It was too complicated to convey in text, and besides, I wanted to gauge his reaction when I filled him in. The last time we'd spoken, Quinn had practically hung up on me.

Could he still be upset because of my crack at the motel about not having a great track record when it came to murder suspects? Ugh. I definitely need to talk to him face-to-face.

I considered, then found the nonemergency number for the precinct where Quinn worked. Two rings later, I was asking if Detective Quinn was in his office. They said he was and asked me to wait while they transferred me. I quickly thanked them and said I'd have to call back later.

"Mungo, let's take a ride," I said. Declan's sisters and their families would all be at Wisteria House in about an hour. If I hurried, I'd have time to chat with Quinn before then.

My familiar obligingly hopped into my tote, and I slung it over one shoulder.

I went into the kitchen and opened the freezer. Leaving Bianca's earrings in a freezer that anyone could come in and open seemed a little sketchy. Not that anyone would do such a thing, but still. I grabbed the jewelry box and zipped it into the deep side pocket next to Mungo in my tote bag.

My familiar's nose jerked up, and a moment later the scent of bacon suddenly filled the air.

"Lucy?"

"Over here," she answered.

I followed her voice to the other side of the central oven and found her frying bacon on the griddle top. "What are you doing?" I asked.

"Prepping for tomorrow's daily special." She reached over and shoved the recipe she was following toward me. "Peanut butter bacon cookies."

"Holy smokes," I said. "These look amazing. Sweet and savory at its best." I looked up from under my eyebrows. "And for the *special* additions?"

"As if bacon wasn't magical all on its own," she teased. "But I'm thinking of dusting them with a bit of cardamom sugar. What do you think?"

"The flavor profile should work, as long as the spice is subtle. But isn't cardamom for lust?"

"It can be," she said. "But I'll focus on its ability to relax the body and clarify the mind."

"Well, I was going to try one of those cookies anyway, but now I will for sure." I made a face. "I could use a little clarity and relaxation."

Lucy put down the tongs she'd been using to turn the bacon. "What's wrong, honey? Or is it the wedding jitters?"

"No, not that. It's only that I have a lot on my plate. The wedding, Rori's ex being murdered, Steve . . ." I trailed off.

My aunt's eyebrows rose. "Steve?"

After a moment's hesitation, I quickly peered around to make sure Ben was still out front. When I was sure he couldn't overhear, I told Lucy about his visit that morning. "I guess an apology was in order," I said when I'd finished. "Since he came by yesterday to try to convince me I was rushing into marrying Declan."

Lucy frowned and turned the bacon on the griddle again. "That poor boy."

"He's anything but poor."

"I wasn't talking about his money," she said, laying down the tongs again and turning to face me. "I really do believe Steve Dawes is in love with you."

"He's done some pretty crazy things to prove it," I mumbled.

"He really has, hasn't he?" she said, ignoring my sarcasm. "Are you going to tell Declan?"

"Someday," I said. "After—"

"Tell Declan what?" Ben asked, coming around the corner.

"Oh," I said, scrambling to cover. The last thing I needed was Ben getting involved. "Um, tell Declan how hard it was to write my vows. I don't want him to know I struggled."

"Oh, I bet Declan struggled as much as you did. In fact, I know it," Ben said with a wink.

"I won't tell him you told me," I said with a smile. "Listen, Tucker Abbott had a ruby ring that seems to be missing. I need to go talk to Quinn about it. Do you mind if I take off a few minutes earlier than I'd planned? I can drop by the precinct on my way to welcome the rest of Declan's family to town."

Lucy looked away so Ben couldn't see the smile on her face. "Fine with me, dear."

"Sure, hon," my uncle said. "We're a well-oiled machine around here."

I kissed him on the cheek. "Thanks, Ben."

Though I wasn't sure I liked how well the machine seemed to run without me.

Pushing that thought aside, I strode toward the front door. Then out of the corner of my eye, I saw something that made me stop and turn around. I hadn't been mistaken.

Dayleen, the manager of the Spotlight Motel, was sitting in the reading area sipping from an oversized cup and nibbling on a scone while turning the pages of a fashion magazine that was open on the sofa beside her.

I backtracked to where Ben was back behind the coffee counter. "Did you see who's in the library?" I asked.

He nodded. "Sure. I took her order. You did invite her to come see us, after all. I even remembered to give her the Parmesan rosemary scone on the house."

"Oh. Right. I'd forgotten about that."

"You have a lot on your mind, darlin'. Don't give it a thought. Are you going to go say hey?"

I checked my watch, even though I knew what it said. I needed to get going. "I'll have to pass if I'm going to get over to the police precinct." I gave him a half smile. "But if you feel like plying her with your social skills, you might see if she's found out anything else about what happened the other night."

"Hmm. We'll see, but I think she's meeting someone." He lifted his chin toward her.

A woman had entered, and Dayleen was waving to her.

"Oh. Wow," I said.

Ben looked the question at me.

"That's not just someone. That's Effie Glass." For some reason, I stepped back behind the counter. "Tucker's ex-girlfriend. The one Dayleen said she didn't know."

I needn't have worried about Effie recognizing me. She walked right by, gave me a smile, and joined Dayleen on the sofa.

My uncle let out a little whistle. "Is that so? Well, she's bound to want something to eat and drink, so you can bet I'll do my best to find out what's going on there. You head on over to see Quinn and leave it to me."

Chapter 19

I waited patiently while the officer behind the windowed reception desk called the detective and gave him my name. Moments later, the door buzzed, and I was allowed in. Quinn came to meet me, his face an impenetrable mask. Mungo kept his head tucked down in the tote bag as I obediently followed Quinn through the sparsely populated desks, past his own surprisingly messy space in the corner, and into a spare gray room. The door shut behind me with a clang, and I realized we were in an interview room.

Good for privacy. Terrible for atmosphere.

"I don't have much time, Katie. Whatever it is, make it quick."

"Well, hello to you, too." I sank into a folding chair and set my bag on my lap. Mungo popped his head up and grinned at Detective Quinn.

Sighing, Quinn sank into the chair across the table from me. "Hello, Katie. Hello, Mungo. Better?"

"Yes! More of Declan's family just got into town, and I'm on my way over there, so I don't have much time anyway." I held up my finger. "First off, I want to apologize."

He frowned. "Why? What did you do now?"

"What? No, no. I'm apologizing for being so mean to you the other night. At the Spotlight."

He gave a slow blink, and his lips twitched though they were still curved down. "Ah. I must admit, I'd forgotten how much you'd hurt my feelings. So, gosh. Thank you for coming by for that, Katie. Are we done?"

I wagged my finger. "Sarcasm is the lowest form of humor, you know."

"Hmm."

Frustrated, I let my hands drop to Mungo's back. He looked over his shoulder at me. "Quinn, I don't understand. I said in my text yesterday that Tucker's signet ring might have a magical connection to this case. Maybe not in so many words, but still, you knew what I meant. And now, after asking for my help with the Bosworth murder, you don't seem to want to have anything to do with me. Are you that close to solving the case? Have you rethought the wisdom of working with a witch?" I held my palms up. "What gives?"

He watched me as if assessing something.

I barreled on, seemingly unable to stop myself. "Tucker was a con man. And you know what con men are? Charismatic. And sometimes people who are charismatic get a little magical boost, you know? It's called a glamour. From what I've learned, that ring might have helped him in the glamour department." I took a breath, and more words tumbled out. "Rori and I went to see the Gibsons this morning. Gibson Estate Sales? Tucker worked for them, at least until he got fired a few weeks ago. Tucker told his ex-girlfriend, Effie—you met her, right?—that he got the ring at an estate sale, but Jake Gibson thinks Tucker stole it. He stole something else, too, it looks like. A little music box that he gave to Rori. She was going to give it back at the Spotlight that night." I shifted in my chair. "The thing is, we don't know why he would have stolen the music box. It's not worth anything. We checked with an antique dealer. Hudson Prater. Rori said he was a friend of Tucker's."

Quinn's eyebrows raised a fraction.

"I know, I know. But we needed to know if the music box was valuable. I checked to see if the music box had any magical signatures, but it doesn't. Still, it has some kind of value to the family. Family, by the way, that visited Hudson Prater's store looking for a music box like the one Tucker gave Rori. I went to talk to them, too, this morning. Zane and Waverly Wiggins. They're in pretty desperate straits, what with having to pay for their father's medical bills and having three kids in college between the two of them. Still, Waverly seems to think that silly little music box would somehow help. Of course, Rori would be perfectly willing to give it back, I should think. I didn't tell them she has it. See, it's downright strange that Tucker would take it in the first place—and if the Wigginses wanted it back that badly, who knows what they might have done to get it? I don't really see Waverly as a killer, but you never can tell. I didn't get a feeling for her brother. Not a very talkative sort. I really think you need to look into them and—"

Quinn raised his hand like a traffic cop. "Stop."

"But—"

"Katie."

I fell silent.

He took a slow, deep breath, never taking his eyes from my face. "Okay. I get what you're saying. We looked for the ring again but didn't find it in the motel room. It's entirely possible the killer took it." He paused, then seemed to make a decision. "At this point I'm not looking at the ring as the motive for Abbott's murder, though. And I'm not seeing a worthless music box as a great motive, either."

Something in the way he said it gave me a bad feeling. "Don't tell me you're still looking at Rori McCarthy as a suspect."

"Let me ask you this, Katie. Did you happen to hear Ms. McCarthy threaten her ex-husband the afternoon before he was murdered?"

"Um . . ."

"Because the gardener heard her threaten him, and so did a postal delivery worker who was walking by. The gardener was very helpful, in fact. He describes the two McCarthy sisters and their mother to a T. He also described a young woman with short auburn hair who drives a new-generation Volkswagen."

"Okay, so Rori and Tucker had words," I said. "Rori said she never wanted to see him again, as a matter of fact."

"And yet she sought him out that very evening."

"Yeah . . ." I trailed off. "But he asked her to bring him the music box."

He opened his mouth, then closed it again.

"There's something else?" I asked, not sure I wanted to know the answer.

"I'm sorry, Katie. There were security cameras."

I stared at him. "I thought they weren't working."

He suddenly snorted a laugh. "I should have known you'd ask the motel manager about that."

"Actually, it was Uncle Ben," I muttered.

"Either way, you're right. The cameras at the Spotlight weren't working. But the ones at the storage facility across the street were working just fine. They caught footage of a woman who parked down the block from the Spotlight earlier in the afternoon. It was around three o'clock."

My forehead squinched. "Okay. So what?"

"It was Declan's sister."

I wagged my head back and forth. "I don't understand. Rori was shopping with her mother."

At least until she took off by herself to drive around Savannah.

Quinn pressed his lips together, then said, "Not that sister."

It took me a moment. "*Eliza* went to see Tucker?"

He nodded. "I'm sorry, Katie. There are still other suspects, but along with Aurora McCarthy, Eliza McCarthy is now on the list. And that," he said, "is why I haven't been asking for your help. Let's just call your connection to the family a conflict of interest."

I stood. The sudden movement caused Mungo to unceremoniously thump down on his behind in my bag. I sensed him glaring up at me and gave his head a pat.

"It's not a conflict of interest if I'm only looking for the truth. I did it when you tried to railroad Uncle Ben, and I was right. Plus, like it or not, I understand an element of the situation you don't. Come on, Quinn. You know darn well I'm not going to stop trying to find out what really happened." I hitched the tote farther up on my shoulder. "I'll let you know if I find out anything you can use." I took a few steps toward the door, then paused to say over my shoulder, "Don't worry. I won't bother you otherwise."

Quinn sighed. "Katie."

I yanked the door open and marched through to the front door, then yanked that door open and went out to my car.

Yip?

I was tucking Mungo into the passenger seat and paused at his questioning tone. I perched on the edge of the seat and ruffled his ears.

"Don't worry. I'm not really mad. I'm just worried." I rubbed my eyes with the fingers of my other hand. "Lordy, why couldn't all this have happened *after* the wedding?"

It only took a few minutes to get to Wisteria House, but I managed to fit in a few expletives. I parked across the street in what I was starting to think of as my customary spot and sat for a moment to gather my thoughts. Mungo watched me with concern. The holy basil and lemon balm were looking faded and sad by now, and I made a mental note to replace them with something more vibrant the first chance I got.

"Well," I said in a forcefully bright voice. "Get ready to say hello to everyone, Mungo. They've come a long way for this wedding!"

Lauren; her husband, Evan; and their twelve-year-old son lived in California, and Camille and John lived in Colorado. My familiar bounced on his front feet, excited to meet new people. I did my best to shove thoughts of Tucker Abbott—and Rory and Eliza's seeming obsession with the guy—out of my mind for the time being.

As I turned off the engine, Declan's truck pulled up, and he double-parked in front of his family's rental. Aggie had parked her rental by the curb a few spots down. All four doors of the king cab flew open, and half of the McCarthy clan piled out of the vehicle as if it were a giant clown car.

Declan was laughing as he got out. He closed his eyes and threw his head back. My heart gave a little jump, under which there was a little ache as I thought again about how stressed he'd been lately. Seeing him laughing with such abandon made me happy, though, and I knew we just had to get through the rest of the week, and everything would settle down.

Well, get through the week, pull off the perfect wedding, find a murderer, and bring Connell back.

One thing at a time.

Aggie waved to me from the sidewalk in front of Wisteria House. I opened the door in time to hear her announce, "Katie's here, everyone!"

Declan greeted me with a smile that made my heart zing even from across the street. His older sister, Lauren, whirled toward me with a grin. "There's our bride!" She strode across the street without a glance in either direction.

I got out of the Bug, and she enveloped me in an enthusiastic bear hug.

"Good to see you. How was your flight?" I asked when she'd let go and I could breathe again.

Mungo nudged the back of my leg, and I moved aside

to let him jump to the ground. Unlike Declan's sister, he looked both ways before trotting across to join the rest of the family. Declan reached down and gave him a scratch behind the ears.

Linking her arm in mine, Lauren filled me in on her family's travels in great detail. Declan had always said she could make a story out of eating a bag of potato chips, and now I saw what he meant. Her husband, Evan, greeted me as he hauled a huge suitcase out of the back of the truck and directed their son to get it onto the sidewalk.

Camille waited until her sister had exhausted her tale, then greeted me in a quiet voice. Her husband, John, came over and put his arm across my shoulders for a quick squeeze before moving to help his brothers-in-law with the luggage. The sisters born on either side of Declan both had brown eyes and dark hair, though Camille's was long and straight and parted in the middle, while Lauren's was cut in an angled bob that was shorter in the back and curved around her narrow chin. John was a wiry guy, high energy, and a jokester. He was the one who'd made Declan laugh with such abandon. Evan was serious, with prematurely gray hair and obvious affection for his wife. His and Lauren's twelve-year-old son, Joel, quickly retreated to the sidewalk and took his phone out, leaving the adults to their chatter. Aggie stood to one side and watched her family with an indulgent smile.

I spied Eliza and Rori talking in the front garden. Rori nodded to her sister, then came out to talk to her mother. I heard her say something about setting out refreshments as I sidestepped her and made my way to where Eliza still stood. No time like the present to find out why the heck she'd been at the Spotlight the afternoon before Tucker had been killed.

She smiled as I approached. "The gang's all here."

"Looks like." I lowered my voice. "Eliza, before coming over, I stopped by the local precinct to talk to Detective Quinn."

She tipped her head to one side. "You're investigating Tucker's murder, aren't you? Rori won't talk about it, but she's dragged you into this. I can tell."

I lifted my chin. "I'm looking into a few things surrounding the situation."

"Why? Is it just in your nature, or is there something else?"

One shoulder rose, then dropped. "I guess you could say it's in my nature. Rori also asked me to help."

Eliza's nostrils twitched.

"She thinks knowing what happened will help her move on with her life. But it's not just that. Eliza, Rori's a suspect. She found the body, and now the police know she threatened Tucker right out here." I pointed toward the entry. "The gardener and the postal delivery person heard, and the police have talked to both of them."

Her lips pressed together.

I went on. "Now it turns out that's not all. Quinn told me you were seen at the Spotlight Motel the afternoon before Tucker was killed."

Her eyes widened, then she looked away. "I parked down the street."

"That was your mistake," I said. "The cameras at the motel didn't work, but the ones outside the storage facility where you parked did. That's where the police got the footage."

Her swallow was audible.

"What were you thinking?" I hissed, more harshly than I'd intended.

She flinched. "I was . . ." Her jaw set. "I was trying to help my little sister. I went to talk to Tucker, to tell him to leave her alone. You saw him motion that he planned to call her. The last thing I wanted was for him to get her alone. See, Aurora is a bit . . . she can be easy to influence. That's how that horrible man got her to marry him in the first place." Her eyes narrowed. "You saw him. You saw how charismatic he could be. It was like some kind of spell."

I bit my lip.

"He'd always been like that. You know—smarmy. Slick. But when he came by on Monday, it was worse. I could tell there was something off about the man, you know?"

I nodded. "Yes. There was."

She looked relieved. "You saw it, too, then. So you can see why I had to try to get him to leave Aurora alone, can't you?"

"I guess I can." My fingers worked at the bridge of my nose as I thought. I let my hand drop and said, "The problem is that Detective Quinn has added you to his suspect list, along with Rori. And that's another reason I'm going to keep trying to find out what really happened."

"How can I help?" she asked.

"It sounds like trying to help me might have gotten you in trouble already," Rori said from behind me. She must have heard everything.

I glanced toward the street. Everyone except Declan was still involved with gathering their things to bring inside. He watched us for a few moments, then shrugged and got in his truck to move it to a proper parking space down the street.

"What did Tucker say when you told him to leave me alone?" Rori asked.

Eliza sighed. "Exactly what you'd expect. I tried to argue with him, but he was so good at deflecting anything he didn't agree with."

"Did you raise your voice?" I asked.

Her lips twisted. "Oh, yes. I committed the age-old mistake of trying to convince someone by using more volume when all else fails."

That accounts for one of the fights Tucker had with women in the parking lot that Dayleen told us about. But who was he arguing with a few days before?

I already had a feeling the argument with the big blond guy Dayleen had spoken of had been Jake Gibson. It could have been Zane Wiggins, but Gibson simply struck me as more violent. Yet Gibson had seemed genuinely surprised to learn Tucker was dead—and not very happy about it, either. It could have been some kind of an accident, however, if Gibson had gone to try and recover what Tucker had taken from the Wiggins estate. After all, the whole room had been torn apart. Had that happened before or after Tucker had hit his head on the dresser?

Accident or not, Gibson—or one of the Wiggins heirs—might have been looking for the very tchotchke he'd pawned off on Rori.

The music box.

I leaned over to Rori. "Did you put it in the freezer?"

"Yes. Thank goodness no one saw me. I'd have a hard time explaining."

Everyone was moving toward the house, and we let the conversation drop. Eliza ran lightly up the steps to open the front door for her baggage-toting family, then stopped dead. She turned and glared at Rori.

"Not only did you not lock the door as I asked, you actually left it unlatched. What were you thinking?"

"I did not!" Rori protested and hurried up to join her.

Eliza shook her head and made a show of pushing the door open with her fingertip.

"But I locked it!" Rori said. "I distinctly remember, because I was annoyed that you felt you had to tell me to do it in the first place."

Her sister only raised her eyebrows and pointed to the evidence.

"Now girls," Aggie said. She climbed the steps and stopped between them. "Let's get inside."

Eliza made a noise of exasperation, pushed the door all the way open, then went inside. Her mother followed, and the newcomers crowded behind her.

However, Rori hung back, her forehead creased. We exchanged worried glances.

"Something's wrong," she said.

A red-and-black dragonfly chose that moment to buzz leisurely by.

Declan came up behind us just as Lauren shouted a surprised expletive from the entryway. He ran past us and up the steps. Rori and I were close on his heels.

Chapter 20

The foyer was packed with luggage and people. Joel and Evan stood on the stairs, while the others stood in a semicircle around the hall table. It took me a moment to realize the problem. Then I saw that the mirror over the table was broken.

Not just broken. Smashed. Even the stained-glass dragonflies were in pieces on the floor and scattered on the top of the table. The gardenia lay on its side, dirt spilling from the cracked pot.

"Careful," Aggie warned. "There's a lot of sharp glass there."

Lauren skirted around and headed toward the living room.

"Wait," Declan called. "It's not safe. Come back outside, and we'll call the police."

Aggie's lips pressed together as she assessed the situation.

Eliza trailed after Lauren into the living room, followed by John.

"No, don't go in there," Declan ordered. "Whoever did this could still be in the house."

I closed my eyes and sent out all my witchy senses. There was power in the house, a signature that hadn't been here before. It was familiar, like a face you almost recognize but can't quite place. But I did place it—it was the same as the spell remnants I'd felt in Tucker's motel room. Like then, it felt like a vestige, left behind like a whiff of exotic perfume. Whoever had been here was gone.

Ignoring her brother's admonitions, Camille patted her mother on the arm then went with the others. The sounds of voices reached us from different parts of the first floor.

"You guys!" Declan shouted. "Come *on*." He looked at me. "Why don't my sisters ever listen to me?"

I offered a sympathetic shrug, my mind racing.

The music box!

Aggie was still rooted to the spot in front of the broken mirror, but she had her phone out and was dialing. "Shh," she said to her son as she put the phone to her ear. "I'm calling 911."

Evan came down the stairs with a wry grin. "Not to worry, Deck. A pack of McCarthys like this would scare anyone off."

"Here's how they got in," Eliza said from the other room. "Broken window. Rori, you were right. I'm sorry."

"And they left by the front door. Still, better safe than sorry. Stay there," Declan said to Joel, who nodded, his eyes wide with excitement. My fiancé hurried after his family. Rori slid past me, then Joel, and ran up the stairs.

I sprinted after her.

She wrenched open the door to her room and gasped. Looking over her shoulder, I could see why. The room was trashed.

Clothes spilled out of open drawers, the contents of the closet lay on the floor, shoes were scattered across the room. The bed had been stripped and the mattress was half off. In the en suite bathroom, more drawers hung open, and bottles lay on their sides.

"Why?" she wailed. Then, "Oh, *no!*" Rori ran in and picked up a gauzy floral dress from the floor. "It's ruined!" She turned back to me with tears running down her cheeks and held it out so I could see the rip along the bodice. "I was going to wear it to the wedding."

"Oh, honey," I said, stepping into the room.

Declan's hand closed on my arm, and he pulled me toward the door. "Huh-uh, darlin'. We need to leave things so the police can see them. Rori, come out to the hallway."

She ignored him, standing in the middle of the room and turning in a circle.

"Rori," I said. "Come on out here."

She looked up and nodded.

Behind me, Declan sighed. "I'm going to check the other rooms."

When Rori joined me in the hallway, I whispered, "The freezer."

She looked puzzled for a moment, then her face cleared. "The music box? You think that's why someone broke in?"

I gave her a look that said, *Duh.*

Anger suffused her features. "Really? Someone did all this damage for *that*?"

"Your room looks an awful lot like Tucker's motel room did, don't you think?"

The blood drained from her face, and she glanced back into her room. "Oh. God. Yeah, it does."

"They didn't find the music box then because Tucker didn't have it. Somehow, they must have found out you had it." I sighed.

Her chin came up. "Well, too bad for them."

I grinned. "Let's go get it."

We looked at each other, then rushed to the top of the stairs and clattered down them. Sure enough, the music box was still behind a pack of waffles in the freezer. She grabbed it. I nodded toward the parlor that opened off the foyer.

For whatever reason, the intruder had either missed the parlor altogether or decided not to trash it. Eliza rounded the corner as we started inside. I waved her toward us. She tipped her head and started to say something. I shook my head and held my finger to my lips.

"Hurry," I urged. I wanted to take a closer look at the music box and could only hope no one would walk in on us, as it might be difficult to explain what we were up to.

Partly because I didn't know what we were up to. I kept coming back to the suspects I'd been thinking about earlier and wondering if there really might be something about a cheap ceramic knickknack that someone would kill for.

The sisters slipped into the parlor. Mungo came in, too, and I closed the door behind us.

"What's going on?" Eliza asked.

"Rori, can I see the music box?" I nodded toward it

and said to Eliza, "The gift Tucker gave Rori might be the reason he was killed."

She made a noise of derision, but I was pretty sure it was directed at Tucker rather than us.

Rori handed it to me. "It doesn't even work now."

"It sounded pretty pathetic to start with," I said.

Turning the music box over, I peered at the maker's mark again. Then I tried to turn the bottom as I'd seen Tucker and Hudson Prater do, but it seemed to be jammed. I banged it gently against the heel of my hand and tried again. Nothing. I tried harder. A lot harder. I banged it on the table and heard it crack.

Suddenly, the bottom twisted off in my hand in two pieces. Rori gasped, and I opened my mouth to apologize. Then I clamped it shut as I saw the piece of paper wedged into the bottom of the birdhouse. The corner had been chewed up by the music mechanism, but I was able to carefully extract it with two fingers.

The sisters crowded close as I turned it over.

"Oh. My. God." Rori's voice was barely a whisper. "No wonder it was worth a lot of money."

And I remembered what Effie Glass had told Mimsey and me at Belford's.

Oh, and his latest whopper? He said he'd won the lottery. The lottery. *Told me if I came back to him, we'd run away to live on some beach someplace. Just another movie script. Can you believe it?*

Well, I believed it now.

Because there was no reason for a Georgia Jumbo Bucks lottery ticket to be hidden in the bottom of a cheap ceramic music box unless it was a winner.

"I wonder how much it's worth?" Rori asked eagerly.

Frowning, I said, "This is what the elderly Mr. Wiggins left his children. No wonder they wanted this 'worthless' little tchotchke so badly."

Always the practical one, Eliza had her phone out. She leaned closer to see the numbers on the ticket and entered them into the search engine. I heard her breath catch, and she stilled.

She looked up at us. "Two point eight million dollars. That's how much. It was an early jackpot, but someone won the whole thing and never claimed it. There's only a week left to cash it in before it expires."

We stared at each other.

Finally, I rubbed my eyes. "I need to tell Detective Quinn about this."

"But . . . are you absolutely positive we can't keep any of it? A finder's fee or something?" Rori asked in a pleading tone.

"Aurora!" Eliza said.

"I know, I know," she grumbled.

The Wiginses hadn't known when the ticket expired. That's why she thought finding the music box now might be too late.

The sound of car doors slamming came from the street. I peeked out the curtain to see two patrol cars stopped out front and police officers coming up the steps.

Quickly, I pulled my phone out and called Quinn.

"Katie, darn it—"

"The house Declan's family rented for the week has been broken into. Whoever did it trashed the place looking for something, just like Tucker's room at the Spotlight."

"Wait, what?"

Voices sounded outside the door.

"Check your scanner or whatever. The police have already arrived. It's a burglary, only I bet they'll find nothing was taken."

Now voices sounded in the background on Detective Quinn's end of the call. I heard the sound of his hand covering his phone mic, then he came back. "I'm on my way. Are you okay?"

"No one was here," I said. "But Quinn? Now I'm pretty sure I know why Tucker was killed."

"Why?" he demanded.

"Two point eight million dollars."

Detective Quinn took possession of the lottery ticket. The police went through the house, though they didn't process it like I'd seen them do a murder scene. The vacation rental company—not the one Tucker had worked for, it turned out—was called, and one of their representatives came to assess the damage and arrange for someone to come fix the window that same day.

The McCarthys were moved to another house in Midtown, not as grand but big enough for everyone. Aggie and Eliza packed up their belongings, while Rori rescued what she could from her room with Camille's help.

"Don't worry," I heard Camille say. "I have the perfect dress for you to wear to the wedding. I couldn't make up my mind, so I brought two. And we'll go on a shopping spree tomorrow, okay?"

Rori's smile was a little watery, but she handled the situation pretty well.

It was nearly four. Back downstairs, I called the bakery to update my aunt and uncle and see if one of them could pick my parents up from the airport.

"Oh, no worries," Ben said. "They've rented a car, and they're going to drive straight to our town house. That will give them time to freshen up before we all go to Churchill's tonight. Don't worry about a thing. You do what you have to do there, and we'll see you tonight."

Declan was going to help his family get settled in their new digs, while I headed to the apartment to get ready for the big family dinner. I was about to leave when Quinn came down the stairs.

"Katie, can I talk to you a moment?"

I sighed. "This isn't my fault."

His forehead wrinkled. "Who said it was?"

No one had, of course. I felt defensive nonetheless, mostly because I couldn't shake the feeling that all the questions I'd been asking had somehow alerted Tucker's killer that Rori had the music box.

"Let's go in here." He opened the door to the parlor, which had been getting so much traffic.

"Do you believe me now?" I asked when he'd closed the door most of the way. "You surely can't think that Rori or Eliza wrecked this place."

"No. No, I don't. In fact, I've been thinking. If that music box is the cause for all this—"

I broke in. "You mean the lottery ticket."

"Right, but not many people know about that. Did you tell everyone here about it?"

I shook my head. "Rori might have, though."

"I believe I caught her in time. Her older sister, too.

221

See, if we can keep the fact that the lottery ticket has been discovered quiet, maybe we can smoke the killer out with the promise of that charming little music box. Or killers. They both may have done it."

"Zane Wiggins and his sister," I said.

"They had the most motive."

"Jake Gibson might have known about the lottery ticket, too. And then there's Effie Glass. And you know what? She was having a tête-à-tête with Dayleen from the Spotlight when I left the Honeybee this afternoon. Have you looked into them?"

"I've looked into everyone. Including, by the way, Carolyn Becker, who found it very amusing that you quizzed her first."

One half of my mouth turned up. "Yeah. Sorry about that. Anyway, what is this smoke-the-killer-out plan you have in mind?"

"You said Hudson Prater was the antique dealer you went to, right?"

I nodded.

"I'm going to ask him to put the word out to his various connections, including the Gibsons and Wigginses, that he has the music box. Then we see who turns up to get it."

"But the music box is broken."

"It's also evidence. He should be able to bluff with something similar if he needs to."

"Can't you just continue your investigation until you can build a case against the murderer?" I asked. Funny, because normally I'd be thrilled with the idea of setting a trap. However, what Quinn suggested seemed risky. I didn't have a good feeling about it at all, not after seeing the violent vandalism in Tucker's motel room and Rori's bedroom.

"That's exactly what I'm going to do," he said. "But that lottery ticket expires in a week. That ticking clock might be the impetus to push the killer into revealing themselves."

"And closing your case. Tell me, though—why on the good green earth would Mr. Prater agree to such a thing?"

Quinn smiled, and it wasn't entirely pleasant. "Because Hudson Prater is a fence, Katie. That's probably why he was a friend of Tucker's. And he's also a confidential informant, which is what has kept him out of jail until now. Don't worry. He'll do it."

Chapter 21

Back at the apartment, I stuffed the jewelry box that had been in my tote bag the whole afternoon behind a stack of frozen vegetables in our freezer. Heck, it had worked for the music box. Then I showered and put on a flowing green jumpsuit that managed to be dressy and casual at the same time, just like Churchill's. My mother texted that they'd arrived from Las Vegas on time and settled in at Lucy and Ben's. As I fluffed my hair, which I'd allowed to grow out a bit longer for the wedding, and applied blush and lipstick, I considered how my parents and Declan's family would like one another.

Dad was easygoing and pretty much got along with everyone. So no worries there. Mama could be a little obstreperous, however. Now that I'd spent some time with Declan's sisters—and not under the best circumstances, either—I thought they'd handle her just fine. She'd like them, too. And she'd love Aggie. The two of them could commiserate over their offspring. Then there was Eliza. She and my mother would get on like houses on fire, I realized. Perhaps that was why Eliza had pushed my buttons when I'd first met her.

Declan got home from helping his family relocate.

"How are they doing?" I asked when he came out of the bedroom, looking handsome as sin in jeans and a light blue button-down shirt.

"One thing I can say about my family is that they're resilient. The whole situation with Rori and Tucker has everyone chatting, of course. Lauren thinks you should find Tucker's killer and collect the reward."

My eyes widened. "Why would she say such a thing?"

"Hmm. Well, I might, just might, have mentioned to the sisters that you've solved a few crimes in the last few years."

"Great. How about that reward?"

"Yeah. I explained there wasn't one. Lauren probably didn't hear me, though. She was already talking about something else."

I laughed. "Let's go."

Mungo whined.

"You want me to turn the television on?" I asked.

He jumped up on the couch and lay down, facing the blank screen.

Rolling his eyes, Declan grabbed the remote and turned the channel to the soap network. Mungo grinned up at him and settled in to catch up on his favorite show.

"You have the weirdest dog," my fiancé muttered as we left.

"Weird as in awesome," I said with a smile.

On the way over, I brought up the idea of casting a spell to augment our attempts at lucid dreaming.

"Really? An actual mumbo jumbo spell?" he asked.

"Careful," I warned. "You're marrying a witch, so you'd better get used to things like that. Also, no. Not a spell like that. I was thinking I could make a tea with a little boost to help us, is all."

He stopped at a red light and looked over at me. "A tea sounds good. Yeah, let's do that."

I smiled at his enthusiasm and said, "Well, okay then!"

Mama greeted us at the door, ushering us to the table, where everyone was chattering away. She looked resplendent in her summer twinset, a light lavender that perfectly offset her red hair. Sure enough, when I looked between Mary Jane Lightfoot and Agnes McCarthy, the two mothers had to use the same hair color. They'd introduced themselves, of course, and had chosen seats together.

My dad came over and gave me a hug. As always, he carried a subtle scent of leather and wood shavings that instantly settled my soul. His full head of silver hair gleamed under the lights, and he wore his usual chambray shirt, jeans, and cowboy boots. I wondered if Mama would make him fancy it up for the wedding. She would, I was pretty sure, since he would be walking me down the path to the gazebo, but a part of me didn't want her to.

"Hi, baby," he said. "How are you holding up?"

"Okay," I said. "Though I have to admit, I'm looking forward to a little rest and relaxation next week. Not that we're taking a honeymoon. Not yet. Just getting back to normal life will be good."

"Remember to enjoy this, though," he said. "It's a big step, the beginning of something new, and a memory you'll have for the rest of your life."

I smiled up at him. "Thanks for reminding me of that. I get a little caught up in things and forget to appreciate them as much as I should."

He kissed my forehead. "My type A daughter."

Ben came over then, indicating with his eyes that he wanted to talk to me. We moved to the corner, not exactly out of earshot, but it was so loud by then that it didn't matter. He put his head next to mine.

"I managed to have a chat with Dayleen and her new friend."

"Effie's her new friend?" I asked.

"That's what they said. Dayleen was so concerned about her that she tracked her down at Belford's." He gave me a look. "It sounds like she wasn't the only one."

My shoulder lifted and dropped. "Mimsey and I paid her a visit."

"Right. Well, when I left them, Dayleen was trying to convince Effie that Tucker was a good guy who really loved her, and Effie was having none of it. So I don't know that they'll actually be friends in the long run, but I thought I'd report back to you."

I grinned. "Thanks, Ben."

A shout drew our attention, and we returned to the party.

We'd pretty much taken up the whole restaurant, but the staff didn't mind. Churchill's was known for hosting everything from informal gatherings to actual weddings, so they easily handled our crowd. After we'd all eaten, our party moved into the pool room, where the conversation stretched into the evening. The subject of Tucker Abbott's death came up a few times, but no one said anything about the lottery ticket, so that seemed to still be under wraps.

Rori was quiet almost to the point of being morose, picking at her food and barely engaging in conversation. This garnered a few sympathetic looks and the occasional pat on the shoulder, and I guessed everyone thought she was upset about Tucker. However, I saw my mother eyeing her a few times.

Finally, Declan and I begged off, pleading exhaustion. Hugs and kisses later, we made our way onto Bay Street and Declan's truck.

We'd barely pulled into traffic when Declan asked, "Can we do it tonight?"

Confused, I raised my eyebrows.

He shook his head and grinned. "The spell, Katie. The *spell*."

"Oh. For lucid dreaming. Right. Um . . ." I looked at my watch by the light of the dash. "It's kind of late, isn't it?"

He was silent for a few beats, then, "Please?"

My heart melted. "Of course we can."

His hand found mine. "Thanks. I can almost feel Connell. Maybe that's my imagination, but I like to think he's not that far away. Even if you can't bring him back, contacting him would make me feel better."

I squeezed his hand. "We'll try the spell. And if that doesn't work, we'll try something else."

I changed my clothes and came out to find Declan in the kitchen with Mungo.

"I brought you a bite of sausage roll from dinner," he

said to my familiar as he placed the morsel in a dish on the dog's place mat.

Yip!

It took three seconds for Mungo to scarf it up. He sat back and eyed my fiancé.

"You know you ate before we left," I said. "That was a bonus."

His response was a baleful look at me followed by an eagerly expectant one directed at Declan.

"How about some ice cream," he said, opening the freezer door and pulling out a pint of French vanilla.

"Oh, for heaven's sake. You spoil him more than I do."

"It never hurts to have your witch girlfriend's familiar on your side."

"Witch wife, soon enough, my dear. And if you don't stop feeding him sweets, I won't be able to lift him—forget about carrying him around in my tote bag."

"I still can't believe I'm marrying a woman who carries her dog in her purse." Declan set a tiny bowl of ice cream on the floor, and the terrier began to delicately lap at it with his tiny pink tongue. Declan returned the ice cream to the freezer as I opened the spice cabinet to start assembling ingredients for the tea to encourage lucid dreaming.

"Katie?" Declan looked at me around the open freezer door. "What's this?" He held Bianca's jewelry box in his hand.

I laughed. "That's my something borrowed. Amethyst earrings. Bianca said the safest place to keep jewelry was in the freezer. Normally, I wouldn't worry about it, but they don't belong to me."

"Ah. I've heard of that. Freezers can protect things from fire, too. I've seen it."

"Shall we try a little lucid dreaming now?"

He nodded. "Absolutely. What do I need to do?"

"Take Mungo out while I get ready."

So Declan took my familiar for his last walk of the day, and I prepared for the lucid dreaming spell I'd concocted. Lucy had been intrigued when I mentioned it to her over the morning baking and had given me some advice about herbs to add to the tea.

An entire room on the third floor of Lucy and Ben's town house was devoted to preserving the herbs she grew in her rooftop container garden. They hung in bunches and stewed in oil or alcohol, depending on what medium best extracted their various constituents. Some of those herbs had made it into my own collection, which was much more modest. I'd added herbs from my gardens at the carriage house, from the tea shop down the street from the Honeybee, and had even purchased a couple things online. The box of jars and vials sat in the bottom of the bedroom closet, one of the remaining things that would have to be moved into the carriage house after the wedding.

I changed into my nightclothes, then dragged the box out onto the floor and sat down cross-legged to paw through it.

We'll need valerian, for sure. And there: mullein. A bit of mugwort . . .

I considered some of the other names for mugwort with a smile as I sorted through the jars—*felon herb, naughty man, cronewort.* There were other names for mullein as well, including *feltwort, hag's taper, Quaker rouge*, and *graveyard dirt*. Heavy lifting for a plant with leaves as fuzzy as a teddy bear surrounding a stalk of bright yellow flowers. In magic it could be used in place of graveyard dirt, though, making it handy if one didn't have time for a trip to a cemetery before casting a spell that called for it.

Ah, there's my burdock root. Now, where's the peppermint?

I searched, but there was no peppermint in the box. Sighing, I hauled myself to my feet, returned the box, and took the jars of herbs I'd selected out to the kitchen counter. A quick rummage through the cupboard netted a few bags of peppermint tea. Since I was making a tea anyway, that was perfect.

I set the kettle on and got to work. First, I combined the herbs in equal parts in a mortar. As I added each one, I invoked the individual powers that I intended to brew into the mix.

Valerian root to guide sleep deeper.

Mugwort to relax the body and heighten consciousness, divination, and protection during travel—in this case, astral travel.

Mullein not in place of graveyard dirt but to prevent nightmares and keep our dreams focused on Connell.

Burdock root to keep the dreams positive and, I hoped, useful in locating Connell.

And finally, peppermint for clarity, to keep our dreams vivid, bright, and focused.

After I'd triggered the elements of each herb that I wanted to bring out, I muttered a quick spell under my breath as I gently pounded the leaves and roots in the mortar with the pestle.

This tea to drink
Into sleep to sink
Connell to find
His spirit to bind
With Declan's again
And home in ten.

Declan and Mungo came in then. My familiar settled into his bed on the floor with his head on his paws and watched me work.

My fiancé eyed the mess I'd made on the counter. "What's that smell?"

"Valerian, mostly. It's pretty stinky." I'd always likened it to the odor of sour dirt.

"Do we have to actually ingest it?"

"The others will offset the flavor a bit. Except the burdock." I shrugged. "It's a small sacrifice if the spell works."

"Okay," he said, but his nose was still wrinkled.

He joined me at the counter. The kettle whistled. I turned off the heat and placed the spell-enhanced herbs in a small teapot. Glancing at Declan, I poured the hot water over the herbs while repeating the spell.

This tea to drink
Into sleep to sink
Connell to find
His spirit to bind
With Declan's again
And home in ten.

He didn't bat an eyelash, which was a good sign. Declan hadn't seen me practice magic often, and I needed him to be totally on board with what we were doing, or it wouldn't work.

I told him as much, adding, "If you want to get out of your dream for any reason, count to ten and you'll wake up. That's what the last line is about."

"Gotcha. Now what do we do?"

"We drink the tea, and we try to visualize what we want to dream."

He looked a bit disconcerted at that.

"Tell you what. When it's finished brewing, we can settle in and simply chat back and forth about what we hope to accomplish."

"Finding Connell."

I smiled. "Maybe more detailed than that. Why don't you change your clothes?"

He returned wearing pajama bottoms and no shirt. I allowed myself a lingering look, but then sternly told myself to focus and turned back to strain the tea into two mugs. We took them into the living room. Declan sprawled on the sofa while I curled into the old recliner that would soon be going to the thrift store. After taking a tentative sip of tea, he made a face but didn't comment. I had to agree that it wasn't the tastiest brew, but I had a good feeling about it.

"Can you feel the power from the plants?" I asked him.

"Um, maybe."

"Try. Close your eyes and try."

He obeyed, inhaling the steam and taking another swallow. His eyes popped open. "It's really hot."

I laughed.

"I'm sorry. I don't have your, you know." He made a

finger-flutter gesture I took to refer to some kind of magic.

A huge yawn overcame me. "Okay, let's make sure we're on the same page. Close your eyes again."

He did, and I followed suit.

"I've been thinking about this. Last night we focused on remaining lucid when we were dreaming but didn't direct ourselves to dream anything specific. When Dad took me on my shamanic journey, he was helping me to find part of my lost spirit—my magic. Connell is your lost spirit, so let's try designing a dream kind of like that. That journey felt like a dream, really, even though I was awake. Sort of. It's hard to explain. But I did see Connell under the tree of life." I settled farther into the chair. "Dad told me to imagine a tunnel leading to the lower world."

Declan didn't say anything.

I cracked an eye open, then sat up. My darling fiancé was lying on his back on the sofa, and his deep, heavy breathing and slightly open lips testified that he'd already fallen into a deep slumber.

"We'll try again another time, sweetie," I whispered as I got up and covered him with an afghan.

Mungo came over and looked up at me with laughing eyes.

Shrugging, I took Declan's tea, which he had barely touched, and downed it. Back in my chair, I closed my eyes again, debating whether to go to bed and leave my honey on the sofa. The image of Connell as he looked in Declan's ancient family photo album came to mind. Spry, wearing breeches and riding boots, a stove pipe hat, lively eyes set deeply into a wrinkled face. I thought of his loud brogue and how he'd first made himself known to us in a séance.

Katie . . .

I felt more than heard my name, but I recognized it was Connell calling to me. My first instinct was to tell Declan, but instead I kept my eyes closed and tried to relax.

Where are you?

Don't know. Lost. No bearings.

Declan stirred on the sofa, and I felt my tenuous contact with Connell waver and then resolidify.

How can we find you? I asked.

I need some breadcrumbs ter follow, lass.

How do we do that? I hoped the desperation and frustration I felt didn't come through.

Send another spirit . . .

The connection was fading again.

Another spirit? How?

He didn't answer.

I concentrated and reached out with my mind. There! Just a pinprick of his consciousness, but it was enough to hear him.

Not suffering, lass. Only want ter come home.

And then he was gone.

I gathered all my energy and tried to reach him again. It didn't work. I tried harder. Suddenly, I realized I had my hand out in front of me, physically reaching in reflection of my mental searching. Letting out a whoosh of air, I opened my eyes and dropped my arm.

Declan was sitting up on the couch, staring at me with wide eyes.

"Were you there?" I asked. "Did you hear him?"

Then I realized my skin was still faintly glowing with blue-tinged light. Suddenly shivering, I rubbed my arms with my hands. "Oh. That's why you're looking at me like that. Sorry."

He ran his hand over his face, then gave a nervous laugh. "Don't be sorry. It's a bit . . . disconcerting. And no, I didn't dream during that little nap." His head tipped to the side and he looked over my right shoulder as if trying to remember something. "No, that's not right. I did have a little dream there. Just a flash. I can't say I was aware of dreaming at the time, but I do remember Connell." He pushed the afghan aside and leaned forward. "What did he say?"

"He's still lost," I said. "He wants us to send another spirit to him to, as he put it, drop breadcrumbs for him to follow back to us."

Declan's jaw slackened. "Another spirit?"

I held up my palms. "Just the messenger here."

"But how do we do that?"

"No idea. I'll check in with the spellbook club and see if they have any ideas."

Frowning, he stood and held out his hand to me. "It couldn't be easy, could it?"

I took his hand, letting him bring me to my feet. "Maybe not, but we'll figure it out. At least there's hope."

He pulled me into an embrace and nuzzled my hair. "Yes. I feel a lot better knowing there's hope." Pulling back, he cupped my face with his hand. "Thank you, darlin'."

I kissed him so he wouldn't see the tears that suddenly threatened.

Because it was sweet that he was thanking me, but he never would have lost Connell in the first place if it hadn't been for me.

Chapter 22

The herbal spell had worked. Not the way I'd thought it would, but still. Now Declan was sleeping peacefully, and I couldn't help but wonder whether the tea might augment my ability to sense his dreams. Actually, his weren't the ones I was worried about. I didn't need another food dream from our neighbor startling me awake with a craving for fried green tomatoes or some such.

Nonetheless, I allowed myself to relax enough to welcome slumber. Relieved when I didn't get a hint of any thoughts except my own for nearly half an hour, I snuggled deeper into my pillow and miraculously began to drift into sleep despite the knowledge that in less than forty-eight hours, Declan and I would be married.

Tomorrow is the big day. The beginning of our new lives together.

Rather than making me worry about all the wedding details, the thought brought with it a sense of peace and a confidence that everything was handled and the next days would be smooth as silk.

Two thoughts floated through my mind before unconsciousness overtook me.

I thought everything was handled, and then Judge Matthews canceled.

And:

But that worked out better than ever with Uncle Ben marrying us. Whatever happens, it'll all be fine in the end.

The smell of fresh water, bright with minerals and promise, teased my nose. Inhaling deeply, I slowly walked down the stone passageway, trailing my fingertips over the wet rocks. The light at the other end beckoned to me. Everything felt strange and familiar at the same time. I was in a place that was both extraordinary and homey. A part of me was aware that I'd been there before.

My long velvet skirt swished around my ankles. My light slippers made no sound on the stone floor. I looked down and saw I was carrying a large, elaborately scrolled key. It had let me into this place, and it would let me out again.

I reached the end of the passageway. An open door invited me into a room I'd always known. I stepped inside and smiled as my gaze ran over the shelves lined with all manner of bottles and jars, lidded boxes and hanging herbs. A scarred wooden table flanked with two long benches took up the center of the room. Another door led out to a lush garden and the world of possibility, but my attention was drawn to the fire crackling cheerfully in the fireplace and the woman who sat on the stool by the spinning wheel there, her face lit up with pleasure as she watched me.

Nonna?

And then . . .

I'm dreaming. This is a dream. Wait! This is a dream! I did it!

My grandmother's face broke into a wide smile, and she nodded. "Yes. This is a dream."

"Are you real?" I asked.

"What do you think?" She rose and walked toward me.

She looked the same as when I'd last seen her when I was nine years old. Her hair was long, a dark red like mine but with vibrant white streaks in it. It fell over her shoulders and the brocade bodice of her Renaissance-style dress. Her laugh lines deepened, and her bright green eyes danced as she held out her arms to embrace me.

Stepping back, she looked down at her dress. "This is a nice touch," she said.

"I don't understand."

"This is your dream." She waved at my own gown and what I suddenly realized were my own long red locks. "You apparently have a hidden romantic streak."

My fingers stroked my sleeve, appreciating the soft pile of the velvet. "Hmm. Maybe." I looked up. "I've been here before. On the shamanic journey Dad brought me on to recover my magic."

She nodded. "This is your hedgewitch's kitchen."

"Is it real?"

My grandmother shrugged and settled onto one of the wooden benches. "We're here, aren't we?"

I sat across the table from her. "Why are we here?"

"Well, you did prime the pump for lucid dreaming with your spell."

"That's all I needed to do to reach you?" I let out a breath. "I wish I'd known."

"Hmm. It might work again. I don't know. But you needed help, even if you didn't know you were asking for it."

"Are you talking about finding Tucker Abbott's murderer?"

"Pfft."

I blinked. "You don't think that's important?"

"It's not why you called me here."

"Do you know who killed him?"

Nonna sighed. "I find you when you need me, Katie. Your mother and aunt as well. They don't get into the shenanigans you do, however, so they're not as much work."

"Sorry."

She waved that away. "You have been asking for my help without realizing it. That's why I'm here." She stood and walked over to one of the shelves. After perusing several items, she took down a box and brought it back to me. "This is what you need. Put it on your bedside table, and it will disrupt the flow of dreams from others to your mind."

I opened the box. Inside was a necklace. Puzzled, I drew it out. The silver spirals interlocked, creating a chain. The spirals were dotted with amethyst and another type of stone. Gray, shiny, metallic looking.

Pointing to one, I asked, "What are these?"

"Polished hematite," she said. "It works well with amethyst crystal. Lucy might have told you this, but you never really confided in her about your new ability."

It was true. I hadn't told Lucy about being able to sense dreams after I'd regained my magic.

I returned the necklace to the box. "Can I bring it back from here?"

Nonna smiled. "You darling thing. No, but you don't have to. I've taken care of it." She moved to look out the door.

I rose. "Wait. Don't go yet."

She turned back.

"I, um . . . I don't know if I want to block the dreams. Not yet."

A frown graced her high forehead. "Why not?"

"Because it's the only way I can contact Connell."

She came back and sat down at the table. "Ah, that Connell. What a hoot he is!"

"He's gone."

She frowned. "What do you mean, gone. Where did he go?"

I explained that he'd helped me retrieve my lost magic, but in the process had been whisked away to who-knew-where. "Do you know where he could be?"

She shook her head. "I'm sorry. I don't."

"I can read him in Declan's dreams. I thought you knew."

She shook her head. "You didn't call on me for that."

"Maybe I did," I said. "We were in contact earlier this evening. He said he's lost. It sounds like some kind of purgatory. He can't get back. He says he's not in pain, but he wants to come home. And Nonna, Declan needs him to come back. I need him to come back *for* Declan. And it sounds like there might be a way to make that happen."

Obviously curious, she leaned forward. "How?"

"He said he needed some breadcrumbs to follow back. That we needed to send another spirit, I assume to leave the breadcrumbs, whatever those might be."

Nonna sat back. "Breadcrumbs? Good goddess. What was the man talking about?"

I felt my shoulders slump. "I thought you'd know."

A speculative look settled across her face. "I might. Let me do some checking. I wouldn't want to attempt such a thing without a tether of some kind, but I think it can be done."

"A tether?"

"Something to keep me from getting lost while I'm trying to find Declan's leprechaun."

I felt the blood drain from my dream face. "Oh, no. I hadn't thought of that."

"We'd need to find the right anchor. Someone who is comfortable on both sides of the veil."

"Like a medium? I don't know where the one who triggered Connell in Declan the first time is right now."

"I'm not sure exactly what we'd need. Let me do some checking."

"Checking?" I asked. "With who? Is there, like, some kind of spirit organization over there in spirit world?"

"Pfft. Don't be silly." She stood. "You might be right. You might have called me in order to help you find Connell for Declan. I'll see what I can do." She gestured at the box containing the necklace. "But that will work, too. Try it. I have to go now."

I ran over and hugged her again. "I don't want you to go."

She patted my back. "I know, honey. But I have to."

"Can I bring you back with the spell again?"

"It's only one of the ways you've called me. I must say, I do prefer it over the life-and-death situations in the past."

I laughed. "Me, too, Nonna . . ."

But she was already out in the garden, then down the path and out of sight.

Thinking I could check what kinds of supplies were on the shelves, I turned back. I was still dreaming, still lucid. And then I realized, I could stay here if I wanted, in this perfectly wonderful kitchen with the fire and potions and anything I might want or need outside the door.

Without Declan. Without Mungo. Without all my friends.

The prospect suddenly terrified me, and I held up the key I was still holding in my hand and willed myself to *wake up!*

I sat up in bed with a start, and Mungo bounded to his feet. Declan turned over and reached out a hand to me in the dark.

"You okay?" he mumbled.

"Yeah," I answered in a soft voice. "Go back to sleep."

Mungo nuzzled me. I drew him close and put my lips by his little ear. In almost no voice at all, I whispered, "I did it! It works!"

The next morning, I woke before Declan as usual. I was anxious to tell him about the lucid dream and what Nonna had told me. I had coffee and fresh muffins ready for him when he finally got up at six. Lucy had told me she and Iris had the Honeybee covered for the day, so I could pop in and out as I needed to stay on top of the wedding preparations. She'd actually tried to get me to take the day off, but I'd insisted on coming in.

Just not for the first baking of the day. It felt odd, but

I was happy to hang out with my guy. We hardly ever got to do that. Tomorrow I'd take the whole day off.

As Declan ate and caffeinated his system, I had a second cup of coffee and related what had happened after he'd gone to sleep the night before.

"You think that was real? The thing about getting some kind of medium to help find Connell?" he asked.

"The dream was a dream," I said. "But I think the advice from Nonna was real. After all, it was a medium who brought Connell to the forefront of your consciousness in the first place. The séance?"

He gave me a look that said he didn't need to be reminded.

"She thinks it can be done. Honey, that's real progress. We're going to find Connell and bring him back."

His gaze shifted to the side. "You really think so?"

I realized he was reluctant to allow himself to hope. It broke my heart that he missed Connell so much. Reaching over, I took his hand in both of mine and squeezed. "Look at me."

He did, his eyes searching.

"Yes. I really think so. As soon as we're married and things settle down a tad, I'm going to bring in all the expertise of the spellbook club and Nonna and anyone else I can think of, and we're going to find that crazy leprechaun spirit of yours and haul him home for you." I held his gaze. "I promise. Hear me? I *promise*."

I felt him relax and knew he believed me. Now I only had to figure out how to keep my promise. But I would. Somehow, I would.

Letting go of his hands, I sat back. "I'm going to try putting hematite and amethyst on the bedside table for a few nights and see if that works." I held up my hand. "I won't keep them there all the time, not until we get Connell back, but I want to test them."

Declan said, "I dreamed of Connell last night."

"You did?" I leaned forward.

"But he didn't give me any information. He was walking through a thick forest on a tiny little path. I tried to talk to him, but it didn't work. I don't think it was a lucid dream."

"Did you know you were dreaming at the time?" I asked.

"Kind of. It's different than before, though." Suddenly he shook his head and rose. "I have to get going. John still needs to pick up his tux."

Declan's groomsmen included Randy Post and Scott Lynde from the firehouse as well as his brothers-in-law, both of whom he'd been friends with for years. It fit with Eliza's idea of tradition but didn't help my case of having the spellbook club stand up with me.

I kissed him goodbye and went to shower before going in to work.

Chapter 23

I arrived at the Honeybee luxuriously late, played with some of the decorations planned for the cupcake wedding cake we'd be making the next morning, and caught up on some of the office work that had been piling up. In the early afternoon, I headed over to the Hair Connection to hang out with everyone getting mani-pedis and facials.

The next two hours were spent among the women I liked best in the world while we were being exfoliated, smoothed, plucked, soaked, scrubbed, buffed, and polished. Vera Smythe, the owner of the salon, and her assistant Zoe moved among us with practiced ease.

Even though I'd arrived after everyone else, they finished with me first—at my request. That morning I'd received word from Vintage Event Rentals that they would be delivering the furniture and awnings at two that afternoon. Declan would be there, too, but I wanted to make sure everything ended up just right.

"Are you sure you have to go?" my mother asked.

"Yeah," Lauren said. "This is supposed to be for you."

Donning my flip-flops so as not to disturb the fresh coat of polish on my toenails, I said, "This is supposed to be for everyone. I'm as pretty as I can be for right now—and I don't want to leave the setup responsibility entirely on Declan's shoulders."

I'd said goodbye to the giggling gaggle of ladies—Vera had broken out the wine by then—and was leaving when Eliza came up.

"Katie? Mind if I go with you? I'd love to help if I can."

I hesitated.

She smiled tentatively. "I promise I won't get in the way or try to boss anyone." Her fingers gestured subtly to where the others were talking and laughing. "But I need a little more quiet than this."

Of course. She's an introvert through and through.

"Sure. Come along. You haven't been in the carriage house yet, have you?"

Relief infused her features. "No. I'd love to see it. Thank you, Katie."

I gave her a one-armed hug. "Of course. We have to stop by the bakery and pick up Mungo on the way."

A burst of laughter followed us out the door.

The delivery van was already at the carriage house, and men were ferrying items from it through the open back gate to the backyard. We got out and went around the house to see how things stood.

A long table was set up in front of the far garden. They'd already arranged a white trellis-looking fence between it and the vegetable garden behind it. As I watched, an awning came up over by the fence that separated our yard from the Coopersmiths next door. Declan was supervising the operation, and I went over to join him. Eliza went off to look at the gardens, though I saw her watching the setup and trying to look like she wasn't.

"Hey, darlin'," Declan said, slipping his arm around me.

"Hey. This looks great."

"Yeah. It's all coming together. I think the other awning should go over in that corner, don't you?"

I considered, then nodded. "That should work. The company is providing strings of old-fashioned Edison bulbs. We can string some in there."

"Katie! This is so exciting!"

I turned to see Margie barreling toward me. "What can I do to help? Anything?"

"Thanks," I said. "I think we have it under control. I'll let you know, though." I looked around. "Where are the kids?"

"Playing in the backyard." Margie waved in the direction of her house. Then she snapped her fingers. "Oh! I know! I'll make lemonade for everyone!"

"Um, you don't have to—"

She cut me off. "Don't worry. It's a mix. Even I can do that." With a grin, she turned and marched back home.

Declan laughed. "Well, I could use something cold to drink."

One of the delivery guys approached. "Miss? Where would you like the chairs lined up?"

"Ah, let's not line them up," I said, moving away from Declan. "Let's arrange them in conversation

249

groups. Oh, and I see you brought extra tables. Those small ones can go along the edge with more chairs, so people will have someplace to put their drinks."

The next hour I spent directing and arranging and rearranging. Mungo took one look at the chaos and went next door to play with Baby Bart and the JJs. Margie brought out the lemonade, which was cold and sweet and tart in the heat of the day, and I thanked the drink mix gods that she'd thought of it. Once things were settling down, I realized I hadn't seen Eliza for quite a while.

Probably checking out the carriage house.

I opened one side of the French doors and went inside. "Eliza?"

There was no answer. In the living room, I paused and peered toward the kitchen. A small noise above made me look up.

Eliza was gazing down at me from the loft with wide, surprised eyes. She stood in front of the secretary's desk Lucy had given me. The front was open, and there was my altar for all to see.

Well, not all. But Declan's oldest sister had certainly seen it. The sister I'd joked to Mungo only a couple days earlier about what she'd think if she knew I was a witch and he was my familiar.

Not sure whether to be angry or try to explain to her what she was looking at or try to diffuse the situation with humor, I climbed the stairs to the loft. Mostly I was tired. When I reached the top, she moved aside. I pointedly closed the desk and faced her.

"Oh, Katie. I'm so sorry," she whispered. "I didn't know. I was looking around the beautiful little house, and I came up here." Her hand went to her throat. "I wasn't snooping, honest I wasn't. I just love this kind of desk and wanted to see . . . I'm so sorry."

I sighed. "It's okay."

Before I could say more, Declan called from below. "Eliza? Mother's on the phone. She wants to talk to you."

In a low voice, she said, "Please don't worry. I'd never tell a soul." Quickly, she started to scramble down the stairs. When her head was level with the floor, she turned back.

"It does explain a lot, though." And then she was gone.

I opened the desk and surveyed what she'd seen. If she knew anything at all about magic or Wiccan practices, it was enough to know I was a witch.

A witch about to marry her little brother. Did I need to worry?

There wasn't much I could do, though. I'd have to trust that she'd keep her word and hope for the best.

That evening Declan and I grabbed a pizza and took it to the carriage house. We sat at one of the tables under an awning in the backyard and ate our pepperoni, black olive, and mushroom pie, crunched on Caesar salad, and sipped red wine. Mungo took the fat leavings of a crust to a back corner and gnawed on it like a bone.

When we'd finished, we put on some music and tidied the inside of the carriage house, making sure everything was right for the next day. Then we walked around the backyard, arm in arm, Mungo trundling along beside us. The gardens looked fantastic—lush and green. I deadheaded a few flowers, and Declan re-arranged a couple of the seating areas to be more invit-ing to wedding guests.

Suddenly, I snapped my fingers.

"What?" Declan asked from across the lawn.

"The sundial," I said. "I'll be right back."

I went inside and rummaged through my tote until I found the sundial that I'd bought at Vase Value. It was remarkably heavy, and I rolled my eyes at myself for hauling it around in my tote. Taking it outside, I searched the yard for the right spot.

There. By the birdbath.

Walking over, I set the sundial on a rock that pro-truded above the plants around it. It had a flat top, al-lowing the piece to rest evenly. I stood back, and two dragonflies promptly landed on the copper gnomon.

Declan joined me, and when he saw my totems on our new yard art, he laughed. "An auspicious sign, don't you think?"

I did. The dragonflies didn't always portend drama, and in this case, I could tell they were offering a blessing.

The next morning we dawdled over a tasty breakfast. It was the big day, which was exciting and nerve-wracking and delicious all at once.

"Everything's set on my end," Declan said. "Unless there's something I don't know about?"

"I don't think so," I said. "I need to check in with the salon. The ladies are supposed to start in on hair and makeup right after lunch. Oh, and I should get over to the Honeybee and see if the wedding cake needs any final touches."

As my maid of honor, however, Lucy had already checked in with Vera Smythe at the salon and left a text on my phone. Everything was set up there. I just needed to get to the bakery to put the final touches on my wedding cake.

Still, I couldn't help texting Quinn before I left.

Any word from Hudson Prater?

Not so far. Looking into the Wiggins family now. You were right about how badly they need the money.

I sent an "okay" emoji and put my phone away. Today was my wedding day, and I needed to leave the investigating to Quinn. If all went well, he'd find the killer, Rori would have her closure, and that would be that. I'd certainly done my part.

As for what would happen to the lottery ticket, there were still six days to figure that out. Someone would get that money. The Wigginses, I assumed.

And hoped. Two point eight million dollars would solve a lot of problems.

Because Quinn wouldn't let a winning lottery ticket go to waste because it was evidence, would he?

Stop thinking about it, I admonished myself. *At least for today.*

Chapter 24

I stood back and surveyed the cupcake-crowded countertop. Lemon whipped cream nestled on top of carrot cake, each topped with tiny piped carrots. The frosting on the German chocolate version was topped with thick coconut shavings. Strawberry boasted pink frosting and candied hearts that looked like stained glass. The devil's food was chocolate all the way, and more chocolate ganache dripped from the lemon-soaked orange sponge. Caramel buttercream whirled up from the bourbon pecan cupcakes, and the banana and pineapple hummingbird cupcakes were slathered with cream cheese frosting and wheels of dried pineapple.

"Do you think we have enough?" Lucy asked in an amused tone.

I gave her a look. "No need to be sarcastic. I want there to be plenty for the guests."

"There will be plenty—for the whole neighborhood," Iris quipped. "Maybe the whole town."

"Hush," I said.

"It's fine, honey," Lucy said. "There are five graduated tiers to the stand, and the strawberry will look nice interspersed with the devil's food on the lower layer. On the next one up, we can mix the hummingbird and German chocolate. That way, the pineapple wheels on top of the hummingbird cupcakes won't crowd each other. Then each of the other layers can hold a single variety."

When I'd embraced the idea of the cupcake wedding cake, it had surprised the heck out of my mother, since we'd argued about everything from my dress to the venue to whether my old pastor should marry us. After spending a week trying to help me, Mama had finally thrown up her hands and left me to my own devices.

The idea of a wedding cake made up of different kinds of cupcakes really had been inspired, though. Iris and Lucy had been baking and decorating most of the morning, and though I'd come in late to check on things, I'd frosted my share as well.

"It's really going to be beautiful," Iris said. "And we'll pack up all the extras so the caterers can keep the tiers full during your party."

"You're coming, aren't you?" I asked Iris.

"Of course."

"And you're bringing your new beau, aren't you?" Lucy asked.

Iris blushed and ducked her head. "Yes. He's coming, too."

"Good," my aunt said decisively. "It's about time we met him."

"Well, hello, you two!" Ben called from out front where he was juggling customers at the register between making coffee drinks. "Are you ready for some caffeine? It's going to be a long day."

I peeked out and saw that Mama and Dad had come in. My mother kissed Ben on the cheek, and Dad paused to talk with him when she continued into the kitchen. She stopped in front of the myriad of cupcakes, momentarily speechless.

"What do you think?" I asked.

Finally, she said, "Well, you sure don't do things in a small way, do you?"

"Not when it comes to baking," Lucy said.

Mama turned and smiled at me. "It's beautiful. And now I'm on the way to help Mimsey's assistant with the flowers in your backyard, so she'll be free to spend the afternoon at the salon with the rest of the spellbook club. I just wanted to stop by and see if you needed anything."

"Nothing that I can think of," I said. "Everyone is going to bring their clothes to the carriage house, so we can change after Vera does the hair and makeup. I'll bring Mungo by before I go, so maybe you could watch him later?"

"I can take him now, if you want."

I hesitated. "That would save me a trip, but I was thinking I should see the flowers . . ."

She cupped my chin in her hand. "Trust me. They'll be beautiful."

Deep breath. I could feel the tension of the day thrumming under my skin. "Okay. Yes. Thank you. Mungo," I called.

"I've got him," Mama said, and went into the office. Moments later, she came out carrying my familiar in her arms. "He's fine with it, aren't you, Mungo?"

He directed a soulful look my way but didn't protest. *Bacon*, I thought. *He gets lots of bacon tomorrow.*

* * *

"There!" Vera Smythe announced as she stepped back and whirled my chair around to face the mirror.

"Wow," I said. "I look like I have twice as much hair as normal."

She'd curled my short auburn hair, then sprayed it and recoiled it and so on, with the end result that my usual casual 'do was converted into a soft and lovely vintage style—subtly studded with tiny pearls no less.

"Thank you so much," I went on, turning to catch the back with the hand mirror.

Vera smiled and nodded, still looking at my hair. "You're so welcome." She adjusted a curl and gave it another spritz of spray. Tentatively, I touched a carefully arranged lock by my temple with a fingertip. It looked utterly natural, but was crispy to the touch.

Lowering my hand, I appraised my reflection. She'd gone light on the makeup, allowing the sprinkle of freckles across my nose to shine through. My eyes were expertly shadowed and highlighted so that they looked greener and bigger than ever, and there were tiny wings of liner at the corners. I rarely wore lipstick, but this shade was a few perfect tones lighter than the rich plum of my dress. The polish on my nails and toes was lighter still, staying within the color palette but not too matchy-match.

"You're beautiful, honey," Lucy said.

There were murmurs all around.

"Everyone looks beautiful," I said. "Vera, you're amazing. You, too, Zoe."

Vera's assistant blushed.

The entire spellbook club was there, each in their own full makeup and hair for the wedding. I'd gone last. It was late afternoon, and soon we'd all troop over to the carriage house and get dressed there. Ben and Iris had been holding down the fort at the Honeybee for the afternoon, though they'd closed an hour early to transport the cupcakes for the wedding cake tiers. Thanks to Mama, Mungo was already at the carriage house, where Declan was keeping an eye on things along with his mother and mine.

Zoe had curled Mimsey's usual white pageboy into loose ringlets, drawn together on one side with an ornate silver clasp rather than the bow she usually wore. Bianca sported a single fishtail braid down her back. Lucy's gray-blond hair was pinned into an adorable updo that brought out her elegant jawline. Vera had woven a band of enameled leaves into Jaida's short-cropped hair, right at her hairline, and she'd gone all out with the eyelash extensions. Cookie wore her dark mane in long loose curls augmented with a few strands of copper that caught the light when she turned her head.

"Now a few lash extensions for the bride, and we're done," Vera said.

My phone rang, and I reached beneath the cape that covered my jeans and T-shirt to take it out of my pocket. Vera rolled a trolley over, then started checking her supplies as I looked at the number. It was local, but I didn't recognize it. However, with the wedding only hours away, I was afraid not to answer. What if it was the caterer, or the musicians who were supposed to be setting up right this very minute?

"Hello?"

"Is this Katie Lightfoot?"

"Yes, this is Katie."

"This is Hudson Prater. You gave me your number when you brought that music box in? Well, I didn't know who else to call." The words tumbled out of the antique dealer. "I tried to call Detective Quinn, you see, but he didn't answer. I left him a voice mail, but I wasn't sure what else to do. He mentioned your name when he, um, talked me into helping him out with the investigation into Tucker Abbott's death, and I thought perhaps you could help me."

"I'll do what I can," I said once he slowed enough for me to get a word in.

"Well, you probably already know Detective Quinn asked me to put the word out about that music box you and Tucker's ex-wife brought in. And that's what I did, you see. Put the word out. To other antique dealers, pawn shops, my usual, er, suppliers, that kind of thing. Well, it worked."

I sat up straighter in my chair. Vera pointed at the phone, a bottle of lash adhesive in her other hand. I shook my head and turned away.

"What do you mean, it worked?" I asked.

Vera leaned against a sink, looking annoyed. I made an apologetic moue and turned my attention back to Hudson Prater.

"I mean someone called and said not to sell it to anyone. That they're on their way over. Right now, Ms. Lightfoot. That's why I called the detective. Someone is on the way to buy that music box, and I don't have it to sell them. And when Detective Quinn spoke with me, well, I got the feeling that whoever might be interested in it might not be the friendliest sort if crossed. I was about to call 911, but I didn't know if I should . . ."

My mind raced. "No, no, don't call 911." The last thing we needed was for a bunch of lights and sirens to show up and scare off Tucker's murderer forever.

"Did you call the general number or Quinn's cell phone?"

"He gave me his cell number."

I suppressed an oath. Would it be better to tell Hudson to stall while I tried to get ahold of Quinn myself? The murderer, assuming that's who was coming to buy the music box, might realize what was up and scamper. Or worse. I thought of the unnecessary destruction at Wisteria House, the violently broken mirror, Tucker's room at the Spotlight Motel, utterly torn apart—not to mention Tucker himself, dead on the floor.

I didn't really see any other choice. Reaching for the Velcro clasp of the nylon cape, I said, "Keep trying to get ahold of Detective Quinn, and I'll be right there. Was the caller a man or a woman?"

"The connection was bad. I couldn't really tell."

My internal alarms clanged louder. Bad connection? That seemed unlikely. What seemed more likely, oddly enough, was someone using magic to disguise their voice. This whole case had revolved around things not being quite what they seemed.

Vera made a noise of protest as I loosened the cape and took it off.

"If the person shows up, tell them the music box is on the way."

"Are you bringing it?" He sounded worried.

"I'm sorry, but I don't have it. The police are holding it for now. But I'll do what I can."

I felt badly that Quinn had hooked the elderly antique dealer into this case, even if he was a fence. The detective knew Tucker's murderer was dangerous, but once again, he didn't understand the possible paranormal danger.

However, to be honest, I didn't, either. Maybe I was overreacting.

I hoped so.

Ending the call with Prater, I stood.

"I don't know who that was," Vera said. "But you sit yourself right back down and let me finish your lash extensions. They're the pièce de résistance of your wedding makeup."

"Sorry," I said. "I'll have to go old school. Mascara will have to do the job. I've got an unexpected errand I have to run."

I turned to find the entire spellbook club regarding me. Lucy looked pensive, Jaida thoughtful, Bianca resigned, and both Cookie and Mimsey looked excited.

"Katie, can't you skip it this time?" Lucy asked in a pleading voice. "Let someone else take care of whatever's going on? It's your wedding day."

"That was the antique dealer. He tried to get ahold of Quinn but couldn't." I gave a little shrug. "I feel responsible that he got dragged into this whole mess. Don't worry." I looked at my watch. It was after four thirty. "I should be able to get ahold of Quinn, and he can take over. In the meantime, I'm going to pop by the antique store."

And find out who the murderer is.

That part I didn't want to admit out loud. If Quinn's plan worked, then we'd finally know who killed Tucker Abbott. I'd be able to tell Rori, and she'd have the closure she'd been looking for.

"I'll drive," Jaida said, looking around at the others. "My vehicle can fit us all."

Everyone nodded.

Relief swooshed through me. I'd known going to Prater's alone wasn't a great idea and had been hoping my friends might jump on board. And bless them, they had.

Mimsey eyed Cookie's baby bump. "I'm not sure . . ."

I nodded. "Cookie? Would you mind going to the carriage house and letting Declan and Ben know what's going on?"

She pouted, then she looked down and rubbed her belly. Her eyes softened. "Yeah. That might be better." She looked back up. "You should call Declan, though."

"I will at some point. In the meantime, you fill him in."

She looked amused. "Coward."

"I'll be there. I will. I'm not going to miss my wedding."

Vera looked alarmed. "What? Where are you going? Who the heck is Quinn?"

Her assistant looked on, wide-eyed.

"I'll tell you all about it when I get my next cut." My hand went to my fancy hair. "Thank you for everything. You're an artist. An absolute virtuoso with scissors and spray and makeup."

She didn't appear impressed with my praise. "I want to see the wedding photos," she said.

"Deal," I said.

Chapter 25

I gave Jaida directions, and she drove quickly and efficiently to Prater's Antiques. On the way, I called Quinn and immediately went to voice mail. I texted him that Prater had called me about the person who wanted the music box, adding that I was on my way to the antique store.

Then I quickly filled the spellbook club in on Quinn's plan, not sure whom I'd told what over the last few days. They all seemed up to speed already, which I credited to the constant chitchat between the members of our coven.

Finally, I texted Declan, who I knew was already at the carriage house with his family and my parents. The caterers would be getting ready to set up, and Ryan would have finished with the flowers.

Will be there soon. Cookie on her way. She'll give you the details.

He texted right back.

Details? What details? What are you doing?

I responded.

Will be there soon. Just get things going if I'm a little late.

We pulled into the parking lot, and I put my phone away but not before I saw his response.

!!! Katie?

Jaida parked and we all got out. The sun had warmed the asphalt of the parking lot, and now it radiated heat. "Let's go inside and see what's going on." I looked around at the group. "No one's going to try anything with five women standing around as witnesses."

Mimsey touched one of her curls. "Five very well-coifed women, I might add."

Jaida grinned. "Piece of cake."

The old Buick and an SUV crossover were in the parking lot. We got out and quietly closed the doors. I eyed the small SUV, trying to remember if I'd seen it before. It could have been one of the vehicles that had passed on the street when Tucker had been at Wisteria House, but I couldn't be sure. Those cars all looked the same to me. Then I remembered it had been in the parking lot when we'd left Prater's on Wednesday.

The woman with the sunglasses and hat.

We crossed the parking lot to the entrance and stopped. The sign in the window was turned to CLOSED. I cupped my hand around my eyes and leaned my forehead against the door, trying to peer inside. It was impossible to make out anything in the dark interior through the dirty glass. I tried the door. It was locked.

"Maybe he was frightened and decided to close before they got here," Bianca said.

"His car's here," I said. "At least I think so." But I didn't know for sure the Buick was his. And what about the crossover?

I struggled to remember the other customer who had been in the store when Rori and I had visited Prater to ask about the music box. The mysterious woman in the big hat and sunglasses. She came in right after us. She could have overheard our discussion with Prater. If so, she would have known Rori had the music box, and might have been able to figure out where to find her. But how? The same way Tucker had? Through his contact at the vacation rental company?

I tried to remember what she'd looked like, standing in the shadows of the antique store, but all I could recall were the dress and hat and sunglasses. Then I realized why.

"She was employing a glamour," I said out loud.

"Who?" Mimsey demanded.

"There was another customer in here when Rori and I asked Hudson Prater to appraise the value of the music box. I'd forgotten about her until now. But those same two cars were here when we left, and I have to wonder if one of them isn't hers." I started to rub my face, but Lucy grabbed my hand.

"Honey. Your makeup."

I dropped my hands and looked around at them. "I think our murderer might already be in there with Prater."

"Who is it?" Jaida demanded.

Shaking my head, I stepped back to take another look at the building. "I don't know. She hid herself behind a glamour."

"But it's a woman," Jaida said, slipping into interrogation mode.

"Yes. So it's not Jake Gibson or Zane Wiggins." I

started around the side of the squat brick building to the back. Maybe there was another door.

"So we're looking at Waverly Wiggins, who knew the lottery ticket was in the music box and knew Tucker must have taken it. Also, she and her brother really needed the money."

"But you said she didn't seem like a murderer," Lucy said, padding along on my heels. The others were following, too.

"She could have fooled me. A lot of that going around," I said. "Who else? Effie Glass, I guess. She's blond and could have been one of the women Dayleen heard Tucker arguing with at the motel. Also, Tucker came right out and told her he'd won the lottery. Maybe she believed him more than she let on to Mimsey and me."

"I think she was telling me the truth," Mimsey said from behind me.

I stopped and looked at her. She meant because she'd used her Voice when we'd talked to Effie. I kept silent about that detail, simply saying, "I think so, too. I did see her with Dayleen in the Honeybee, though. Maybe she told Dayleen about the lottery? But that doesn't make sense. Not unless they knew each other before Tucker's murder."

I sighed. What other women were involved in this case? Carolyn Becker, but she had a rock-solid alibi. *Who else?*

The day was warm, and I could feel perspiration glistening at my hairline. The sun made me squint as I headed for the shadows on the east side of the building, and I wished I'd brought sunglasses.

Sunglasses.

The woman in the antique store had been wearing big sunglasses that hid most of her face. So had Serena Gibson when she'd come into the Gibson Estate Sales office. Baseball cap, dark ponytail, big blue eyes—and not only sunglasses, but the same sunglasses as the woman Rori and I had seen in Prater's.

What had Rori said after seeing her in the antique store?

I just got the strangest shiver. I hope I'm not coming down with something.

The exact same sunglasses. She might be a master at glamour spells, but she hadn't changed her sunglasses.

"There." Lucy pointed. "The back door."

We sidled down the back wall toward where she pointed. My mind was racing.

Serena had known Tucker and had worked with him. I only had her word that she'd not been involved with the Wiggins estate. Jake had left by the time she told Rori and me that. She easily could have known about the hidden lottery ticket if she and Tucker were working together. And what if Tucker crossed her? Took the ticket and tried to hide out at the Spotlight Motel? She'd try to find him, that's what. He'd kept looking over his shoulder when he was at Wisteria House talking to Rori. He'd wanted to come inside, and she wouldn't invite him in. If he'd been trying to dodge Serena, and Serena was looking for the music box, he might have given it to Rori for safekeeping. And if Serena did track him down and he no longer had the music box? She'd be furious.

I thought of the hole in the plaster in the Gibsons' office. I'd assumed Jake had made it. Now I wasn't so sure.

"It's Serena Gibson," I whispered as we gathered by the thick metal door. In a few short sentences, I told them my reasoning. "And if I'm right, she's angry, desperate, and prone to violence."

"Also a witch," Mimsey pointed out.

"That, too."

Jaida tried the door. The knob didn't turn.

Lucy looked relieved. "We'll have to wait for Detective Quinn to get here."

Then Jaida yanked on the door, and it opened a few inches. She grinned at us. "There's no lock in the knob. This locks with a deadbolt only." She pointed.

"Nice work," I said, and slowly pulled the door all the way open.

"We should wait," Lucy said.

A crash sounded from inside, then a man groaned.

"Why don't you stay outside until Quinn gets here, Luce," I said, and slipped inside.

Jaida followed, then Bianca and Mimsey. Lucy propped the door open and brought up the rear, looking determined. We were in a short hallway. An alcove off to the side held a furnace, silent this time of year, and beyond that was a small bathroom. I glanced inside, absently noting its lack of cleanliness, and moved quietly to where the hallway opened out to the main shop.

I crept forward, grateful for the carpet that masked my footsteps. The clothes rack I'd spied at the back of the store on my previous visit came into view. The smell of mothballs was nearly overwhelming so close to it, but I could use it to orient myself in relation to where the register counter was in the middle of the store. Pointing in that general direction, I gestured the others forward.

"Where *is* it?" a woman screamed. "Where have you hidden it, old man?"

Beside me, Lucy gasped. I didn't blame her. The voice was horrible. Not just angry but wildly unstable.

Great.

We heard the groan again, and my stomach twisted. Hudson Prater was hurt, and who knew what Serena was doing right this moment. We couldn't wait for Quinn to get his messages and decide to show up. I deeply regretted telling Prater not to call 911.

But I still had my phone. I pulled it out, made sure the ringer was off and the volume was as low as it could go, and made the call. The operator answered, and I put the phone back in the pocket of my jeans, leaving the call open, hoping they could trace it.

Jaida moved up beside me with an approving nod. She pointed to Lucy and Bianca. Then she gestured for them to move to the right. Next, she pointed to Mimsey and herself and indicated they'd go to the left. She pointed at me and made the straight-ahead sign.

We all understood. I'd confront Serena, while the rest of the spellbook club flanked her position. Jaida's military precision would have been amusing in other circumstances, but there was nothing funny in this situation.

The others slunk away, and I tiptoed down one of the narrow aisles bordered by furniture piled higher than my head toward Serena Gibson and Hudson Prater. As I did, I realized the aisles were spokes that led out from the center rather than arranged in a grid. That might make it easier for the spellbook club to circle around. I hoped so. I had a feeling I was going to need all the help I could get.

"You hid it, didn't you?" Serena screamed again in that voice that made my prettily done hair come to attention on my scalp. "You know what's in there! Well, it's not yours." There was a sickening sound of something striking something thick. "It's not yours. It's mine. Give it to me!"

I stepped out from behind a hulking credenza. The sight that greeted my eyes stopped me in my tracks, stunned. Hudson Prater lay on the floor in front of the counter. He was rolled into a ball, with his hands over his head and his eyes squeezed shut. Standing over him was a woman. That's all I could tell—that she was female. The air around her shifted and wavered, playing with my vision so that I couldn't focus on the figure for more than a second or two at a time. Was she blond or brunette? I couldn't even tell skin color or what she wore. The atmosphere reeked of the magic I'd smelled in Tucker's motel room and Wisteria house.

The veil around her crackled with power, almost audibly snapping as she moved. She drew her foot back to kick Prater again.

"Serena," I said.

She whirled toward me, eyes blazing. They altered in flashes, so that I couldn't tell their color or shape. Her glamour was so out of control, it was as if I wasn't facing a real human being anymore.

"Leave him alone," I said. "He doesn't have the music box."

"You," she hissed. "I knew you'd be trouble. Asking after that ring. You've known all along. And now you have the box." She drew the word out, sounding for the world like Gollum.

I made myself take a step forward. "No. I don't have it, either. The police do. And they have the lottery ticket. They'll be returning it to the rightful owners in time for them to cash it in and use the money to pay for their father's medical treatment."

She shrieked in rage.

I cringed but managed not to run. She was crazy and very dangerous. The crazy was part of her power, I realized. And I had to wonder if it hadn't been caused by misusing her power in the first place.

"No!" She picked up the lamp from the desk and threw it at me.

I ducked.

Next came the card holder, then a small table from behind her. She was enormously strong, but her aim was terrible, and I managed to avoid all the projectiles. Then came the soup tureen.

I sidestepped it, and it crashed into an old sewing machine table and smashed into pieces. I'd avoided the tureen, but in the process stumbled into a china hutch stacked with end tables piled high with old magazines. The magazines slid off, raining down on my head, followed by one of the end tables. I fended them off with my arms and wasn't hurt, but a cloud of old, sour dust rose all around me. I looked down to see my arms were streaked with dirt. I could only imagine what my face and hair looked like.

Turning back toward Serena, I advanced.

She was panting. "I waited for years to have that kind of money. I groomed Tucker for a year. I showed him how to use his own natural charisma, and then I gave the gift of more!"

"The signet ring enhanced it," I said, stalling for time. If I could keep her attention away from Prater long enough, the police would get here.

The air crackled again, and she became more recognizable as Serena Gibson. "Yes. The ring." She raised her hand, and I saw she was wearing it. It throbbed with power.

On either side of her, Jaida and Bianca emerged from their own aisleways, but Serena didn't see them. Then I saw Mimsey right behind her. The diminutive witch who usually resembled Cinderella's fairy godmother shone with a deep presence. Her clear blue eyes held speculation as she studied Serena.

"Did your husband know about the lottery ticket?" I asked.

"Jake? Of course not," she scoffed. "He'd give it back. He doesn't realize how much it costs to live the way we do. To have all the pretty things. For him to drive a Cadillac."

While you drive a what? A Subaru?

"I did it for him. I do it all for him." There was a new plaintiveness to her voice. Her face wavered. An audible pop sounded. She turned, took a couple steps, and grabbed a cast-iron Dutch oven off the top of a dresser and flung it at me with all her might.

Her aim was much better this time. Without thinking about it, I flung up my arm and, in an instant, drew on the energy being offered to me by my coven mates, the four elements, and surprisingly, Serena's own power. There was a blue flash of light, and the heavy metal pot fell to the ground at my feet.

Serena hissed in a breath, and her eyes grew wide. She turned to run.

Mimsey stood between Serena and the front door. She drew herself up to her full height and stood her ground. Serena advanced toward her.

No, no, no. Stay away from Mimsey.

"Did you follow Rori and me here the day after you killed Tucker?" I asked, desperately trying to distract her. "Or was it dumb luck that you were here?"

She stopped and turned. "I don't believe in dumb luck."

I tried my Voice, just a little. "Serena, what happened at the Spotlight Motel? Did you mean to kill Tucker?"

She blinked. Frowned. "Of course I didn't mean to kill him. I'm not a killer! I wanted the music box. Correction: I wanted the lottery ticket." Her voice sounded flat and dreamy as she remembered. "Tucker said he didn't have it. That he'd given it to his ex-wife."

So Rori's ex had thrown her under the bus. A coward as well as a con man.

Serena continued. "I didn't believe him. Who would do something like that? I didn't think he'd let it out of his possession. We struggled. He fell and hit his head. While he was unconscious, I searched the room, but the music box really wasn't there. By then I realized he wasn't merely unconscious. He was dead. I didn't mean for that to happen, but I couldn't undo it. I took the ring and left.

"But I'd figured out where he was staying and had been following him until I could decide how to handle his betrayal. So I knew where the ex lived. I followed her—and you—here, and came in as she was talking to

Hudson here about the music box. I knew the lottery ticket was going to expire soon. I had to get the music box back from her."

"So you broke into the house where she was staying."

Serena frowned again. Blinked as if coming out of a haze. Fear sparked in her eyes. "*Witch*," she hissed. "Leave me alone." She whirled to face Mimsey.

In a flash, I realized that all the physical damage she'd done, as much destruction as she'd caused, including Tucker's death and Hudson Prater's injuries, had been fueled by an impressive anger and possibly desperation but nothing magical.

"You're a one-trick pony, aren't you, Serena?"

I saw Mimsey smile as Serena turned back to me. "How dare you judge me."

"Oh, I'm not judging. I'm just figuring it out. The glamour thing you do." I waved my hand. "That's all you know how to do, isn't it? I mean, it's good. It's really good. Too good. I might not have noticed Tucker's if it hadn't been so over-the-top."

A sneer played on her lips. "I fooled you, didn't I? And I know how to get away from you. How to hide." Her lips curved in a truly disturbing grin. "I know how to hide better than you can imagine."

"Ha!" I said. "I bet you can. With being able to change your appearance and all."

On the floor between us, Hudson Prater moaned, and his eyes fluttered.

"I'm done talking," she said. "You won. This time, that is. But I take revenge. I always take revenge. And you'll never know who you can trust, because you'll never know if it might be me."

Her words struck deeply. "Oh, please. You're good at glamours, sure. But you can't change into someone else."

Suddenly, it felt like I was looking at Rori. It wasn't her, of course. And it didn't really look like her. Not really. But enough that, for a moment, I doubted.

"Is that so?" Serena said, and turned back toward Mimsey.

Jaida, Bianca, and Lucy stepped out from the piles of furniture.

Serena paused, then her nostrils flared, and her head came down. She'd run right over Mimsey if we didn't stop her.

"Serena Gibson, do not move," I said in my Voice, doing my best to target just her, to use my Voice as Mimsey had, carefully as a scalpel. "You want to wait until the police come. You want to pay for your crimes."

She paused. "I do not want to . . . crimes . . ." She trailed off, looking confused.

Mimsey stepped forward. "Honey, for some reason you think you need to be someone other than you are." She was using her Voice, too, so much stronger than mine, and subtler at the same time.

The other women exchanged surprised looks. Then they all advanced toward Serena. I walked forward, too. She slowly turned in a circle as we approached.

"Honey, you don't have to fool anyone. You're a beautiful, wonderful person," Mimsey said.

Her Voice is more powerful because it doesn't command. It allows.

We stood to the side of Prater now, protecting him, surrounding Serena. Jaida raised her arms to her sides, and we all followed suit, forming a circle though our fingertips did not touch.

"Not beautiful," Serena whispered. "Not wonderful."

"Oh, but you are, sweet thing. Someone told you that you weren't, but they were wrong."

I tipped my head, watching Mimsey. Was she right? Had something happened to Serena to turn her into a monster?

"They were wrong," the older witch said again.

"Wrong," Serena whispered. Then she shook her head. "No, I have to. Jake only loves beautiful things. I have to be beautiful, or he won't want me anymore."

I felt anger and sadness blossom in my chest. Toward Jake Gibson for making his wife feel so small and worthless, toward a society that advertised and airbrushed and Photoshopped until real people felt they weren't good enough anymore.

"You're beautiful," Mimsey said firmly. "To your core, darlin'."

"Core," Serena repeated.

"You don't need your glamour. You don't need to fool anyone."

Serena looked into Mimsey's eyes for a long moment, then finally nodded. She took off the ring and let it drop to the floor. I felt her power drop away. First the strong power of the ring, and then the finely honed glamour she'd learned to maintain all the time.

The woman who stood in our circle was Serena Gibson, but different. She wore the same makeup and had the same mouth and eyes, but she was a tiny bit heavier, and a little older. A thin scar, barely visible, traced down one cheek from her temple to her jawline. She shuddered and looked away from Mimsey.

"There you go," Mimsey said gently. She'd been using her Voice the whole time and still was. "Doesn't that feel better?"

"I don't know," Serena whispered. "I haven't been like this for a long time."

My heart wrenched in my chest.

Banging on the front door drew our attention. Lucy hurried to let the police in. Serena looked frightened, then angry again.

"You don't need the glamour," Mimsey said again. "You won't ever need it again. Do you understand?"

Serena nodded. I could sense her power waning. Mimsey wasn't taking it away from her. She was giving her permission to let it go. And as Serena let go of her power, she let go of the psychosis that seemed to fuel it in a never-ending loop.

"And you're going to tell the police everything about Tucker and the lottery ticket, right? But not about the ring. You're going to give me the ring right now."

I stared at Mimsey. But of course, she was right. The police wouldn't understand about the ring, and it would be best to deal with it on our own.

Serena didn't even hesitate, reaching down and picking up the ruby ring off the floor and handing it to Mimsey as uniformed officers came through the doors. The older witch tucked it into her pants pocket and winked at me.

The police took Serena into custody. As they were leading her away, Quinn strode through the door.

"About time," I said.

"Hmm. I'd cleared Zane and Waverly Wiggins and was giving them the lottery ticket. They're over the moon." He quirked an eyebrow. "Besides, you seemed to have managed all right."

"Hudson Prater didn't. They're loading him into an ambulance as we speak."

Regret passed over Quinn's face. "Yeah. That was a miscalculation on my part. I take full responsibility." Then he looked closer at me. "What happened to you?"

My hand flew to my hair. "Oh, no! I have to go."

"Lightfoot . . ."

"I know, I know. But Quinn, I'm getting married! In, like—" I looked at my watch. "An hour. Oh, God. Declan is going to kill me!"

"I doubt that. Well, I know where you live. In fact, I'll be there as soon as I can as one of your guests. You can give me a full statement about what happened here tomorrow. Or the next day."

I grinned. "Thank you." Going up on tiptoe, I gave him a kiss on the cheek.

"Come on," Jaida said, already heading toward the front door with the other ladies. "We have to get you cleaned up!"

Chapter 26

The back gate was open, and the caterer's truck was in the driveway when we arrived. Cars lined the street out front, and music and the sound of voices floated toward us from the backyard.

My party had already started.

"There's no place to park," Mimsey fretted.

"There." Lucy pointed. "Margie's waving at us to park in their driveway."

Relieved, Jaida turned off the street and pulled up behind my neighbor's Subaru. We tumbled out of the car. Margie ran toward us on tiptoes to accommodate her high heels.

"What are you doing?" she demanded. "Where have you been? And Katie—oh, dear." She looked me up and down.

"I'll fill you in later," I said.

"Right." She snapped her fingers. "They haven't opened the carriage house to guests, so all we have to do is get you inside to dress." Her lips pursed. "And get you cleaned up. Hurry!"

Mrs. Standish and Skipper Dean were parking down the street, and I rushed across to the porch of the little house so I wouldn't have to answer their questions. Lucy moved even faster than I did and was pounding on the door by the time I got there. It swung open, and Cookie peered out.

"Cutting it kind of close, aren't you? Quick. Get inside."

"You have everything under control?" Margie called to her.

"Yes, thanks!" Cookie waved and closed the door behind Bianca.

"Oh, my God! Katie! What happened?" Mama hurried toward me, worry etched into her face. She cupped my cheek with her hand. "Are you all right?"

"I'm fine." I looked down at my dust-streaked clothes. "Can you fix me up in time?"

"Of course." She sounded confident, which made me feel better.

"I need to talk to Rori first," I said.

"*Now?*" Mama asked.

I nodded. "Tucker Abbott's killer has been arrested. I have to tell her."

"Cookie, go get Rori," my mother demanded. "And hurry."

In less than two minutes, Cookie had returned with Declan's little sister in tow. She looked like a spring flower in the dress Camille had given her to wear. When she saw me, her mouth dropped open.

"Katie! What happened to you?"

"A little altercation at Hudson Prater's antique store. Some of his merchandise sort of fell on my head," I explained.

She looked concerned. "Are you okay?"

"Yep. But you can have your closure now. Serena Gibson killed Tucker."

Rori sucked in a breath. "Serena!"

I nodded. "They'd been working together to rip off the Gibsons' clients, and she knew about the music box and what it contained. Tucker betrayed her by taking it—I imagine they were going to share the proceeds, but that didn't come up in the conversation. She went to get it back from him, but he'd given it to you."

Rori's eyes widened. "He wanted the music box to give back to her. If only—"

I cut her off. "No. Don't think like that. Tucker told her you had it."

"He told her . . ." She trailed off and her lips pressed together.

"She didn't believe him." I told her the rest, leaving out everything about glamours and magical rings and Voices. It didn't take long.

When I was done, Rori swallowed hard, then said, "Oh, Katie. I'm just glad you're okay. Thank you."

"Do you feel better now that you know what happened to your ex?" I asked her.

"I'm . . . I'm not sure." Her chin came up. "But yes, I think I do. Tucker was a jerk until the very end, wasn't he?"

"Pretty much," I agreed. "Though he didn't deserve to die."

"Of course not. But if he had lived, he wouldn't have ever stopped being a jerk. I guess that answers a lot of my questions."

Mama had been listening. "Any chance we could

have the rest of this chat after the wedding? We're getting down to the wire here."

"Of course!" Rori flushed. "I'll see you out there, Katie. Good luck," she said over her shoulder as she left.

"Let's see what we can do to fix your hair," Mama said. "And we'll have to reapply some makeup, because you have dirt all over your face. Good heavens. Come with me."

I padded behind my mother like an obedient duckling, and the rest of the spellbook club followed. They hustled into the bedroom to change, while Mama steered me into the bathroom. Cookie, who was already wearing a soft green chiffon number that elegantly disguised that she was seven months along, came with us.

"You're a mess, Katie," Cookie said. "Maybe you should consider using a glamour. Between all of us, we could keep it up for the duration."

I shuddered. "No way. I want to be the real me at my wedding, even if I am a mess."

"Don't worry. I've got this," my mother said. "Let's get your face washed."

And she did, fixing my makeup down to the eyeliner wings, getting the dust out of my hair, and fussing with the style until it looked nearly as good as when Vera had done it. The rest of the spellbook club was in the living room by then, and I ran into the bedroom to change into my dress. The club members trickled in to sit on the bed as I finished.

In front of the mirror in my closet, Mama tucked a strand of hair behind my ear, stepped back, then reconsidered and returned it to curl around my temple. "Declan brought your earrings."

"Oh, Lordy. I totally spaced. No wonder I love that man." I put them on.

Mama surveyed me in the mirror. "Perfect. Lucy? Do you have Mother's necklace?"

"Right here," my aunt said, and came up behind me to clasp it around my neck.

I gasped. It was a beautiful set of interlocking silver spirals, set with amethysts and what I now knew was hematite. It was the necklace Nonna had shown me in my dream.

"You were right," Lucy said as she examined me in the mirror. "It's just right with this neckline."

"And it's yours to keep, Katie," Mama said. "She would have wanted you to have it, and what better time to give it to you."

I quickly blinked away the hint of tears that threatened. The last thing I needed was to smear my mascara right now. Leaning forward, I took a closer look at the necklace in the mirror.

"That's hematite," Mama said. "Your grandmother's favorite."

I glanced upward, as if Nonna was watching me from above. "I know." And she'd just passed along the cure for my dream eavesdropping that she'd told me about in my hedgewitch's kitchen.

Thank you, Nonna.

"And here's the dragonfly," Lucy said.

"What dragonfly?" I asked.

"You have something old now, and something borrowed—from Bianca—and now you need something blue." She held out a tiny blue enameled dragonfly, less than a third of an inch across, then nestled it into my hair near one of the pearls Mama had managed to reposition, and gave it a spritz of hairspray to keep it in place.

"Thank you," I said with a smile.

"What about something new?" Mimsey asked.

The door opened, and Eliza slipped in.

I gestured at my dress. "This is brand new. That will have to do."

"Katie?" Eliza said.

"I'm almost ready," I said. "I need a couple more minutes to gather my thoughts."

"Okay, I'll tell them, but first I wanted to give you something." She held a small box in her hand. Then she looked around at the others and seemed to hesitate. Taking a deep breath, she took a step forward and thrust the box toward me. "It could be your something new. If you like it, I mean."

Curious and slightly apprehensive, I opened her gift. Nestled into a puff of cotton was a small silver key chain with a single key on it. I took it out and saw the round fob was designed in three concentric circles, and inside them a tiny pentacle gleamed. Surprised, I looked up at her.

Understanding flashed between us. She was letting me know she accepted me for who I was, even if she wasn't sure what that might be after seeing my altar in the loft.

I was deeply touched by the gesture. "It's lovely. Thank you."

"It's a wedding tradition." Eliza grinned. "And you know how much I like those. The key is to this house, which is new in a way, and where you start your new life with my brother. The idea is that you can tuck it into your bouquet." She held up her palm. "Not that you have to do that, Katie. Not at all. But it's there if you want to."

I gave her a hug, which seemed to surprise her. "This something new is absolutely going into my bouquet."

Mimsey held out her hand, and I gave her the key ring. Her eyebrow quirked when she saw the design, but then she expertly attached it to the flowers she had at the ready. "Remember to take this out before you throw the bouquet," she said, her tone laughing.

Eliza looked around at us all. "You are all simply lovely. And Katie, you're a stunning bride. I'm so happy to welcome you to the family." Tears welled in her eyes, and she quickly turned back to the door. "I'll let them know you're on your way."

As the door closed behind her, I turned to my friends. They stood side by side, each dressed in styles that suited them, each in a different pastel color. Cookie in green, Mimsey in pink, Jaida in peach, Bianca in yellow, and Lucy in blue. Each individual, each unique, each special. Around each of their necks, an identical silver locket hung, my gift to them. The lockets contained herbal spells I'd invoked for each of them.

I thought back to when I'd given them the lockets at my bridal shower. We'd gathered together in Lucy's rooftop garden, and I'd insisted on handing them out before opening my own gifts. They all contained holly and snakeroot for good fortune and basil and hyssop for protection, but each contained a little something tailored to the wearer.

My heart filled with love. "She's right. You're all so beautiful."

Mama came to stand beside me. "As are you, daughter. Now, let's get this ceremony started."

The ladies went out to take their places, and my father came to stand by me at the end of the moonlit path of white rose petals. He looked spiffy in the suit Mama had made him wear, and I gave him a kiss on the cheek. The backyard had been transformed into an enchanted space with twinkling lights, pristine white tablecloths, and gorgeous flowers. Mimsey and Ryan had gone all out with the red roses on the gazebo, festooning the railing and creating an arch over the entrance. Ben stood in front of that arch, with Declan to one side wearing a gray tux. His groomsmen also wore gray, except the two who were in uniform. Facing me, Mungo sat quietly at his feet. He wore a purple bow tie, and the simple platinum wedding rings we'd chosen hung around his neck on silken cords.

I suppressed a grin and swept my gaze over the yard, taking in our guests, who were perching on mismatched vintage chairs arranged in conversational clusters, quiet now that I'd appeared. The photographer stood to one side, ready for my entrance. Quinn had managed to show up and stood with his tall, elegant wife by the fence. A movement to my right drew my attention. Steve stood to one side. I met his gaze, and he gave me a small nod and a smile. I inclined my head slightly, then looked back toward where Declan waited by the gazebo.

The light from above dimmed, and my heart sank as I looked up to see a cloud had skittered across the moon.

Not now!

Desperate, I looked at Bianca. Her eyes were closed, and she stood with her fingertips pointing toward the earth. A moment later, the cloud moved away, and the scene glowed with moonlight again. She opened her eyes and looked right at me with a grin.

No . . . she didn't. Did she?

"Here we go," Margie whispered, ushering the JJs over with their baskets of flowers. "You guys know what to do?"

"Yes," they answered in unison, and grinned up at me.

I leaned down. "All righty. Start your engines."

They giggled but didn't start walking until Margie gave them a little push. They walked slowly, scattering red rose petals on top of the white ones. Dad and I followed behind. The musicians began to play an instrumental version of John Legend's "All of Me," which Declan had suggested.

This is it. This is really happening.

I wanted to savor every moment, but my mind was a whirl, and before I knew it, I was standing by Declan and my father had gone to take his seat by Mama. The music stopped, and everything was eerily silent.

Ben looked so handsome, and his eyes crinkled as he smiled at us and then looked beyond to our guests. "Welcome, everyone, as witnesses to the union of Katie and Declan. Their love is strong and will nourish their futures as well as the lives of those they touch. However, I'm just here to make things official, and they've written their own vows to tell each other, and you, how they feel. Katie?" He stepped back.

I'd written the vows weeks ago, and efficiently memorized them. I opened my mouth, and nothing came out. Adrenaline from all that had happened that day added to the enormity of standing right here, right now, and I couldn't remember a thing.

Declan grinned. His eyes laughed. "Want me to go first?" he murmured.

Then it all came flooding back. "No. I've got this." I took his hands in mine.

"Declan McCarthy, you are the love I've looked for my entire life. You are my best friend, and you will always be my family, my heart, my partner. I pledge to be there when things are amazing, when things get tough, and everything in between. No matter what happens, together we can figure it out. I love you, Declan. I love you with all that I am and all that I can be. I can't wait to spend the rest of my life with you." My voice was a little wavery at the end, but I made it through.

Declan's eyes were full of tenderness, and he squeezed my hands. "And I love you, Katie Lightfoot. I vow to spend my life strengthening that love and caring for you with honesty, faith, and patience. For the rest of our days I will be your loving husband and steadfast partner. I am so grateful to have found you, and I'm never letting you go."

My knees were a little weak by the time he'd finished, but I managed to take the ring Ben handed me after he'd retrieved them from Mungo.

Declan said, "I give you this ring as a symbol of my love." He slipped it on my finger.

I almost dropped his but managed to get it on his finger as well. "This ring has no beginning and no end, representing my love for you."

We turned back to Ben, and he said, "So do you two take each other as husband and wife?"

As one, we said, "I do."

And then Mungo chimed in with his approval.

Yip!

Acknowledgments

A heartfelt thanks to Jessica Wade, my insightful and wise editor at Berkley Prime Crime, as well as to the rest of the terrific team there who shepherded my manuscript into book form and got it out into the world: Miranda Hill, Megan Elmore, Joan Matthews, Dache Roberts, Natalie Sellars, and everyone else who contributed their talents and hard work. Another thank-you goes to Kim Lionetti at BookEnds Literary Agency for all she does on my behalf. Hugs and gratitude to the Lauras—Pritchett and Resau—of the Old Town Writers Group for valuable feedback, encouragement, and traveling arm-in-arm with me on this ongoing writing journey. Steve Delinger helped with accounting research, and Linda Jaffee filled me in on how estate sales work. I couldn't manage without my cheerleaders—Mindy Ireland, Jody Ivy, Natasha Wing, Teresa Funke, Amy Lockwood, JoAnn Manzanares, and Mom and Dad. As for Kevin—I can't express how much I appreciate the right questions at the right time, the kitchen cleanups, the cups of tea (even when you use the saucers we use to feed the cat), and the love. Especially the love.

Recipes

Hummingbird Cupcakes

Classic Southern fare. Makes 24 cupcakes.

2 cups all-purpose flour
½ teaspoon baking soda
¾ teaspoon salt
¾ teaspoon cinnamon
½ teaspoon ground ginger
3 sticks (¾ pound) butter, melted and cooled
1¼ cups granulated sugar
2 large eggs
1⅓ cups mashed bananas
⅔ cup crushed pineapple
⅔ cup toasted and chopped pecans
⅔ cup shredded coconut (unsweetened if possible)
1½ teaspoons vanilla extract

FROSTING:
12 ounces cream cheese
½ cup butter at room temperature
2 teaspoons vanilla extract
2 cups confectioners' sugar

   Preheat oven to 350 degrees F. Line muffin tins with paper liners. Whisk together the flour, baking soda, salt, cinnamon, and ginger. In another bowl, cream the butter and sugar together on medium-high speed. Add the eggs, one at a time, beating on medium speed until each is thoroughly mixed in. Continue beating until light and fluffy. Add the bananas, pineapple, pecans, coconut, and vanilla extract, and mix until combined. Fold in the flour mixture, one third at a time, mixing until all streaks are gone.

Fill muffin cups three-quarters full. Bake for 20 minutes or until a cake tester comes out clean, rotating the tins halfway through baking. Allow to cool completely, still in the tins, before frosting.

FOR THE FROSTING:

Beat the cream cheese and butter together on medium-high speed until fluffy. Add the vanilla extract. Reduce speed to low and add the confectioners' sugar gradually until it's all incorporated. Increase speed to medium and whip the frosting until light and fluffy.

Peanut Butter Bacon Cookies

Gluten-free! Makes about 15 cookies.

1 cup all-natural chunky peanut butter
1 cup sugar
1 tablespoon molasses
½ teaspoon baking soda
1 egg
6 slices of bacon, cooked and diced

Preheat oven to 350 degrees F. Line a baking sheet with parchment paper.

Mix together the peanut butter, sugar, and molasses until combined. Add the baking soda and egg. When thoroughly incorporated, fold in the diced bacon. Roll into balls a little smaller than a golf ball. Place on the cookie sheet and press flat with the tines of a fork. Sprinkle with a little more sugar—or if you prefer, sprinkle with just a dash of smoked salt. Bake for 10 minutes until lightly browned. Cool on the baking sheet. Will keep in an airtight container for 3 days—if they last that long.

If you love Bailey Cates's *New York Times* bestselling Magical Bakery Mysteries, read on for an excerpt from the first book in Bailey Cattrell's Enchanted Garden Mystery series,

Daisies for Innocence

Available now wherever books are sold.

The sweet, slightly astringent aroma of *Lavandula stoechas* teased my nose. I couldn't help closing my eyes for a moment to appreciate its layered fragrance drifting on the light morning breeze. Spanish lavender, or "topped" lavender—according to my gamma, it had been one of my mother's favorites. It was a flower that had instilled calm and soothed the skin for time eternal, a humble herb still used to ease headache and heartache alike. I remembered Gamma murmuring to me in her garden when I was five years old:

Breathe deeply, Elliana. Notice how you can actually taste the scent when you inhale it? Pliny the Elder brewed this into his spiced wine, and Romans used it to flavor their ancient sauces. In the language of flowers, it signifies the acknowledgment of love.

Not that I'd be using it in that capacity anytime soon.

But Gamma had been gone for over twenty years, and my mother had died when I was only four. Shaking my head, I returned my attention to the tiny mosaic pathway next to where I knelt. Carefully, I added a piece of foggy sea glass to the design. The path was three feet long and four inches wide, and led from beneath a tumble of forget-me-nots to a violet-colored fairy door set into the base of the east fence. Some people referred to them as "gnome doors," but whatever you called them, the decorative miniature garden phenomena were gaining popularity with adults and children alike. The soft green and blue of the water-polished, glass-nugget path seemed to morph directly from the clusters of azure flowers, curving around a lichen-covered rock to the ten-inch round door. I wondered how long it would take one of my customers to notice this new addition to the verdant garden behind my perfume and aromatherapy shop, Scents & Nonsense.

The rattle of the latch on the gate to my left interrupted my thoughts. Surprised, I looked up and saw Dash trotting toward me on his short corgi legs. His lips pulled back in a grin as he reached my side, and I smoothed the thick ruff of fur around his foxy face. Astrid Moneypenny—my best friend in Poppyville, or anywhere else, for that matter—strode behind him at a more sedate pace. Her latest foster dog, Tally, a Newfoundland mix with a graying muzzle, lumbered beside her.

"Hey, Ellie! There was a customer waiting on the boardwalk out front," Astrid said. "I let her in to look around. Tally, sit."

I bolted to my feet, the fairy path forgotten. "Oh, no. I totally lost track of time. Is it already ten o'clock?"

The skin around Astrid's willow-green eyes crinkled in a smile. They were a startling contrast to her auburn hair and freckled nose. "Relax. I'll watch the shop while you get cleaned up." She jammed her hand into the pocket of her hemp dress and pulled out a cookie wrapped in a napkin. "Snickerdoodles today."

I took it and inhaled the buttery cinnamon goodness. "You're the best."

Astrid grinned. "I have a couple of hours before my next gig. Tally can hang out here with Dash." She was a part-time technician at the veterinary clinic and a self-proclaimed petrepreneur—dog walker and pet sitter specializing in animals with medical needs. "But isn't Josie supposed to be working today?"

"She should be here soon," I said. "She called last night and left a message that she might be late. Something about a morning hike to take pictures of the wildflowers." I began gathering pruners and trowel, kneeling pad and weed digger into a handled basket. "They say things are blooming like crazy in the foothills right now."

Astrid turned to go, then stopped. Her eyes caught mine. "Ellie . . ."

"What?"

She shook her head. "It's just that you look so happy working out here."

I took in the leafy greenery, the scarlet roses climbing the north fence, tiered beds that overflowed with herbs and scented blooms, and the miniature gardens and doors tucked into surprising nooks and alcoves. A downy woodpecker rapped against the trunk of the oak at the rear of the lot, and two hummingbirds whizzed by on their way to drink from the handblown glass feeder near the back patio of Scents & Nonsense. An asymmetrical boulder hunkered in the middle of the yard, the words ENCHANTED GARDEN etched into it by a local stone carver. He'd also carved words into river rocks I'd placed in snug crannies throughout the half-acre space. The one next to where Dash had flopped down read BELIEVE. Mismatched rocking chairs on the patio, along with the porch swing hanging from the pergola, offered opportunities for customers to sit back, relax, sip a cup of tea or coffee, and nibble on the cookies Astrid baked up each morning.

"I am happy," I said quietly. More than that. *Grateful.* A sense of contentment settled deep into my bones, and my smile broadened.

"I'm glad things have worked out so well for you." Her smile held affection that warmed me in spite of the cool morning.

"It hasn't been easy, but it's true that time smooths a lot of rough edges." I rolled my eyes. "Of course, it's taken me nearly a year."

A year of letting my heart heal from the bruises of infidelity, of divorce, of everyone in town knowing my— and my ex's—business. In fact, perfect cliché that it was, everyone except me seemed to know Harris had been having an affair with Wanda Simmons, the owner of one of Poppyville's ubiquitous souvenir shops. Once I was out of the picture, though, he'd turned the full spectrum of his demanding personality on her. She'd bolted within weeks, going so far as to move back to her hometown in Texas. I still couldn't decide whether that was funny or sad.

I'd held my ground, however. Poppyville, California, nestled near the foothills of the Sierra Nevada Mountains, was *my* hometown, and I wasn't about to leave. The town's history reached back to the gold rush, and tourists flocked to its Old West style; its easy access to outdoor activities like hiking, biking, and fly fishing; and to the small hot spring a few miles to the south.

After the divorce, I'd purchased a storefront with the money Harris paid to buy me out of our restaurant, the Roux Grill. The property was perfect for what I wanted: a retail store to cater to townspeople and tourists alike and a business that would allow me to pursue my passion for all things scentual. Add in the unexpected— and largely free—living space included in the deal, and I couldn't turn it down.

Sense & Nonsense was in a much sought-after location at the end of Corona Street's parade of bric-a-brac dens. The kite shop was next door to the north, but to the south, Raven Creek Park marked the edge of town with a rambling green space punctuated with playground equipment, picnic tables, and a fitness trail. The facade of my store had an inviting, cottagelike feel, with painted shutters above bright window boxes and a rooster weathervane twirling on the peaked roof. The acre lot extended in a rectangle behind the business to the front door of my small-scale home, which snugged up against the back property line.

With a lot of work and plenty of advice from local nurserywoman Thea Nelson, I'd transformed what had started as a barren, empty lot between the two structures into an elaborate garden open to my customers, friends, and the occasional catered event. As I'd added more and more whimsical details, word of the Enchanted Garden had spread. I loved sharing it with others, and it was good for business, too.

"Well, it's nice to have you back, sweetie. Now we just have to find a man for you." Astrid reached down to stroke Tally's neck. The big dog gazed up at her with adoration, while I struggled to keep a look of horror off my face.

"Man?" I heard myself squeak. That was the last thing on my mind. Well, almost. I cleared my throat. "What about your love life?" I managed in a more normal tone.

She snorted. "I have plenty of men, Ellie. Don't you worry about me."

It was true. Astrid attracted men like milkweed attracted monarch butterflies. At thirty-seven, she'd never been married, and seemed determined to keep it that way.

"Astrid," I began, but she'd already turned on her heel so fast that her copper-colored locks whirled like tassels on a lampshade. Her hips swung ever so slightly beneath the skirt of her dress, the hem of which skimmed her bicycle-strong calves as she returned to the back door of Scents & Nonsense to look after things. Tally followed her and settled down on the patio flagstones as my friend went inside. I saw Nabokov, the Russian blue shorthair who made it his business to guard the store day and night, watching the big dog through the window with undisguised feline disdain.

Basket in hand, I hurried down the winding stone pathway to my living quarters. "God, I hope she doesn't get it into her head to set me up with someone," I muttered around a bite of still-warm snickerdoodle.

Dash, trotting by my left heel, glanced up at me with skeptical brown eyes. He'd been one of Astrid's foster dogs about six months earlier. She'd told me he was probably purebred, but there was no way of knowing, as he'd been found at a highway rest stop and brought, a bit dehydrated but otherwise fine, to the vet's office where she worked. Of course, Astrid agreed to take care of him until a home could be found—which was about ten seconds after she brought him into Scents & Nonsense. I'd fallen hard for him, and he'd been my near constant companion ever since.

"Okay. It's possible, just possible, that it would be nice to finally go on an actual date," I said to him now. Leery of my bad judgment in the past, I'd sworn off the opposite sex since my marriage ended. But now that Scents & Nonsense wasn't demanding all my energy and time, I had to admit that a sense of loneliness had begun to seep into my evenings.

"But you know what they say about the men in Poppyville, Dash. The odds here are good, but the goods are pretty odd."

A hawk screeched from the heights of a pine in the open meadow behind my house. Ignoring it, Dash darted away to nose the diminutive gazebo and ferns beneath the ancient gnarled trunk of the apple tree. He made a small noise in the back of his throat and sat back on his haunches beside the little door I'd made from a weathered cedar shake and set into a notch in the bark. Absently, I called him back, distracted by how sun-warmed mint combined so nicely with the musk of incense cedar, a bright but earthy fragrance that followed us to my front door.

Granted, my home had started as a glorified shed, but it worked for a Pembroke Welsh corgi and a woman who sometimes had to shop in the boys' section to find jeans that fit. The "tiny house" movement was about living simply in small spaces. I hadn't known anything about it until my half brother, Colby, mentioned it in one of his phone calls from wherever he'd stopped his West-falia van for the week. The idea had immediately ap-pealed to my inner child, who had always wanted a playhouse of her very own, while my environmental side appreciated the smaller, greener footprint. I'd hired a contractor from a nearby town who specialized in tiny-house renovations. He'd made a ramshackle three-hundred-twenty-square-foot shed into a super-efficient living space.

There were loads of built-in niches, an alcove in the main living area for a television and stereo, extra foldout seating, a drop-down dining table, and even a desk that tucked away into the wall until needed. A circular stair-case led to the sleeping loft above, which boasted a queen bed surrounded by cupboards for linens and clothing and a skylight set into the angled roof. The staircase par-tially separated the living area from the galley kitchen, and the practical placement of shelves under the spiral-ing steps made it not only visually stunning, but a terrific place to house my considerable library of horticulture and aromatherapy books.

Most of the year, the back porch, which ran the seventeen-foot width of the house, was my favorite place to hang out when not in the garden or Scents & Non-sense. It looked out on an expanse of meadow running up to the craggy foothills of Kestrel Peak. Our resident mule deer herd often congregated there near sunset.

After a quick sluice in the shower, I slipped into a blue cotton sundress that matched my eyes, ran fingers through my dark shoulder-length curls in a feeble attempt to tame them, skipped the makeup, and slid my feet into soft leather sandals. Dash at my heel, I hurried down the path to the shop. I inhaled bee balm, a hint of basil, lemon verbena, and . . . what was *that*?

My steps paused, and I felt my forehead wrinkle. I knew every flower, every leaf in this garden, and every scent they gave off. I again thought of my gamma, who had taught me about plants and aromatherapy—though she never would have used that word. She would have known immediately what created this intoxicating fragrance.

Check her garden journal. Though without more information it would be difficult to search the tattered, dog-eared volume in which she'd recorded her botanical observations, sketches, flower recipes, and lore.

A flutter in my peripheral vision made me turn my head, but where I'd expected to see a bird winging into one of the many feeders, there was nothing. At the same time, a sudden breeze grabbed away the mysterious fragrance and tickled the wind chimes.

Glancing down, I noticed the engraved river rock by the fairy path I'd been forming earlier appeared to have shifted.

For a second, I thought it read BEWARE.

My head whipped up as I wildly searched the garden. When I looked down again, the word BELIEVE cheerfully beckoned again.

Just a trick of the light, Ellie.

Still, I stared at the smooth stone for what felt like a long time. Then I shook my head and continued to the patio. After giving Tally a quick pat on the head, I wended my way between two rocking chairs and opened the sliding door to Scents & Nonsense.

Nabby slipped outside, rubbing his gray velvety self against my bare leg before he touched noses with Dash, threw Tally a warning look, and padded out to bask in the sunshine. A brilliant blue butterfly settled near the cat and opened its iridescent wings to the warming day. As I turned away, two more floated in to join the first. As the cat moved toward his preferred perch on the retaining wall, the butterflies wafted behind him like balloons on a string. It was funny—they seemed to seek him out, and once I'd seen two or three find him in the garden, I knew more blue wings would soon follow.

Ready to find
your next great read?

Let us help.

Visit prh.com/nextread